Advance Praise f

"There is an unmistakab⋯ ⋯ ⋯ ⋯ how Orlando Davidson writes in capturing those tumultuous times"
Garrett Hongo, author of *The Perfect Sound*

"Cops and crooks, babes, bombers, and bikers—all the idiosyncratic denizens of California in the Seventies come to life in this delight of a novel. The music of the time provides a rich, nostalgic accompaniment to a plot that winds and twists its way through highways and byways to a satisfying conclusion."
Vicki Lane, author of *And The Crows Took Their Eyes* and of the Elizabeth Goodweather Mysteries

"With tight, well-paced plotting, Davidson transports the reader to Baseline Road and Southern California of the 1970s. It's a worthwhile trip! Historical facts and figures are expertly woven into a twisty-turny ode to a culture and landscape filled with well-drawn characters who are flawed enough to be believable and interesting enough to keep the reader engaged well past bedtime."
Tena Frank, author of *Final Rights*

"Orlando Davidson is a gifted writer, and his first novel *Baseline Road* is riveting, complex and intriguing. It's a book full of compelling action and irresistible tension, and at the same time is grounded in empathy and compassion for its characters, including its hired killer. In that way Baseline Road is a rare thing – a moving crime novel with emotional depth and real heart."
Tommy Hays, author of *The Pleasure Was Mine*

"Bombs, babes, and burning rubber. Buckle up! It's 1972, and that's cordite you smell with the patchouli oil and pot smoke. With this delightful detective boogie, Davidson hits all the right notes—sex, thugs, and rock and roll!"

Ed Davis, author of *The Last Professional*

BASELINE ROAD

by

Orlando Davidson

Artemesia
Publishing

ISBN: 978-1-951122-44-7 (paperback)
ISBN: 978-1-951122-54-6 (ebook)
LCCN: 2022941202

Artemesia Publishing
9 Mockingbird Hill Rd
Tijeras, New Mexico 87059
www.apbooks.net
info@artemesiapublishing.com

Content Notice: This book contains descriptions of drug use, mental illness, police actions, and physical assault and trauma that may be disturbing to some people. The book also uses racial slurs and derogatory terms that were in use at the time that this book is set. We have kept this language to reflect its usage at the time, but the author and the publisher condemn the usage of such language whether it was used in the past or today.

Dedication

To my wife, Dana Hinze Davidson, and our children, Daniel Davidson and Shannon Davidson, whose collective love and support motivated me to finish this novel.

CHAPTER ONE

Monday, May 25, 1970

I'LL CALL YOUR OFFICE at 4:45 Monday afternoon. No cops.

Rebecca Meadows stared down at the note on her office desk, her fingers drumming a nervous beat, still only half believing it. Holding her manuscript for ransom? That just didn't happen... but it was gone, leaving her with no choice but to wait for Mark Collins, the thieving bastard, to call.

What had she been thinking? Collins had shown up five days ago, during the evening panel presentation on the financial impacts of continuing the Vietnam War. The topic was too broad for the Economics faculty to tackle on short notice, but she and her Claremont Graduate School colleagues had soldiered through it. The panel had told the audience—still angry and bruised from Nixon's Cambodia debacle and the resulting Kent State/Jackson State murders—what they wanted to hear, namely, that the costs of the war were insupportably high.

Collins had approached her afterward as she organized her papers. He'd asked good questions, showing he'd understood the nuances of her talk. She'd been intrigued, not least by his looks. He was handsome, ridiculously, movie-star handsome. He'd told her he was an army veteran, now disillusioned with the war, and that religious faith was guiding his actions.

On Saturday night, after two lovely dates, Rebecca decided to sleep with Mark. It was a whirlwind affair by her standards. She knew it was a fling—that this mystery man would probably vanish in the air—but it sure was fun. It had been work, work, and more work since January, made more depressing by the endless Vietnam War and now all the student unrest and heartbreak. Rebecca figured she deserved to have the sexy stranger in her bed.

After their lovemaking, she reached over to him. At first, he resisted, seeming nervous, then relented. Rebecca felt a long, jagged scar along his lower back, and something else near the base of his neck. He answered before she could ask. "Too many wars, too many battles," he murmured. "I'm so tired."

She then felt him fully relax as he allowed her to hold him. It was more intimate than the sex. Intertwined, they both drifted to sleep. Rebecca woke up in the morning in a dreamy haze, wanting him again. But Mark wasn't in bed. Maybe he was making breakfast. Did the guy cook too? She got up, hoping to find him in the kitchen. No luck. The apartment was empty. Throwing on a robe, concerned now, she made a check of the parking area from her front balcony. His convertible was nowhere to be seen. What the hell?

Still hopeful that he would return with bagels or pastries, Rebecca made coffee and took a cup into her study. Her eyes went at once to her desk to enjoy the sight of the finished manuscript, her journal article titled "A Macro-Economic Analysis of the the 1919 Paris Peace Treaty" by Rebecca Anne Meadows, Ph.D., neatly typed and awaiting a mailing envelope.

"Holy Mother of God," she gasped, her hands shaking, spilling the coffee. The manuscript, the work that had consumed her life for the past two years, was gone. She'd planned to make a copy before mailing it off—pricey but necessary. And now the only copy was gone. Had Mark stolen it? Had he played her? She steadied herself against the desk, almost fainting. That's when she saw the note, written on a single sheet of paper and wedged under the lamp. *I'll call your office at 4:45 Monday afternoon. No cops.*

"This is crazy," she muttered. The journal article was due at the University of Chicago next Friday. No publication meant no tenure track job at Claremont Graduate School for the fall semester.

Okay, stop and think. Some perverted creep had humiliated her; she could handle that. Nobody knew of their affair, anyway. But she needed her work. The article was good, possibly even groundbreaking. Her thoughts churned furiously. Christ, her research notes and early drafts were scattered all over hell, some in her office, some at her library work station. Could she put the whole thing back together? Sure, but not by the freakin' deadline. Rebecca began to cry. The sexy stranger had been a total fraud, and a thief. But why?

Waiting for her office phone to ring on Monday afternoon, the thought of those tears put her in a rage. She would find out what this slimeball wanted and deal with it. She stared down at the phone with loathing. At 4:45 exactly, it rang.

"What in God's name are you doing?" she asked without waiting for him to say anything, surprised and annoyed that a wave of sadness had crept into her voice. She realized that she was wounded. That she'd cared for the man. That she was no good at flings.

"Listen, the boss wants you to understand something. You're not in charge. You can't dictate terms. That's all. I'm just the messenger. Sorry about all the subterfuge, babe, but we did enjoy ourselves, right?"

"The boss..." Rebecca struggled for the right words. "Now what?"

"Simple. The manuscript is in the departmental mail room. Consider it a lesson learned. Have a nice life."

"Wait... just wait. Who is your boss? What did you get out of this horrible, cruel trick?"

"Well, aside from the obvious, I must admit to a souvenir, those black panties of yours. I'm putting them to good use right this minute, thinking of you naked in the shower, that thing you did. It was so—"

"Fuck you!" She slammed down the phone, shaking the desk. Flinging open her office door, she reeled toward the mail room, her heels clattering on the polished wood floor.

A chill. She knew suddenly who the "the boss" was. That crazy night. Its memories clung to her. The bad sex, fumbled apologies, and then the sudden violence. He'd slapped her, hard. After that, she'd refused to see him again, despite his pleadings. And to think it was all because of a bad toothache and too much nitrous oxide. Never again, she'd swore to herself.

Was he stalking her? The man she'd jilted. She'd recently felt eyes on her at the apartment. But all that was tomorrow's problem. First, she needed to reclaim her life, her future—all wrapped up in the journal article.

The second-floor mail room, cool and elegant like everything at Harper Hall, was deserted in the late afternoon, the department secretaries having left promptly at four. The high ceiling and thick stucco walls kept out the heat of the day. A fat manila envelope was stuffed into her named mail slot above the common worktable. Rebecca practically wept with relief as she stretched her five-foot frame to remove the package. There was a click, and a blinding white light.

****

Collins watched from nearby. The pay phone was located on the north portico of the Claremont Colleges' main library. It offered a perfect view of Harper Hall. The sex talk had been a ruse, something to keep the target off balance, to keep her from asking any more questions. He saw the flash before he heard the explosion. Now smoke was billowing from two second-floor windows. For a moment, the smoggy Southern California air smelled like Nam. He breathed it in, and it made him tingle. People were running in all different directions. "Not again," a young woman wailed.

Collins fired up a Marlboro and checked himself out in the reflection of the library's big revolving glass doors, seeing himself and his Dodgers baseball hat again and again in the shadowy light as the doors spun round and round, faster and faster, students spilling out from the library to find out what had happened. He looked good.

He heard the first sirens. The colleges still were jumpy on account of that other bombing two weeks before. It was time to split. His blue Corvette convertible was parked close by on Dartmouth Avenue, facing south, away from Harper Hall. He headed toward it, not too fast, not too slow, and careful to keep a serious expression on his face. After all, he was as shocked and concerned about a campus bombing as anyone.

A gust of hot desert wind nearly blew his hat off. Dirty brown leaves swirled in the almost combustible blast of air. Collins pulled his hat tighter, noting that the Santa Ana winds had come early this year. He got in the car, thankful that the convertible top was on, and pulled away from the curb, failing to notice a piece of stiff paper—a parking ticket—that lay in the gutter buried among the leaves and gritty debris. He drove through Claremont village, then down toward the San Bernardino Freeway. A fire engine blazed past him, heading toward Harper Hall, followed by two cop cars. Those damn campus radicals! It made him laugh out loud.

Mission accomplished. More complicated than he would have chosen, but he got extra pay for his time and trouble. The client somehow had known about the journal article and had insisted upon its theft, after the seduction. Humiliation definitely was a part of this gig. Collins made a quick stop at the Chevron station near the freeway, found the pay phone, and made his brief after-action report, using all the correct code words. The client was pleased.

Turning his Corvette east toward the desert, Collins began to relax. He could be home in an easy four hours, going fast but not too fast. He wasn't carrying—no weapons, no coke—but still didn't want the Highway Patrol to pull him over. At this precise moment, Collins did not exist, except to a small chosen few, and even they had no clue as to who he really was. He was a specter, a shadow, possibly your worst nightmare, and that's the way he liked it.

He put *Sketches of Spain* in the tape deck, digging on Miles Davis's haunting trumpet. It was a tradition of his after completing an assignment. Maybe he'd hit some golf balls at the club tonight, pounding long arching shots into the neon-tinged sky. They kept the driving range lit up all night. Las Vegas was groovy that way. The city didn't sleep much, and neither did he.

Later, as Collins drove through the twilight, it hit him like a punch; the familiar stirring of feelings and thoughts, half-formed and confused, remorse for the dead woman, remembering the way she'd held him after the sex, her kindness, so different from his usual, joyless couplings. Briefly, in the dark, as he'd stared at her ceiling while she slept, her body turned toward him, she'd made him regret all the things he wasn't, made him wonder if he could ever find a better, less feral, version of himself. But...

Forget it. He refused to let this jumble of emotions take hold of him. It was post-job blues, nothing more. No room for weakness in his line of work. Collins stopped at a diner in Baker, wolfed down two cheeseburgers, and flirted with the waitress. Sipping coffee, he breathed deeply, closed his eyes, and let all the negative thoughts drift away, replaced by plans and calculations, anything concrete, technical, and capable of implementation. Feelings were a trap.

Walking back to the car, his step lighter despite the heavy food, Collins was free again, as if absolved from sins to which he hadn't confessed. He removed the convertible top, choosing the starry night as his roof. The vast Mojave Desert, keeper of secrets, stood in mute witness, its harsh landscape offering a perfect refuge for fractured souls.

CHAPTER TWO

January 1972

I WAS AT THE urinal in the club's dark, putrid bathroom, thinking about Papa John Creach—that fiddler who played with the San Francisco hippie bands—and wondering if I should change my style, when a man sidled up behind me, too close. I felt his presence, even his breath on my neck. Christ! I tensed up and reached for my sidearm, which of course wasn't there since I was off duty.

"Nice playing, Jimmy," the man rasped.

"Thanks. Gimme a little room, will you?"

"You're the law, right?" he asked, backing off some.

"Not tonight, dude."

"We know who you are, man. Here's a news flash for you, Sergeant Sommes. The Claremont bombings, the FBI pigs got it all wrong."

I zipped up and faced the man. In the dim light provided by the single naked bulb dangling above the sink, I recognized him as "Acid Bill" Dixon, a Pomona College lifer who showed up at some of our gigs. He had a late-night weekend show on college radio, broadcast from a funky little shack on the Pomona campus. I listened sometimes, when I was too wired to sleep after playing two sets. He preached Peace, Love, and LSD, mixed in with conspiracy theories and really good album cuts. A stone freak to be sure, but he knew his music.

"Not my case, Bill. In fact, not even my county—I work San Bernardino, not LA." The notorious Claremont Colleges bombings had taken place in May of 1970, during the whole Cambodia/Kent State business. One person had been injured when a bomb went off at the Pomona College administration building. Two weeks later, a female economics professor was blown up at the Claremont Graduate School. My best friend, Carol Loomis, of the Claremont PD was first on the scene and the horror of it bothered her to this day. But like I told Bill, not my jurisdiction. Claremont was just over the county border, a rich college town. Perfect for LA County.

Acid Bill stayed in my face and said, "You're the only lawman I know that can play 'Mr. Bojangles' on his mandolin so, by my reckoning, you can't be a complete asshole. And if you care anything about justice, man, you should take another look. There might still be a bomber out there. Nice hat, by the way." I wore a battered old black Stetson at our shows, anything to not look like a cop. Bill started to shuffle away in a fog of patchouli oil—that hippie smell—mixed with a richer, earthier scent: high-quality Mexican weed. A real goddamn spice rack.

I remembered something. "Anyway, they caught the guy and he confessed. Score one for the FBI," I said to the retreating back and the salt-and-pepper ponytail.

Bill turned and sad-eyed me like I'd really disappointed him, like I'd failed a test. "He confessed to the first one, Jimmy, where the secretary got hurt."

With that he was gone, leaving me oddly irritated that I'd disappointed a spaced-out old hippie. What did I care? But I had music to play.

Which brought me back to...Creach. His fiddle playing with Jefferson Airplane, long psychedelic runs and leads, was not my style at all. But the kids dug it. Our band, Salton Sea, had finished the first set at Baldy Village, and my playing was off tonight. The rhythm and fills were okay, which was mostly what I did since we were more rock than country. But my leads didn't have any flow, any magic. I'd seen people drifting away toward the bar as I played. Hell, even the bass player gave me a look. It was a constant struggle. I wanted more Bakersfield honky-tonk country in our sets. The singer and drummer wanted to be The Rolling Stones.

What the hell. Maybe it was time to rock some more and give the crowd some cheap thrills—easy to do on Neil Young's "Down by the River," one of our staples, with me and Tom Sokoloski, our lead guitar player, trading licks. After all, our band was playing country rock to California college kids, not auditioning for the Grand Ole Opry.

I gathered myself, dismissing all thoughts of Acid Bill's dark ramblings, and headed for the door. Time to let my fiddle screech like Creach.

****

The telephone woke me up the next morning, after a short night's sleep. The second set had gone better—I'd even pulled out my mandolin and played "Mr. Bojangles." It was my mother on the phone reminding me of our monthly brunch date at Walter's down in Claremont. As always, she asked me if I was bringing "someone" with me. In other words, had I met the woman of my dreams that would result in marriage and children and a house in the suburbs? "Just me, Mom," I said. "See you in an hour."

Being a cop and a musician was a great way to meet the ladies—one-night-stand-type ladies, mostly at bars—and a lousy way to meet a future wife. That's the way it was. Also, I was thirty-five years old. The women I had gone to high school and college with were happily married, or bitterly divorced. And the younger ones I met, often at gigs, seemed so different in terms of life experience. Sometimes, I'd say "Buddy Holly" to my date, out of the blue. A blank look spelled trouble. It happened a lot.

The weird episode with Acid Bill Dixon was bugging me. Over coffee, I took a quick look at a *Time* magazine story I'd kept about the bombings. Richard Manning, an admitted student radical and member of the Claremont Chapter of the SDS, Students for a Democratic Society, had been arrested after the second Claremont Colleges bombing, the one in which the college professor had been killed. I thought he'd confessed, but he hadn't exactly. Instead, he'd issued a statement through his lawyer saying, "Death to all pigs that support Nixon's Killing Machine. Civilian casualties are to be expected during the revolution. Power to the people." Then he'd clammed up. It certainly wasn't an outraged claim of innocence. His statement sounded like bullshit to me. I had friends dying in Vietnam. I doubted that he or his SDS buddies could say the same.

Time for breakfast. I left my Palmer Canyon cabin, tucked in among the live oaks, my boots resonating on the wooden steps, and took a deep breath of sunny winter. Scrub jays were gathering above in the oaks and pines, having some sort of raucous meeting. The rain had finally stopped two days ago, but snow remained on the higher peaks of the San Gabriel Mountains. There was no smog, and it was just cool enough for my jean jacket. This was Southern California at its sneaky best, trying to convince the doubters, myself included, that its best days lay ahead—that its golden promise still could be kept.

Climbing into my '71 Dodge Charger, I resolved to take a quick look at the Manning thing tomorrow at the office, provided some poor soul didn't get stabbed in a back alley along old Route 66, in which case I'd be too busy.

CHAPTER THREE

AT 20,000 SQUARE MILES, San Bernardino County was larger than New Jersey, Connecticut, Delaware, and Rhode Island, combined. The bosses liked to trot out this fact, especially when they'd lost a prisoner or suffered some comparable calamity. The dividing line with Los Angeles County was more than just a boundary. "San Berdoo" had a long history of untamed lawlessness, was almost proud of it. It remained the wild, wild, west.

I worked as a homicide investigator for the San Bernardino Sheriff's Department, SBSD to us, and was based at the small, relatively sleepy Alta Loma substation. We shared the building with the county fire department. On paper I had a partner, but he was long gone, unofficially transferred to the higher crime Fontana area, near the speedway, where more bad guys hung out. This sleight-of hand maneuvering was needed to keep the accountant types happy, since all investigators were required to partner up.

Working alone suited me. Fewer personality hassles. We were a relaxed crew at Alta Loma. I mostly wore jeans, except on court days, and nobody cared if my hair came down over my collar. If things got tricky on my Cucamonga, Etiwanda, and Alta Loma beat, I called the patrol guys to back me up. Laurie, our dispatcher/secretary—one of those California blondes the Beach Boys wrote songs about—ran the office and also made good coffee. Which

I was drinking Monday morning while reading the sports page of the San Bernardino Sun. The Lakers had finally lost, ending a record winning streak, the Bucks' Abdul-Jabbar outplaying Wilt Chamberlain. Ah, basketball. I'd actually tried out for my college team at Cal Poly, but wasn't good enough or, at six feet even, tall enough. It still was my favorite sport.

"Call on line two," Laurie yelled out at me. Our intercom system was busted, had been for quite a while. Yelling worked. I picked up.

"Is this the intrepid homicide detective?" a familiar female voice asked.

"You bet. Got any dead bodies?"

"Only the mayor, but he doesn't know it yet, like that zombie movie."

It was my best buddy, Carol Loomis, who worked for the tiny Claremont Police Department as its only detective. I'd called her earlier. "Actually, I have a question for you. You know the famous Claremont bombings—"

She laughed. "Do I know the bombings, only the biggest deal that ever hit this sleepy little burg?"

"Yeah, I know, but I had a weird conversation, if you can call it that, with a stoner type over the weekend. About the bomber, saying he'd only confessed to the first one. Does that ring any bells?"

Carol hesitated a moment before answering. "Kind of. Buy me lunch at La Paloma and I'll tell you more."

****

I was ten minutes late to lunch. Carol was already seated and made a show of pointing at her watch as I approached, giving me the good-natured grief that was customary in our relationship. She often remarked that nobody remembered what she looked like on account of her regular and unremarkable features. She wore her brown hair short, cut just above her neck. Her mouth and nose were small, surrounded by light freckles. She had a figure that was best described as trim as opposed to sexy and she dressed to avoid unwanted attention.

Carol thought of herself as a plain Jane, but her flashing brown eyes told me a different story. They sparkled when she was happy, broke your heart when she was sad, and were downright scary when she was mad. I knew all three emotional circumstances well. She also was the smartest person I knew.

We ordered and dug in. It was way too much food, as always, at La Paloma, but I didn't let that stop me. Tortilla chips, two chicken enchiladas, rice and beans, and iced tea for both of us. Our usual order, except Carol always asked for more hot sauce. Some people said we made a perfect couple, since our features and demeanors seemed to match. Not exactly.

One night about two years earlier, after too much tequila and fast, sweaty dancing at a rock club in La Verne, I'd put the moves on her in the parking lot. Following an unusually fierce rejection, then boozy tears, Carol let me in on her secret. She was attracted to women, always had been. Since she wasn't sure how her superiors would react to this fact, Carol kept it to herself and, as far as I knew, didn't have much of a love life. I often served as her date at official functions, and that worked out fine for both of us.

Small talk and gossip had filled our lunch. Time to get to work. "Okay, what do you remember about the bomber, Richard Manning?" I asked.

Carol drank some more iced tea. "You remember how crazy it was back then? All the college kids marching and protesting, even burning down that bank in Santa Barbara. So when that first bomb went off, the one at the college library, everybody just freaked out. The college presidents met at midnight, demanding action, their assistants screaming at the mayor, who of course then screamed at me. The normal chain of command."

"Yeah, I remember. It was all hands on deck for us too."

"It was a serious freakin' pipe bomb," Carol said, poking her finger at me. "That young woman, the secretary, just about lost her hand, plus her eardrums were ruptured. The entire storeroom at the library was torched."

"Did you take the initial call?"

"For about half an hour, then your buddies from LASD, LA County Sheriff's Department, came rolling in, the arson guys, bomb guys, you name it. My job quickly shifted to coordination and communication—which really meant bringing them coffee—which was fine with me. I didn't know squat about bombs."

"What about the FBI? Did they show up?"

Carol shook her head and pushed her plate away. "Not then. I heard they were getting briefed by LASD. In fact, once things settled down and it was clear that the victim was basically okay—no life-threatening injuries—and the college kids stopped occupying buildings, it was almost business as usual.

"Then it happened, late May, a couple of weeks later." Carol shuddered. "I've got no illusions, Jimmy. I'm a small-town cop, nothing more, and that second bomb scared the living crap out of me."

I signaled for the bill, needing to be in San Bernardino at 2:30 for a meeting with an assistant DA. Carol didn't notice. Her eyes were fixed on something I couldn't see; she was reliving the scene.

"It was almost 5 p.m., just a regular day," she said. "I was thinking about taking my dog to the park after work when the call came in—a man, hysterical, screaming, 'A bomb, a bomb, Jesus! They blew her up.' I got to the graduate school in about five minutes... and, wow." Carol's eyes welled up.

"Sorry, I didn't mean to open up old stuff."

She ignored me. "The room was still smoking. I had to tell the fire department to wait, needed to preserve the crime scene. The woman, the professor... well, she was just blown to bits, body parts, blood on the walls. Who could do shit like that?"

The waitress came with the check. I took it. "My treat."

Carol nodded. "Okay, but I haven't earned my lunch yet. This time the FBI was all over the case, senior people from the LA office, real arrogant pricks. They pushed everybody else away, never even talked to me, probably thought I was clerical if they thought anything. All the Los Angeles TV stations showed up too, helicopters landing at the Pomona College quad. It was chaos."

"What about LASD?"

"They were there, but second string to the FBI. It turned out that Ed Charles of the LA Sheriff's Department had been investigating Richard Manning, this campus radical guy, for the first bombing. In fact, he'd gotten an anonymous tip that Manning was good for it."

I'd worked with Ed Charles. He was solid. "But he hadn't acted on it yet?"

"Nope. He told me later that he didn't have enough evidence to even brace the guy. He was still talking to other radical types, trying to figure Manning out, when the second bomb blew. Then he felt terrible, told the FBI about Manning. The Feds snapped their fingers, a judge gave them a search warrant, and they showed up in force at 3 a.m. the next morning at Manning's cottage in the Claremont barrio and arrested him. I heard he was just sitting there, reading something by Che Guevara, like he was waiting for them."

"Jeez. Did you know about the raid?"

"Not until later, when I read about it in the *LA Times*, which was embarrassing. Maybe the mayor knew. The FBI found all sorts of threats, manifestos, you name it, about pigs, Vietnam atrocities, et cetera, et cetera. And then the big deal. There was bomb stuff in the garage, bags of fertilizer, blasting caps, diesel fuel, and timers. Plus bomb instructions. The Feds had Manning cold. In fact, there even was some kind of half-crazed letter, unsent of course, to the library victim, part apology, part political rant about the revolution."

"Some of that showed up later in his statement," I said, "civilian casualties and such."

"Yeah, what a jerk. That's pretty much it. You know the rest, except, apropos to your question, the evidence on the second bombing was thinner, more circumstantial. And the case never really got worked in any normal way. They'd arrested their man, decided he'd set both bombs, and J. Edgar Hoover was happy as hell. That was it."

I frowned. "Same kind of bomb though?"

"Yeah, that's what the U.S. Attorney's Office said, really hammered on that point, said the bomb experts told them the bombs were identical." Carol shrugged. "We'll know more if there's ever a trial. They're fighting over him, you know, the State and the Feds, each claiming jurisdiction. Hoover and Governor Reagan both want the credit for nabbing the radical bomber. Isn't there some kind of law against just sticking a guy in a cell without a trial?"

"I guess not for him."

I paid and we moved from La Paloma's fake Mexican gunfighter décor into the bright white glare of Foothill Boulevard. It always was kind of a shock, the brightness of Southern California, especially reflecting on all the concrete. I put on my shades, a necessity even in January, and we walked to Carol's shiny cherry-red Chevy Bel Air, her pride and joy.

"When are you going to pop for new wheels?" I asked, trying to tease her into a better mood, away from the bombing memories.

She mock-shoved my arm. "Hell, this baby is on its way to being a classic."

"Let's go to the Fontana drag strip someday. My Charger can take this antique."

"In your dreams, pal. That bananamobile of yours doesn't stand a chance," she said, pointing at my car.

"That's classic gold and black, lady; a lawman's vehicle."

"Whatever." Carol grinned at me, got in the Chevy, gunned the engine, and then peeled rubber out of the La Paloma parking lot, taking a wild left turn onto Foothill. Illegal as hell. Lucky she was the law.

CHAPTER FOUR

I DIDN'T JUST WORK homicides. In fact, I rolled on any violent, or even potentially violent, incident on my beat. Which was why I spent part of that same afternoon at a house in the flatlands of Etiwanda talking down a drunk couple—threatening each other with a carving knife (her) and hedge clippers (him)—instead of meeting with the assistant DA in San Bernardino. These interactions with the public, no matter how nuts, were way more interesting than witness prep with a rookie DA.

After convincing the warring couple to stow their weapons, eat something, and love one another a little better, I departed, leaving a patrolman to monitor the situation. Reflecting on my lunch with Carol, I didn't see much to argue about with the FBI. The bomber sounded guilty to me. I planned to call Ed Charles, time permitting, to close the loop, but that was it.

Back at the office, I wrote up an incident report on the Etiwanda thing, then shot some hoops with the firemen. Some of them were really pissed about Nixon's new wage and price controls. Not me. I never could get worked up over collective bargaining type stuff, which had disappointed my father, a strong union man. Driving home that night, I realized it had been over a year now. My dad had put down his cigarette, took a sip of Pabst Blue Ribbon, and dropped dead of a heart attack at his local tavern in Pomona. He did enjoy a cold one with the boys after finishing his shift at General Dynamics—building some sort of missile to launch at the Russians—so not a bad way to go. But he was too young to die, and I missed him. So did my mom.

****

I reached Ed Charles at home a week later, surprised as hell to find out that he'd retired from the Los Angeles County Sheriff's Department. He didn't remember who I was at first and almost hung up the phone. Then it clicked. "Oh yeah, the kid sheriff fiddle player."

It sounded sarcastic, but I let it pass. I needed information from him. He agreed to meet me on my turf, at Bodene's, a barebones beer bar on East Foothill between Claremont and Upland. SBSD operated in these no-man's-lands between the incorporated towns. On occasion, I'd had to bust rowdy bikers in this bar for various offenses against the public order, but things were quiet at 3p.m. in the afternoon.

Ed Charles had arrived first. He looked washed out and smelled like the bottom of an ashtray. He'd gotten a head start on me too, an empty beer glass in front of him. Since I'd last seen him, muscle had turned to fat on his frame. His once eagle-sharp blue eyes were cloudy.

I bought a pitcher of Miller High Life, which cheered him up. "How's retirement, man?" I asked, pouring him another glass.

He pulled a sour half-smile. "I got a trailer in Rialto, a color TV, cold vodka in the fridge, and a friendly lady next door. What more does a man need?"

It sounded rehearsed. "Don't you miss the job?"

"Only when I'm sober, kid."

Just then Mike, the owner, walked by our table. He clapped Ed on the shoulder. "How ya doing, man?"

"Bring me another pitcher, Mike, and I'll tell you."

I don't usually drink on duty but make exceptions for circumstances of investigative necessity. Like now. A vagrant thought hit me. Was I working? Reports needing attention were piling up on my desk. What did an old bombing in Claremont have to do with me? I must be bored. Mike came back with another pitcher and some salted peanuts, barely looking at me, since ordinarily my presence was bad for business. I threw a ten-dollar bill on the table to ease his pain.

Ed was inhaling the beer and had two cigarettes going at once. He paused, burped, and headed toward the bathroom. I chugged one glass to keep up.

"Is he here often?" I asked Mike, who was fiddling with an ashtray at a nearby table. Our table was tucked toward the back of the bar. A Rolling Stones song pulsated through the speakers, the live version of "Jumpin' Jack Flash."

"No more than my other regulars. You still playing music?"

"Yeah, when we get the gigs. Things are a little slow." He'd never hired us. I heard there was some history with our lead guitar player and Mike's wife.

Ed rejoined us. "Hey, Mike, bring me one of those pickled eggs?"

"The girl will bring it to you. Take care, guys." Mike moved toward the bar where a group of off-duty county ambulance drivers were waiting for their beer.

"You said you wanted to know about the bombings," Ed started, attacking the second pitcher. "Not much to say. The Feds got the asshole that set them off."

Now came the awkward part. "I heard you were tracking the guy."

He glared at me. "I figured that was your angle. You

ever been one hundred percent right and dead fucking wrong at the same time?" he asked me, not really wanting an answer. "Well, that was me. Playing it by the book, keeping our DA's office in the loop, building my case against Mr. Manning on the attempted murder charge, and then BOOM", he slammed his beer glass down, breaking it, "he kills her."

It got quiet. The barmaid, not making eye contact, brought over a broom and a dustpan, swept up the glass, and then gave Ed another one along with the pickled egg. Mike was shooting the shit with the guys at the bar, his dark eyes now watching us with that special look reserved for trouble. "It was bad luck, Ed," I said. Pretty lame, but the best I could do.

"I know what you see when you look at me, kid—a failure." I started to protest that statement, but he ignored me.

"And the funny thing—not so funny really—is that it's true," Ed said, wiping some blood—he'd cut a finger on the broken glass—on his jeans. "Sometimes I dream it. Sometimes I'm awake. I'm at the graduate school. I'm looking at the body, what's left of it. The smell of cooked flesh. I dropped the ball. She's dead. So as soon as I qualified, I pulled my pension."

"Did you, uh, try to see somebody, get some help?"

"You mean a shrink." He pounded down another beer. "I don't do that shit."

"What about the call you got, the tip on Manning?" I figured I'd better ask before Ed got too far gone. How was he going to drive home? Maybe I'd take him. Now the Stones were playing the bluesy "Love in Vain," with Mick Taylor doing his freight train slide guitar.

"We got lots of calls after the first bombing, but one was weird. He wouldn't give his name, and I think he was disguising his voice, using a phony accent. He said, 'Look at the SDS guy, Manning, the wild one with red hair and the big mouth. He's your bomber. He learned how in Cuba.' Of course, we'd already been looking at Manning, even the Cuba angle. He was that obvious."

"Find anything?"

"Started to. The SDS had an office at the grad school, can you believe it, an office. They'd put out flyers, all kinds of anti-war stuff, saying that Castro was the answer, dump Nixon, empower the unions. But the main thing I learned, Jimmy, was that it was all talk, talk, talk. Man, they never stopped shooting off their mouths. But Manning, he was different. We had a kid on the inside who talked to us sometimes, not exactly a snitch, but reliable. He said there was this endless debate among the radicals whether violence was justified. Manning always led the charge on violence, saying deadly force was all the pigs would ever understand."

Ed lit another cigarette, then resumed. "We were close, maybe one day away on a search warrant, trying to find a witness who had seen Manning at the library, still trying to lock down the Cuba angle. But we were too late." His face went slack.

Time to go, nothing left to say. I could hear the big rigs outside on Foothill, downshifting for the light. The peanut shells on the floor were sticky with spilled beer. Suddenly, the whole joint smelled like despair. I took Ed home. He kept his trailer neat. The friendly lady next door saw me as I was leaving. She said she'd drive him back for his car when he sobered up. "This isn't the first time," she said.

I resolved to give Al Sevilla, Ed's former partner, a call to see if there was help available for him. LA County had money. But I knew it wouldn't do any good. Those of us in law enforcement weren't supposed to crack. I'd learned my trade in the army, an MP in Germany. "Don't give an inch," they'd ordered. No pussies or wimps allowed, only tough guys who could handle anything the job threw at us. So, the nightmares we all had seldom were shared.

Talking to Ed Charles had put me in a dark mood. Screw it. This whole Claremont bomber thing—none of my business to begin with—seemed like a dead-end street. But it was hard to let go. That look on Carol's face at lunch. She was still in pain. Then I thought of something that lifted my spirits. Maybe, just for the hell of it, Carol and I should pay a surprise visit to Acid Bill Dixon. After all, he'd started it with the Manning tip. Rousting Bill would be fun.

CHAPTER FIVE

"WHERE ARE WE, JIMMY?" Carol said, staring out into the darkness.

"Almost there," I replied. We were driving slowly on a narrow dirt road in the hills above Claremont on a clear, cool Saturday night. The neighborhood, San Antonio Heights, was a weird mix, always had been. Big fancy houses with great views—you could see all the way to Catalina Island on clear days—mixed in with bungalows that weren't much more than shacks. Newcomers came face to face with grizzled locals, cabernet sauvignon versus Budweiser.

I figured Acid Bill Dixon's place to be more on the shack side of things. I was wrong, sort of. The house didn't look like much, but the large flat lot contained a beautiful old lemon grove, sadly hard to find these days. The property was tucked in a hollow just below the Baldy Dam. There was a hint of the big mountains above us, even in the darkness.

It was close to midnight when I killed the lights, rolled to a stop along the road, and got out. A fast shadow passed above us, maybe an owl. Good music, the Allman Brothers' "Statesboro Blues" was playing loud on outdoor speakers. We were at the edge of the grove, peering in toward the house. I could already smell the tangy scent of marijuana.

"None of your weird cowboy stuff, just a friendly chat," Carol said. "And we don't care about their dope. Besides, we're unarmed and in civvies."

"Agreed, I'm a lover, not a fighter," I said, just as a massive German shepherd came bounding out the grove right at me, teeth bared, growling like he meant it. Unprepared, I reached down, looking for a rock.

"Hey boy, good boy," Carol called out in a high-pitched, singsong voice. She repeated her greeting and then pulled a large dog biscuit out of her jacket and offered it to the animal. The dog accepted Carol's treat, still eyeing me with evil intent.

"Wow, that was nifty," I said, impressed by her forethought. "Got any more?"

A big man, wearing overalls with no shirt underneath and sporting a full biker beard, appeared from behind one of the lemon trees to our left and whistled for the dog. It retreated, after giving Carol a quick thank-you glance. "Who the fuck are you?" Big Man demanded. "This is private property." So much for the Age of Aquarius.

"Friends of Bill. Is he around?"

"Friends? Well, that might be stretching it." Acid Bill, in a Woodstock Nation sweatshirt, made his own appearance. "They're okay," he told the burly biker, who shrugged and retreated to the shadows, taking the dog with him.

"Why the security, Bill?" I asked. "You running dope?"

"No. I'm not. But the sad fact is that you can't be too careful these days. Lots of evil characters lurking 'all along the watch tower,' as Dylan says. Who's your partner?" He gave Carol the eye.

"I'm Carol Loomis, Bill. Claremont PD, just a social call."

Acid Bill broke into a slightly demented laugh. "Two cops at midnight, prowling around. A social call. Okay, I'm cool with that." He paused. "I'm assuming a little recreational marijuana is not going to offend your legal sensibilities, correct?"

"Not our concern," Carol said.

"I'm liking you more and more. Come meet my other guests." We trailed behind him through the grove to a large stone patio. There was a fire pit in the middle; a woman was tending to the blaze, adding pine branches. The warmth was welcome in the chilly night air. The music had changed to the Grateful Dead, a song I knew called "Uncle John's Band." Our band had rehearsed it some but couldn't pull it off, we didn't have enough singers.

Six people—three men, three women—all much younger than Bill, were seated around the fire pit, trying to stay warm, passing joints and drinking wine. They were using one of those weird animal skin holders for the wine. The kind you hold above your head and squeeze. Never saw the point myself. A bottle worked fine. The young folks were pointedly ignoring us, waiting for a cue from Bill, like he was their guru or something.

He raised a guru-like hand and announced, "Jimmy and Carol have joined us, brothers and sisters, representatives from law enforcement as a matter of fact, but they're cool and come in peace."

The woman tending the fire pit turned and looked at me—and took my breath away. She was wearing jeans and a purple sweater, her black hair pulled back in a ponytail. Her face was beautiful... and ugly... a large nose and mouth, flashing dark eyes, and a hint of a smile. She looked like Mona Lisa, only better, with a full figure that jangled me. She turned away and busied herself again with the fire.

"You like this Grateful Dead tune, Jimmy?" Bill asked. "Let's talk in the kitchen."

I didn't answer, distracted, still looking at the woman. Carol followed my gaze, then gave me a soft nudge toward the house. The kitchen was warmer. My focus returned.

"Yeah. Garcia's a good player, for an acidhead."

Bill stroked his salt-and-pepper beard. "Nothing wrong with acidheads. It takes all kinds. Although many of the young ones out there," he gestured toward the people around the fire, "don't fully appreciate this fine, acoustic music. All they want is 'Dark Star' and that other acidhead stuff, as you call it, getting as high as they can. Well, I tell them, from vast experience, that you've got to mellow out some too, listen to the river run, so to speak. Otherwise, you'll fly into the sun and burn out."

We contemplated this sage advice for a while. Then Carol said, "Mr. Dixon—"

"Please, please, call me Bill. Nobody's called me Mr. Dixon since the last time I was in jail."

"Okay. Based on your recent conversation with Jimmy here, both of us have been taking another look at the Claremont bombings, but—"

"I didn't do it. Is that why you're here—" He looked surprised.

"Cool it," I interrupted him. "We know you didn't do it."

"So what do you know about this bomber, Richard Manning?" Carol asked him.

"Not much." Bill reached for a pan on the kitchen drain board. "I'm hungry, got the munchies. Would you like a hash brownie? I baked them myself. They might change your life for the better."

"Come on," Carol said. "Don't change the subject. I looked you up, summa cum laude graduate of Pomona College, Honors in Philosophy."

Bill looked up from the brownies. "Don't hold that against me. It was a long time ago." He selected a perfect dark square and popped it in his mouth.

"My point is, you're way smarter than me. So fill me

in. What have you heard about the bombings? You're connected to the movement, hear stuff we don't. And why did you talk to my partner here about Manning, after all this time?"

Bill's expression was pained. "Too many questions. You're bringing me down, just like Richard Manning used to. Always too intense, too wired, saying we needed an armed revolution and other violent shit. Not my scene at all. In fact," Bill turned and looked straight at me, "I started thinking that maybe he was one of yours, you know what I mean, an agent provocateur."

"No chance," I said. Why was I so sure?

"Whatever. But like I told you before, I believe in justice, of the cosmic variety. There's this vibration, hard to pin down, that he's getting framed for the murder."

"Who's saying?" Carol asked.

"I don't know, it comes in whispers on the wind. But it's real. Why not ask Allie out there?" He pointed toward the patio. "She used to hang out with Manning. They lived together for a time."

It was going to be her, Mona Lisa. I just knew it.

Acid Bill shifted to a happier subject. "The key to a good brownie, Carol, is the right mixture of dark chocolate, wheat flour, brown sugar, organic vegetable oil, and hashish. Remember that," he said, strolling outside. "Now let me introduce you to Allie."

She stood facing us, her back to the fire as we approached, the flames creating dancing shadows behind her on the old house's wall. Fire and stone—it could have been anytime, anyplace, any century.

"I don't talk to pigs," she said, quickly breaking the spell.

Usually the word grated on me. Not tonight. "Not a bad strategy," I said. "People often tell us all kinds of stuff they don't have to, just because we make them nervous. Right, Carol? What does Allie stand for?" I asked, studying her face, her olive skin, every detail. Her complicated looks, not conventionally pretty, held my gaze and wouldn't let go.

"Allessandra. What's it to you, Columbo?"

"I'm Jimmy Sommes, homicide investigator for the San Bernardino County Sheriff's Department, and this is Carol Loomis of the Claremont Police Department. Don't get on her bad side, or she'll eat you for lunch."

I heard Carol sigh. "Don't listen to him, Miss...?"

"D'Amico. Allessandra D'Amico. That's all you get, end of discussion."

"That's a beautiful name, High Renaissance," I said to her. It got me a small smile, a big victory.

"Ah, Christ." Carol sighed. "Miss D'Amico"—switching to her cop voice, thrown off balance by my reaction to the woman—"I'm going to give you my card," she said, handing Allie two. "I would very much appreciate it if you could write your telephone number on one of these. Sometime next week I'm hoping we can discuss your relationship with Richard Manning and—"

Allie threw the cards into the fire. They burned blue and green, some sort of chemical in the ink. We all watched the cards burn. Behind us, someone lit another joint, smoke wafting through the now quiet group. It was a stalemate. We had no legal right to ask Allie anything, and she knew it.

"Okay, thanks. I think we're done here," Carol said, and turned toward the lemon grove to leave. "You coming?" she asked and started walking, not waiting for an answer. Luckily, I had the car keys, or she might have left me behind.

I looked at Allie. "I'm in a band, Salton Sea."

Her glare softened. She even smiled a little. "I know. I've seen you guys. I like the sound. Kind of a heavier Nitty Gritty Dirt Band."

Good answer. "We're playing The Corral next Saturday night. It's a small club on Baseline in LaVerne."

"I know where it is." The smile stayed.

"Why don't you come?"

Allie didn't answer, but I didn't expect her to. She'd come, or she wouldn't. I was betting she would.

"Bye, Jimmy," Acid Bill called out. "Be cool, brother."

I stumbled through the grove, the glorious scent of lemon blossoms, early this year, clearing my head. Carol was standing by the car, smoking a cigarette, when I got back. She ground it out. "What was all that nonsense? You blew that interview."

"Come on, that was on purpose," I lied. "She wasn't going to say a word to us up there in front of Bill and those kids. I'm hoping she'll show up at my gig next weekend. I invited her."

Carol's eyes rolled. "Wow. So, Mr. Hotshot is going to charm the pants off Miss D'Amico and get her to talk to you in bed."

"That's the plan, exactly."

She burst out laughing. "My God, Jimmy. You're a piece of work. 'High Renaissance.' Gimme a fucking break."

I drove Carol home, a small Claremont bungalow on College Avenue wedged between old wooden two-story houses. Her house probably was built for the help in the old days. Pulling into her driveway, I flushed a raccoon from its perch on a nearby trash can. The time was tickling 2 a.m., a fingernail moon hung in the sky.

"You're not mad at me, right?" I had to ask.

"No. We were freelancing. Nothing ventured, nothing gained. Anyway, I'm off tomorrow." Carol unfolded a napkin I hadn't noticed on her lap. Inside was a hash brownie. "I guess I'm a little hungry after all."

It was my turn to laugh. "Okay, kid. Don't do anything I wouldn't do."

I headed for home, thinking about Allie, wondering if I was out of my mind for wanting her.

****

4 a.m., sitting out on my deck, unsettled and sleepless; what in God's name was I up to? Allessandra D'Amico was a radical college student who'd likely shacked up with the bomber two years before. She needed to be interviewed, not wooed. I could pretend this little charade was for work, like I'd told Carol, but that was bullshit. Something about Allie had burned through all my usual defense mechanisms. I wanted her to like me, to respect me. Even though I wasn't sure I liked her... she'd called me a pig. But I wanted her, right this very second, in my arms. That Mona Lisa face, breasts straining against the sweater, tight jeans. Christ. I was getting aroused like a high school kid.

"Okay, Jimmy, enough of this nonsense," I said out loud, pacing the deck. It was precisely this type of confusion I sought to avoid with the ladies, choosing bachelorhood and meaningless encounters instead. I finished my bottle of Coors, threw the empty into the metal trash can where it smashed to pieces, and went inside. It was all academic, anyway. Allie wasn't going to show up at the gig next weekend. I breathed a sigh of relief that was weighed down by sadness. Maybe I'd been lonely for so long I didn't know the difference.

CHAPTER SIX

THE CALL CAME IN late Wednesday afternoon, Laurie yelling out, "Jailbreak at Glen Helen! Jailbreak at Glen Helen! All deputies report to the West Fontana substation ASAP."

I grabbed my gear, including my shotgun, and hightailed it. As we filed into the Fontana squad room, Undersheriff Sam Fuller moved to the podium. Sam was my mentor in this business, the best cop I knew. There was an actual sheriff out there somewhere, a numb-nuts politician we almost never saw, but Sam, in the number two job, ran the show for San Bernardino and had for my twelve years with the department. He began the briefing.

"Listen up. Three armed men wearing masks stormed the Glen Helen facility at lunchtime today just when the shift was changing. They shot one guard in the leg and got the others to lay face-down in the holding area. Using the guard's keys, they busted three guys out and left in two military-style jeeps. Only three inmates—that was their dumb mistake in an otherwise well-planned operation." Sam shook his head. "If they'd let more guys out, we wouldn't know what this was about. Now we do. Show the pictures," he said to the projectionist. "Based on some damn fast research by our crime library folks, we believe these might be the geniuses who broke them out."

The faces of three men flashed on the screen behind Sam.

"Jesus, I know those guys," one of the deputies yelled out. "That's Booger Willis."

I knew them too. The men were well-known "gearheads," guys who hung out at the Fontana Drag Strip, less than a mile from this substation. When they weren't under the hoods of dragsters or racing stock cars on Foothill at three in the morning, these miscreants were dealing hard drugs, heroin and especially methamphetamine—speed freaks in more ways than one.

Other faces flashed on the screen, the mug shots of the escapees. Same deal, gearheads. "We've got a pile of photos to take with you," Sam said. "So, haul ass, work your sources, and find them."

"Sam, what if they're in Mexico already?" another of the squad asked.

"Could be, but we're on this pretty quick. If it was the Hells Angels, I'd be worried. But these fellows are not that sharp. My guess is they'll split up and go underground right here in county, or maybe try to reach Death Valley. Their pictures will be everywhere, including tonight's television news."

As I started to leave, Sam called me over. "Jimmy, work with Hank Files on this. No solo stuff. These men are dangerous as hell now that they've put their foot in it."

"Okay, Boss. As long as I don't have to eat with him. He's a real pig." What was I going to say? Files was a racist and borderline psycho. But since the perps were white, I didn't expect too much trouble with Hank. And he was good in a fight. Sometimes he'd even bite guys.

"Good," Sam said. "Pick up Sergeant Files at the drag strip, and you guys stick to the Rancho Cucamonga area, especially the mountains. They might be up there."

****

Hank Files and I spent the next two days hitting every car repair joint, beer dive, and greasy spoon in the region, showing the photos and coming up empty. Hank was well-behaved, except when he kicked one of his snitches in the balls for disrespect. A great new cop movie had come out late last year, *The French Connection*, starring Gene Hackman as a wild, violent New York cop named Popeye Doyle. I liked the movie, but Files loved it—kept raving about it. Clearly, he thought of himself as a West Coast version of Popeye Doyle. My tastes ran more to Steve McQueen in *Bullitt*.

After eating at a taco joint on Saturday afternoon—Hank insisted, then spilled red sauce on his shirt—we caught a break. One of my informants had called Laurie at the office with a tip. "Tell Jimmy to look for a red Ford 150 truck up in Ice House Canyon, at one of those stone houses. It might be them."

We drove up Baldy Road, parking at the old inn, which was now closed, maybe for good. Our band had played there last year before the owner went broke. Hank and I walked fifty yards back into the canyon. There were five or six old stone houses scattered in the scruffy forest, all deserted. A red Ford truck was tucked in behind one of the houses, right where my snitch said. It might be nothing, a couple having a romantic interlude or kids smoking dope, but I didn't want to take any chances.

"Hank, go back to the car, call for backup, and then try to get behind the house, in those pepper trees." We had walkie-talkies. "Give me a 10-4 when you're set up." He moved off, staying low.

He called in ten minutes later, all set. But we must have spooked them. Two rifle shots rang out over my head. Getting shot at really pisses me off. It had only happened a few times and, unlike TV shows, most of these jerks were bad shots. I'd never been hit and wanted to keep it that way. I moved behind some larger boulders and stayed down.

I had my shotgun trained on the front entrance to the stone house. It was not the ideal weapon at thirty yards, but it was all I had. Files had the tear gas canister and planned to fire it into the house, if needed, when the backup units showed up. Unfortunately, Ice House Canyon was a long way from anyplace, so we waited. If the sons-of-bitches inside the hut got antsy and moved early, we'd have a gunfight on our hands, a damn cowboy movie.

The bad guys' house was in a little bowl below my position, which was good. I didn't know how many of them were in there, and hopefully they didn't know there were only two of us.

"Hey, cop," a rough voice yelled. "We've got a hostage. Drive off, and we'll let her go."

"Let me see her," I yelled back.

A young woman in cut-off jeans and a skimpy halter top appeared at the doorway and did an awkward pirouette. She stood there squinting into the sun until a tattooed arm pulled her back in. "Satisfied?" Rough Voice asked.

Actually, no. Somebody should have told her that grinning—like she was at a picnic—and happily displaying her impressive figure was not appropriate hostage behavior. Most likely, the "hostage" was a girlfriend. Still, I had to respect what the man said, especially if these idiots were all cranked up on speed.

"What do you want? Money? A plane to Cuba? Justice for Oppressed Rednecks?" Trying to buy time.

"Just drive the fuck off, asshole," was his response. So much for small talk.

So far there were two of them, a gearhead and his girl. I figured there were more. "I can't leave until the boss says

I can. I'm just a deputy, man, not some kind of bigshot. How many of you in there?"

"None of your business." Muzzle flashes: four more shots over my head. Two shooters.

Shit! I fired my shotgun, two shells, ten yards wide of the house and away from where Files should be.

"What're you doing?" Hank's voice crackled over the walkie-talkie.

"Keeping them pinned down," I replied. "There're at least two armed men in there."

There were no more shots. Then I heard tires crunching on the gravel, as our backup units arrived, including Undersheriff Sam Fuller. Sam crouch-walked over to the my boulders.

"You think I'm going to miss all the fun?" He narrowed his eyes and stared at the now quiet house. I quickly filled him in and he nodded. "Is Sergeant Files in position behind the house?"

"Yeah. He's got a tear gas launcher."

Another deputy crawled up to Sam. "The LA County Special Armor Unit contacted us. Do we want them here?"

"Hell no," Sam scoffed. "This is our collar." He turned on his megaphone. "You, in there. Come out with your hands up immediately. Let's get this over with and nobody gets hurt."

"We've got a hostage," Rough Voice yelled back.

"Bullshit. She's your girlfriend, Booger. Time to give it up."

Two more gunshots, and a stinging pain erupted in my right temple. I reached up and felt blood, but not much. It wasn't a bullet wound, or I'd be dead.

Sam turned and checked me out. "A ricochet. Enough of this nonsense. Tell Files to hit them with the gas."

I gave Hank the order. We heard the bazooka shot

and a metal cylinder flew out from behind the house. He'd angled it wrong.

"Holy shit!" Sam cried.

The tear gas canister missed the house completely and landed about twenty yards in front of our position. With the prevailing wind, the gas was blowing right at us. I stepped from behind the rocks, a bad idea, and got a blast of gas right in the face. I could barely see, my eyes were burning so bad, and I was about to puke. Fucking Files!

I hit the deck, giving the gearheads a smaller target, and rolled to my right toward a small pine tree. Then I took aim and blasted the tear gas canister with my shotgun. I'd spent my youth shooting at cans and the same rules applied here. The canister would move.

The result was even better than I'd anticipated. Not only did the canister get blown away from us, it bounced into the bowl surrounding the shooters' house and clunked down a set of old cement steps. Lo and behold, the canister rolled right inside the opening. Nothing but net! A shot I couldn't replicate if I tried all day.

"Great shooting, Jimmy!" Sam hollered and clapped me on the shoulder when I scrambled back behind the boulders. We could see the gas enveloping the enclosed house space. If anything, the holes made by the shotgun pellets made the device even more toxic.

"Don't shoot! We're coming out." And they did. Two shooters, two of the men who had led the jailbreak, and two girls. A double date gone wrong.

That was the end of it for me. Hank drove me to Pomona Valley General Hospital for treatment, apologizing all the way for the missed tear gas shot. First, I got my burning eyes washed out, but the left one was red and itched like crazy. The doc stuck an eyepatch over it to keep me from scratching it. The gouge to my right temple was messy and full of dirt, requiring five stitches to close up. The doc said to watch out for infection. I started to relax, helped by the pills, and then remembered. Christ! I needed to get to the gig!

****

I showed up at The Corral fifteen minutes before show time, looking like a pirate with a black eyepatch covering my left eye and a butterfly bandage on my right temple. "You should see the other guy," I told our bass player, who just grunted. Nothing fazed him.

Tom Sokoloski looked at my face. "What the hell happened to you?"

"Long story, I'm pretty messed up. Play 'Grapevine,'" I told him. "No fiddle leads tonight." They'd pumped me full of painkillers, more than I needed for the stitches. Sokoloski and I had been playing together in one band or another for almost ten years. We didn't socialize away from the band but trusted each other completely on stage. He was Salton Sea's sex object, the lead guitar player with long, flowing blond hair that was always spilling into his face. I never knew how he managed that, but boy could he play, everything from Eric Clapton to Chet Atkins, clean as a whistle.

Shaky as hell, I'd almost passed on the gig, except, of course, *she* might show up. It had been a good week to deal with a jailbreak. Otherwise, I might have obsessed over Allie the entire time. By now I'd convinced myself that the whole thing was a joke, an illusion. Allessandra D'Amico had no interest whatsoever in me. She was this fine-boned radical angel—probably a spoiled rich kid— who detested everything I stood for, especially law and order, which meant I didn't much like her either. She was likely in Malibu hanging out with movie stars, or running guns in from Mexico, or marching with the farmworkers in the valley. Anyplace but a small rock club watching a spaced-out, wounded, off-duty deputy sheriff trying to execute the simplest rhythm chords on his fiddle, and failing.

Later, toward the end of the set, I saw her, standing alone in back, leaning against a wooden post. Her black hair was down, flowing over the blue work shirt that topped her white jeans. My fugue state vanished. I signaled Sokoloski and mouthed *Orange Blossom Special*. We often did a rocked-up version of the old bluegrass standard. He looked puzzled, given my earlier malaise, but then shrugged. We hit it full stream. Ten minutes later, I was sweaty and exhilarated. I'd played the song better than I ever had. For her.

The set ended and I sought out Allie. She came up to me, gave me a quick hug. "That was groovy."

"Thanks." I'm normally pretty good at a glib, "aw shucks" style that works with the ladies, at least at first. That was out the window. Tonight, I was speechless, standing there like a dope. The silence was louder than the music.

A look of irritation, or maybe embarrassment, crossed her face. "Well, it was good to see you," she said, starting to turn away.

"No, please stay. I got shot in the face today with a rock which, together with the tear gas, has me kind of out of it." Shit! The last thing I wanted to talk about was the job, but it just spilled out.

She turned back to me and smiled. Have I mentioned her smile? It can light up even a dingy joint like The Corral. "Well, all I did today was work on a history paper," she said. "No tear gas."

Wow.

After the second set, we went to a coffee house in Upland and talked and talked, mostly about rock music with some European art thrown in. The previous October, my sister and I had taken our mother to Italy, a life-long dream of hers. It was part of the cheer-up-Mom-on-account-of-Dad-being-dead plan. We did the Rome/Florence/Venice tour, and I'd liked it way more than I'd anticipated.

My Italian journey was paying dividends now with Allie, an art history major at Pomona. She'd been to all those places more than once—a rich girl. We avoided three subjects, her politics, my job, and particularly a bomber named Richard Manning. It was time to pop the question.

"Would you like to come up to my place? I live in Palmer Canyon."

She hesitated, gave a quick shake of her head, and then touched the bandage on my forehead. "You better go home and get some rest."

As we walked to our cars, I was struggling again, not sure what to say. She bailed me out. "When's your next gig?"

"Back at The Corral next Saturday night. The pay sucks but it's steady, every Saturday this month and next."

"How about I come see you next Saturday night? Pretend I'm your special groupie."

"If you were my special groupie, we'd be on our way to my place." Her face clouded. I'd made a mistake.

"Unless you also were a deputy sheriff investigating my former lover."

"Allie—"

"I know less than you think, by the way. Richard was a mystery to me, too, especially his fucking bombs. See you next week. I'll be there—I think—but don't you dare crowd me." She turned away to leave, then paused, came back, and kissed me, her lips lingering. "See ya, cowboy."

I watched the taillights on her Fiat fading into the distance, searching for clues, coming up empty. I didn't even know where she lived or how she lived. She came at me like magic, and then disappeared.

Everything began to hurt when I went to bed. I'd barely noticed the cuts on my arms from rolling through the rocks and gravel to get a shot at the canister. The hospital drugs had worn off and the aspirin I'd taken an hour before wasn't working. I rolled out of bed, grabbed a Budweiser out of the refrigerator, and dragged a sleeping bag out onto the deck, thinking the cool mountain air might help. I lay there looking up at the Big Dipper.

I could tell that Allie saw through me. She knew that sooner or later I was going to try and steal her secrets. It was a cop's disease. And I knew that she would resist me, with fury. It was her nature. But the kiss stayed with me all night and was still there when I woke up.

CHAPTER SEVEN

I WENT OUT FOR a late breakfast the next day. The Sunday *Pomona Progress Bulletin* carried a fairly detailed account of our capture of the gearheads and their molls. Had that only been yesterday? The story included a quote from Undersheriff Sam Fuller regarding "Sergeant Sommes's remarkable shot redirecting the tear gas canister into the stone house." Good on the resume at salary review time.

One of my sins is that of pride. I just love to see my name in the paper, can't get enough of it. Some folks I knew came over to my table, offering their congratulations. I enjoyed the attention. It *was* one hell of a shot. But thoughts of Allie kept nagging at me, both good and bad. I wasn't used to having a woman in my head like this. I'd wanted her in my bed last night. But she'd said she was coming to the gig next week... so maybe soon. Did I even like her, a campus radical? Well, yeah. She'd gotten to me, big-time.

****

Monday was all business. In the morning, there was a mountain of paperwork to be prepared as a result of our arrest of the gearheads, and I appeared at their arraignment on Monday afternoon, still sporting my bandages. The other offenders had been rounded up over the weekend without incident. Attempted murder was added to the other charges against Booger Willis and his partner on account of their rifle shots at me. The entire SBSD looked good, except for the prison employees who had allowed the break-in. They were in big trouble. Heads might roll.

After the hearing, I got some good-natured ribbing and attaboys from the other deputies, and even some of the lawyers, at the courthouse. Before I could leave, the bailiff told me I had a call. It was Carol.

"Hey, you're famous, man," she said. "Seriously, that was good work, Jimmy."

"Thanks. Yeah, me and Wyatt Earp. *Have Gun, Will Travel.*"

"That was Paladin, Richard Boone, not Earp. Anyway, did your friend show up on Saturday night?"

I couldn't help but sigh. "You wanna meet me at Marie Callender's tonight? I'll buy you a frozen margarita, or three."

"The answer is yes to the margaritas. Does that mean the lady failed to appear?"

"No. It means she showed up. I need a drink, and some advice."

"Okay. See you there at 6:30."

****

I was downing shots of Cuervo Gold, sucking on limes, and topping off with Corona chasers. Frozen margaritas had seemed a little feminine to me, especially since my manhood had taken a hit over the weekend. The result was the same though. Carol and I both were getting loaded on good tequila while I ran off my mouth about Ice House Canyon, then Allie. Part celebration, part confusion.

"Okay," Carol said after finishing her third margarita, "let's accept as a working hypothesis that you're an asshole."

"Hey, that's rude."

"I mean with women. You're so proud of your bachelor ways, of being so tough, invulnerable. Welcome to the real world. This chick just blew your cover. I need to pee."

Carol wandered off to the ladies' room, taking the scenic route. The restaurant had just opened, and the whole town was raving about the margaritas. I watched her getting lost, asking for directions to the bathroom, never losing her dignity or sense of humor. Too bad I didn't love her, and vice versa. Nobody else understood me at all. I downed another shot of tequila. In my experience, tequila had certain illuminating properties, somewhere between booze and those illegal psychedelic drugs I chose not to use. But everybody needed illumination on occasion. I realized I had been running at the mouth, better go home soon.

"I'm sorry if I sounded harsh," Carol said upon returning. "I'm not going to give you any advice about your love life. Look at me, Miss Lonely Hearts. But what are we good at, great at, in fact? Working. Investigating. We both do better when we're working."

"So what?"

"So, if there's a mad bomber out there, somebody that the entire goddamn law enforcement community has failed to find, then let's you and me find the bastard and nail him."

We left it at that and called it a night. Carol hadn't really helped me with my Allie issue, but it was my problem, not her's, and she was dead right about the work.

****

Al Sevilla of the Los Angeles County Sheriff's Department called me back a few days later, offering to show me the Richard Manning file. Carol and I were on the way to meet him at the LASD San Dimas office. Neither of us had anything real pressing at work so it was easy to sneak off. It was pouring rain, a cold, gray February day.

"They're going to build a freeway right through here." I gestured toward the surroundings. We were traveling west where Baseline Road and Foothill come together, mostly residential but some farms were still hanging on. "Too many houses already."

"So, you're the big environmentalist now?" Carol asked.

"Nope. I just like things the way they are. How do you want to play this with Sevilla? We've had our differences. He thinks I'm an Okie from Muskogee." Which I was, sort of. My parents had moved to California from Tulsa when I was a little kid.

"No problem. I'll take the lead. Al's about your age, old man, and he likes me. He thinks I'm cute."

"Good."

"Not good. I'm sick of being cute. I want to be feared, like Dirty Harry, the guy in that new movie."

I groaned. "Don't start me on him. He's a bad cop, makes rookie mistakes all the time. In the real world, he's dead."

"But he's feared."

"Only in that movie. Could we get back to Sevilla? How do we play it?"

"Nothing fancy," Carol said, "just information. We know that he and his partner, Ed Charles, the guy who retired, were building a case against Manning when the second bomb went off. So, let's see what they've got."

Al Sevilla, in a blue LASD poncho, was waiting for us at the front door. The entire Sam Dimas office consisted of one floor in a small office building, a far cry from the Hollywood glamour of the main LASD headquarters in Los Angeles. Sevilla ushered us into a cramped conference room, looking at his watch, already impatient. Two files were on the table. He saw my reaction and said, "Remember the FBI took this away from us the day after the woman got killed, and they haven't shared much since. And," he gave me a look, "Manning is rotting away in jail, so who gives a shit. Don't you guys have enough real police work to do?"

"Maybe not as much as you, Al," Carol said. "We're reacting to a tip we got so we can put it to bed, okay?"

He left us to it. We each grabbed a file. Mine contained the early stuff, nothing new. Carol was studying her file, taking notes. She was great at research, lived for it.

"Hmm. Ed Charles tried to talk to a certain Allessandra D'Amico," Carol said. "She hung up on him. At least she's consistent." Carol gave a whistle. "Did you know that Jason Phillips represented Richard Manning at the time of his arrest?"

"Makes sense, but I didn't know," I said. Phillips was a legend in Claremont. Local boy made good, high school football star, scholarship to Dartmouth, Rhodes Scholar, and then Yale Law School. After a spell at a big Los Angeles law firm, Phillips chose instead to represent the poor, the downtrodden, and the Black Panthers. His Justice for All Clinic was located in Claremont village. He was lefty as could be; he hung out with people like Jane Fonda.

Sevilla returned thirty minutes later. It was time for us to go. But I had one last thing I had to check off my list.

"Seems Ed Charles isn't doing so great, drinking a lot," I told his ex-partner. "Any help he can get from LASD?"

Sevilla shrugged. "He turned it down, won't see a counselor or social worker. Said to bring him a case of beer instead."

Pretty much what I'd expected. But I kept pushing.

"Do you think somebody could check in on him once in a while?"

"I stop by to see him every couple of weeks," Sevilla told me, glancing at his watch.

"Right, I figured you would. Let me know if you need any help."

"Okay. Thanks, man," Sevilla said, the tone more friendly.

"Now that wasn't so hard, was it?" Carol asked me as we hurried through the rain back to the car. "Playing well with others. There's hope for you yet."

Halfway back to Claremont, I pulled off the road into a Vons supermarket parking lot. Something about this case was really bugging me. I kept the engine on, the windshield wipers slapping at the rain.

"What's up?" Carol asked.

"Manning has clammed up from day one, right? Except for his political speeches. He says he won't talk to any pigs, the system is corrupt, and so forth. But assuming, for just a moment, that somebody else did the second bombing—the murder—he's risking the gas chamber for no reason. He could plead out on the attempted murder charge from the first bombing, get it bumped down to some sort of felony assault, do his time, get out on parole, and still have a life."

"But he doesn't think like that," Carol said. "I did some reading. He wants his case transferred to the World Court in Europe—The Hague, wherever the hell that is—says he's a political prisoner. Of course, the Federal Court said no, but the case is a mess, all gummed up, lawyers for everybody filing appeals. That's why this case never goes anywhere."

"And that's my point," I said. "Manning just sits there at the Federal Detention facility not helping his 'revolution' one bit. It doesn't add up." I had an idea. "Why don't we pay a visit to Jason Phillips, Esquire, and ask him what he thinks?"

"He won't talk to us."

"Only one way to find out." I pulled out of the parking lot and got back on Foothill. We were ten minutes away from his office.

"You've heard the stories, right? About Phillips," Carol said, running a comb through her wet hair.

"Wild parties up in Padua, the television actress, what's her name?"

"Beverly Edwards, on that western show. She OD'd on coke in his pool house, lucky to be alive. I was on vacation, visiting my parents, or I would have taken the call."

"Who caught the case?" I asked.

"Our patrol officers. I think the mayor even showed up. Phillips was a campaign contributor. And somehow Phillips made the whole case go away, no charges against him, probation for her. And Beverly Edwards is still driving that wagon train on Saturday nights, just before *The Mary Tyler Moore Show*."

"You watch too much television," I said.

****

The Justice for All Clinic occupied a storefront office on Yale Avenue in Claremont, right next to the drug store. I parallel parked right in front, and we went in. There were posters on the wall, some political, Cesar Chavez and Bobby Seale, and some not, Bob Dylan in a leather jacket riding a motorcycle and Robert Redford as the Sundance Kid. A former girlfriend of mine had put that Redford poster on a wall directly above her bathtub, him staring down on her naked body. So, I disliked the guy.

A machine spitting out punch cards stood in the middle of the large open room next to a portable copier. "FREE ANGELA DAVIS" bumper stickers were stacked on a table in front of us. Young people milled around. Carol was in uniform, and I looked like a cop in my blue sports jacket. Nobody gave us the time of day.

I was thinking about firing my revolver at their ceiling to get some service—except I didn't want to kill some accountant on the second floor—when a woman came out of a side door and approached us. She was tall, with a raw-boned look to her, abetted by blue jeans, leather boots, and a maroon western shirt. What kind of law firm was this?

She looked us both over then directed her words to Carol. "Hi, I'm Annie Hoover, the office manager. Can I help you with something?"

"Sure. I'm Carol and this is Jimmy. We're police officers, but sort of off-duty, and wondered if Jason Phillips is available."

The woman, still looking at Carol, did something fast with her eyes, almost like a wink, but more personal. Then she smiled, and it softened her face. "Sort of off-duty... that's a new one. Anyway, Jason's not here. He's trekking to Machu Picchu. He'll be back in ten days. Is there anything I can help you with?"

I knew that Machu Picchu was an Incan ruin in South America, and decided to pitch in, to be friendly, part of this "playing well with others" thing. "Wow, it must be freezing down there."

The woman gave Carol a "Who's the dumb shit with you" look and said to me, "Actually, it's summer in Peru."

So much for that.

"Can we talk someplace privately?" Carol asked. Annie nodded and they walked off. I wasn't sure if I was invited but went anyway. The woman directed us into her office, and we all sat down. Carol got right to it.

"Although it's technically an FBI matter, we're looking into the Richard Manning case, the Claremont bombings. That's what I meant by sort of off-duty. We just learned that Mr. Phillips represented Mr. Manning at the time of his arrest."

Annie gave this some thought before saying, "That's a matter of public record, so I can confirm it. Jason helped Mr. Manning get through the initial arrest and arraignment process so as to guard against any government misconduct. The FBI can be very aggressive. After that, Mr. Manning's defense went to the McMasters firm in Los Angeles."

Everybody knew who McMasters was. He'd been part of the Chicago Seven defense team in Chicago, defending Abbie Hoffman. Then I noticed the diploma on the wall in Annie's office. Annie Hoover had graduated from Stanford Law School five years before. Appearances can be deceiving. She looked like a Bakersfield rodeo rider, not a lawyer. I jumped in.

"Look, we're hearing some rumors about the second bombing, that maybe Manning didn't do it. What do you say to that?"

Her face was impassive. "Nothing, of course. Mr. Manning is not guilty of either bombing as far as we are concerned, until the government proves otherwise and convinces a jury." She turned to Carol, dismissing me. "Although we no longer represent Mr. Manning, nobody in this office, including Mr. Phillips, would dream of talking to law enforcement about this matter. You must know that. Is there anything else?"

"Thank you," Carol said, getting up. "I appreciate the work you do here, the Alvarez case, restoring their voting rights." She handed Annie her card. "I work just a block over, on Harvard Avenue. Could you let Mr. Phillips know we came by when he returns?"

The two of them shook hands. I just left.

"That was a waste of time," I said as we hit the sidewalk.

"Don't be too sure of that. Look, I'd better get back to the office before the mayor gets back from his chiropractor appointment. I'll walk."

Off she went, disregarding the chilly rain. Was there a spring to her step that hadn't been there before? Maybe. I headed back to my Alta Loma station, going east on Baseline this time, wondering what the bad guys were up to. It was always something. Then I had another idea.

CHAPTER EIGHT

ED CHARLES HAD MENTIONED to me at Bodene's that he'd had an inside source for SDS information back at the time of the bombings, in 1970. This was confirmed in Al Sevilla's notes and now I had a name, Alan Jacobs. He was now a senior at Pomona College. I'd gotten his phone number, but not his address, from Pomona's registrar, who did this for me as a favor since she knew my mother from church. I gave Mr. Jacobs a call and told him the reason for my call.

"That's all behind me now," he said. "I'm graduating this June, then going to law school." He sounded nervous.

"Fine by me, Mr. Jacobs," I said. "I just want to have a little chat about the old days, about your bomber friend, Richard Manning."

"Christ, he wasn't my friend. I never even talked to him. I was just a flunky, bringing them wine and coffee at the meetings."

"That means our meeting will be short. Where do you live?"

"No. Not here. My, uh, girlfriend doesn't know I hung out with those guys. Meet me at Betsy Ross Ice Cream Parlor on Foothill tomorrow at noon. I want to get this over with." He hung up.

I called Carol. It was the day after our meeting with Annie Hoover at the Justice for All Clinic. "You want a hot fudge sundae? My treat."

"Why?"

"Because I'm meeting Ed Charles's snitch there tomorrow at noon. The SDS guy that knew Richard Manning."

"Hell, yes. See you there."

I hadn't been to the old-fashioned ice cream parlor in years.

****

Carol and I each ordered a hot fudge sundae, more for the idea of it than anything else. Alan Jacobs looked startled when he walked through the door at Betsy Ross, not expecting to see two of us. I waved and he came to join us at a corner booth facing out toward Foothill. I introduced Carol, said she was much nicer than me, and asked him if he wanted a sundae.

"No thanks. Just coffee." He gave us an odd smile, more like a grimace. "I actually picked this place since nobody that knows me would think to come here."

"Fair enough, us too." I signaled the waitress, and she brought a pot of coffee for the table. Jacobs lit a Marlboro and that seemed to settle him down some. Carol did likewise to keep him company. I got back to it.

"As I mentioned over the phone, Detective Loomis here and I are taking a fresh look at the1970 Claremont bombings and—"

"I made the call fingering Manning," Jacobs blurted out. "I should have identified myself, but I was pretty freaked out. Not sure what to do. The whole SDS thing, it was a mistake. My sole concern was, and is, that I'm against this fucking war, but they were wrong too, the radicals." His hands were shaking.

"Alan—can I call you that?" Carol actually patted the kid's hand. "That's very valuable information that you just gave us, about the call. You're not in any trouble with us. So why don't you tell us how you got to know Richard Manning?"

"Like I told him," Jacobs pointed at me, "I started hanging around the grad school, going to the SDS office, handing out leaflets, stuff like that, after Nixon's Cambodia invasion."

Jacobs actually hadn't told me any of that but no matter.

He went on. "They had lots of meetings, the radicals, mostly talking about tactics and targets, like going after ROTC. Anybody could come to the meetings, 'the more the merrier,' they said. So that was me, figuring out what I could do to stop the war."

Jacobs paused to drink some coffee. "Then that first bombing happened, at Pomona, my school, and I began to have my doubts, not about the war, but about Manning and his crazy friends."

"Is that when you contacted Ed Charles at the LA Sheriff's Department?" I asked.

A bunch of noisy kids entered the ice cream parlor, all excited, and headed toward a party room. Jacobs paused to let them pass through and then answered me. "Yeah. I'm a criminal justice major, planning to go to UCLA Law School next fall if they let me in, Loyola if they don't. I'd interviewed Detective Charles for a class assignment earlier that year and decided to call him. I'm not sure that was right either." Jacobs hesitated. "Like I said, nothing made any sense to me back then. It's not like I really knew anything, but I did tell him about the planned sit-in at the ROTC building. It was no big secret."

"We heard there were factions among the radicals, the pro-violence and anti-violence groups. Is that right?" Carol asked.

"Yeah, a Martin Luther King versus Malcolm X type

57

of thing. Richard Manning was the big 'let's take it to the pigs' guy. Along with some others. But most wanted to keep it peaceful, disruptive as hell but non-violent. Then Manning stopped coming to the meetings, went 'underground,' somebody said."

Carol made a show of looking through her notebook. "Was there a woman with Manning at these earlier meetings? We have a name, Allessandra D'Amico."

"Allie was one of the leaders," Jacobs said, "especially after Manning left, but, you know, she was way too cool for me. She was like this foxy radical chick, really sure of herself, and she intimidated me. Still does, to tell you the truth. We have a class together this semester."

I was tempted to say that I knew what he meant, but held my tongue.

"Okay, Alan," Carol said. "You've told us today that it was you who called in the anonymous tip about Manning, just before the second bombing, as it turned out."

Jacobs really smiled this time. "I've been in some plays in high school, even here at Pomona. So, I called Ed Charles and did my best Marlon Brando *On The Waterfront* 'I coulda been a contender' voice. All I really said was check out Richard Manning, he might have done it."

"So, you didn't have any hard information that Manning set off the first Pomona bomb, is that right?" I asked him. "And why anonymous, since you were acquainted with Detective Charles?"

"I was fingering a very scary character to the cops, so I didn't want my name anywhere near it. But you're correct, I didn't have any evidence that he did it. But he was so extreme that the cops needed to look at him. He talked about bombs being a good tactic."

We drank coffee while Carol and Alan smoked their cigarettes, and then we thanked him for his time. Off he went, obviously glad to be free of us. Our sundaes had melted into congealed messes at the bottom of the tall glasses. Carol plucked the cherry off hers and ate it. "He's a somewhat confused character," she said.

"Yeah, perfect for a defense attorney. That ties up some loose ends, not much else." I gave Carol a look while waving away all the smoke. "Thanks for the Allie question, by the way."

"My pleasure, Sergeant Sommes. We needed to know."

She was right.

****

"Shoes, fucking shoes," Allie muttered as she reached over my body for her glass of wine on the windowsill, her breasts brushing my arm, setting off another electric charge inside me. "That's the only reason a second-generation wop like me gets to go to Pomona College and study art history."

"You better explain that," I said, not really caring about the answer, but she was edgy as hell and needed to talk. Allie had come to my gig earlier tonight and said "yes" this time to my invitation to come to my cabin. We'd gone straight to bed. The sex had been basic and fast, but really good. No talking until now.

"Simple," Allie said. "Rich women in Beverly Hills and New York City, and even Milan, like to wear D'Amico black leather pumps when they lunch with their friends at the club and D'Amico stiletto heels when they attend the opera later that evening."

"Wow, that's you." Even I had heard of those fancy women's shoes.

"Yup. None other than." She lit another of her smelly cigarettes, unfiltered Camels, and said, "Everything I hate about capitalism, and look who wins. Me."

"Why Camels?" I asked, fanning away the smoke.

"Because they're strong. Just like you, cowboy." She reached down and gave me a little tweak that set off the electricity again. Not quite a full recharge but still...

"I don't even like horses," I said, reaching for her.

She pulled away, slightly. "You know, I tried to stay away from you, and couldn't," she said, "which pisses me off. Lack of control. But then I decided it's not your fault you're a pig." She smiled attempting to soften the words.

I shook my head. "Not even in fun, Allie. I hate that word."

"Nobody's ever accused me of saying the right thing," she said. "I better go." She got out of bed and grabbed her panties, jeans, and blouse all scattered on the floor beside the bed and dressed in the blink of an eye. "See you next week."

I watched her, unsure what to do. "Let me walk you—"

"No, don't move," she said. "This is good, you know, you and me. I just have to go slow, slow, and be careful."

"Okay," I answered as she left. As I lay there in the tangle of sheets, Allie's scents all over me, I felt like the one with no control, but I wasn't fighting it too hard either.

Later, I found a rolled-up dollar bill and a dusty hand mirror on the sink in my bathroom. In her haste to leave, she'd left them behind. Cocaine. It didn't make me happy. But I still wanted to see her next weekend. She was affecting me like a drug.

CHAPTER NINE

WHOEVER THREW THE BRICK through the windshield of Detective Carol Loomis's Chevy Bel Air was a supreme idiot. Carol had walked out on a sunny Sunday morning to get the newspaper and had seen the damage to her beloved car. She called me immediately and I went over to offer moral support and check it out.

She'd preserved the scene and also taken some photographs. The brick was in the front passenger seat, covered with shards of glass. A note was attached to the brick with a rubber band. In childish block letters, it said, "LAY OFF THE MANNING CASE."

Two weeks had passed since we'd gone to the Justice for All Clinic, and Jason Phillips hadn't contacted us. I didn't expect him to. I hadn't gotten any further with questions about the Manning bombing and had begun to mentally put it on the back burner. Then this.

"I don't know if the mayor will authorize payment for this damage," Carol sighed. "He's such a prick."

I could feel eyes from inside the big houses on either side of Carol's bungalow watching us as we surveyed the scene. "Just what have you been up to?" I asked. "Nobody's thrown any warning messages through *my* windshield."

"You're not the only one with natural curiosity," she said. "I went over to the grad school this week, told them I was doing an annual report on the bombings for my boss, and interviewed some folks."

"I'm guessing your boss, the honorable mayor of Claremont, had not asked for said report."

"Well, duh," Carol said. "Aren't you a smart guy?"

"Hey, don't blame me. I didn't throw that brick."

"Sorry. I'm just really pissed off. This is the car I drive for work, so I figure they'll pay, don't you?"

"Yes, and more importantly, Madame Investigator, you've struck a nerve with somebody."

"I'm not sure that's more important," Carol said, pulling her hair back into a short ponytail, "but I'm sure as hell going to keep looking now. I'm mad, not scared."

Carol was a bulldog, and I was going to help her. "You better call the FBI," I said. After all, it was their case.

****

The FBI blew her off, not interested at all, she reported when she called to tell me the news on Monday. "Some guy sounding so bored he might nod off right during the call said, 'Thank you, ma'am, that case is concluded,' like I was a civilian. Jesus, what's with the FBI these days? I'm surprised they catch anybody."

"What about LASD?" I asked, holding the phone tight to my ear. The fire department was moving out on a call, sirens blaring.

"A little better. At least Sevilla wanted copies of the photos I took of the damage, the brick, and the note, so I sent them over."

Carol and I agreed to meet on Friday, as I was in a trial—a particularly nasty child abuse case—until then.

"But not La Paloma. My butt's getting too big," she said, signing off.

I was the chief law enforcement witness in the child abuse trial; a man had engaged in things I could barely imagine a human being doing to two young children. The creep's lawyer went after me, saying I was prejudiced against his client. Damn right, but I had still collected the evidence according to all the rules, gave the pervert his appropriate Miranda rights, and told the truth at trial. How that lawyer could sleep at night was a mystery to me. The perp was convicted on all counts. One for the good guys.

****

Friday was a salad lunch with Carol. We met at an upscale restaurant in Claremont village that seemed to serve very little food. "You order for both of us," I said, not wanting to figure this stuff out.

After Carol did the ordering, she said, "We must be getting somewhere. Nobody would brick my car unless they knew something about the bombings, maybe an accomplice to Manning. The stupidity of criminals never fails to amaze me."

I agreed. "So, what's next?"

"The mayor said the city will pay for a new windshield, but I have to wait until July, the start of next fiscal year, to get my money. They've given me a city-owned loaner until then, a clunky Chevy Nova—no pick-up at all. I better not get into any car chases."

"I mean about the bombing," I said, spooning a mouthful of some type of green garden weed into my mouth. It was topped off with a foul vinegar dressing. Yuck.

"I know that, dumb-ass," Carol said, punching my arm. "I interviewed six people at the grad school last week; the victim's department chair, two secretaries and three other economics professors—one of them is the man that called in the first bombing—and got one good lead. Rebecca Meadows, the one who died in the second bombing, kept to herself, mostly, but sometimes had coffee with Ellen, one of the secretaries."

"And?" I asked, opening my fourth package of unsalted crackers from the complimentary basket that came with our salads.

"A couple of weeks before the bombing, Rebecca complained to Ellen about some creep, an older guy, who wouldn't stop bugging her. She tried to make a joke out of it, saying you know how it's always the guys you don't like who never stop calling, but Ellen sensed that Rebecca was spooked. Unfortunately, that's all Ellen knew, no names or details. Not sure how we look for a nameless creep. What about you, got anything?"

"Not much. During a break in my trial, I called the State Police in Sacramento, where Rebecca grew up. They'd looked into it when she got killed. Not really trusting the FBI." I paused, looked down at the salad, decided I couldn't eat it, and made a face.

"Just like us," Carol said, "not trusting the FBI. They didn't even interview Ellen." She clearly was amused by my discomfort.

"Yeah, anyway, it's puzzling about Rebecca," I continued. "She was an only child, her father worked for the state government as an agricultural inspector, and her mother was a homemaker. They lived on a leafy, middle-class street in Sacramento. Both the parents are dead, natural causes. At school, she was a loner, but there was no indication that she was unhappy. Her entire higher education was at UC, Berkeley. B.S. M.A., and Ph.D., the works. According to my source, all the professors spoke highly of her, but again she kept to herself. Rebecca was a popular mystery woman."

"So, we got zip on the victim," Carol said. "Nobody else at the grad school has even a clue as to why she was killed." She took a fork full from the pile of nameless green stuff on her plate and popped it into her mouth.

I persisted. "Well, we've a creep who was bugging her. And somebody threw a brick through your windshield with a warning to back off. That's a big deal. We also talked to Annie Hoover at that law office. Maybe that set somebody off."

"I doubt it, since Annie's cool," Carol said. "My working assumption is that me nosing around the grad school got somebody nervous."

"Yeah, maybe," I said, not fully agreeing with her. Annie's cool? Where did that come from? "I also made one call to Manning's LA law firm, asking if we could talk to him about the bombings. Got an immediate no. He's not talking to anybody without a subpoena, for which we've got no grounds or jurisdiction. In fact, the lawyer I talked to, some young kid, threatened to call Sam Fuller to complain if I bothered them again. I told the kid lawyer that Sam would put him over his knee and spank him if he did that, so I'd say our call ended in a draw."

"No big deal. We'll work it backwards," Carol said, "when we can."

"What about Jason Phillips?" I asked her.

"He's back from South America but has nothing to add beyond what Annie told us."

I nodded and signaled the waiter and asked for coffee.

"Will that be regular or decaf, sir?"

"Son, decaf coffee is a contradiction in terms," I said. "Gimme the real thing, extra caffeine if you've got it." He scurried off. I tended to go kind of Waylon Jennings country when confronted with uncomfortable things—like everything at this restaurant. Even my chair felt weird, like I'd break through it. The bill came. I handed it to Carol, since I wasn't paying for this.

"By the way, to get paid for the busted windshield, I

had to log it in," Carol said. "Do you want me to leave you out of the reports?"

I gave that some thought. "No. How about I'm assisting you, a fellow officer, with the investigation of a violent assault on your car, and we believe that the perpetrators may frequent the Upland area. It might even be true."

"Works for me," she said, standing. "Gotta run. You might want to try their carob brownie. It's great."

I stayed and finished my coffee but did not order their so-called brownie. Why was Carol so sure that Annie Hoover was *cool*? I remembered the look they'd shared.

Time to roll. My next stop was EZ Burger in Upland for a double cheeseburger. It was right on the way to the station.

CHAPTER TEN

THREE O'CLOCK IN THE morning. Allie was sleeping on her back, one leg draped over me. For such a tough woman, she slept soft, her mouth slightly open. It was our fourth weekend together, each stay getting longer as we built trust, got more relaxed. Thankfully, she'd stopped snorting coke in my bathroom.

I should have been sleeping too, but I didn't want to miss a moment. John Coltrane's *My Favorite Things* was playing low on the stereo. His soprano sax—and Tyner's piano—turning a pretty tune into something complex and powerful, then bringing it back home as a pretty tune again.

Allie graduated in less than two months and already had a job lined up in New York City as an intern with the *Village Voice* newspaper. Her aunt worked there, the only member of her family she liked. After the internship, she was talking about graduate school in Paris, at the Sorbonne. The whole world belonged to her.

Not me. I was rooted, right here in this cabin, in my job, my music, and my places. And I wasn't planning on making any changes.

Allie stirred in her sleep, turning toward me. I loved her body—more than she did. She had a short waist and worried about getting fat. Like most women, she wanted to be skinny. I hated skinny. Allie had beautiful, full breasts and strong hips that I could grab while we made love.

She might get fat. I'd never know. Our brief time was now. She'd said she'd come back to visit me. Maybe she would, once or twice, I thought, and it wouldn't be any good.

I lay there in the dark with her nestled against me, feeling peaceful. Yet, the end of this was coming at me, fast and inexorable, like a hot desert wind. So, I listened to Coltrane, swept in as he played circles within circles within circles within circles... My newly discovered favorite thing was leaving town.

Allie woke me up as the sunlight streamed into the bedroom. "Okay, let's talk about Richard Manning," she said. "I want to get it over with. But I can't do it naked, so you better get up and make me some coffee."

"Yes, ma'am." I was tempted to vote for naked over Manning, but the cop in me won out. I provided the coffee and the donuts, served on the deck. Both of us were wearing sweaters, enjoying the elusive Southern California spring weather.

"This is going to take a while," she warned. "So, no smart-ass comments, please."

I settled back and pretended I was in one of those crummy interview rooms in San Bernardino, listening to a perp telling me a sad story—why he did it—my only questions designed to draw out the tale. Allie sipped her coffee, fired up one of her stinky Camel cigarettes, and began.

"It was February 1970, the start of second semester of my sophomore year. I almost didn't come back to school that fall. My freshman year grades were lousy, mostly C's. My parents were pissed off—especially my dad, complaining about wasting all this money on me. Things were just generally screwed up. One night, feeling restless, I went to a meeting at the Pomona North Quad, and this guy with a red beard was talking, saying really righteous stuff about taking down the establishment. I asked a question about tactics. He fixed his eyes on me. They were wild, like a Russian mystic's or something. I thought he was scary and cool at the same time. But mostly I was ready to hear somebody say we needed a revolution, none of this liberal peace-march bullshit, since it wasn't accomplishing anything." Allie paused

"This was Richard Manning," I said.

"Yeah," she said. "We talked afterwards, that night and into the next day. No sleep. He was a student at the grad school and head of the local Students for a Democratic Society chapter. I joined right away. They had it figured out. I'm still a Democratic Socialist thanks to Richard."

"Did your parents know you joined the SDS?" I asked.

"Sure. They thought, and still think, that my radical views are a phase that I'll grow out of." Allie smiled. "We'll see. Hell, I'm seeing you, an instrument of repression."

"Happy to help," I said.

"Anyway, Richard and I began to hang out, became lovers. After a while, I moved into his cottage in the barrio. But it's not like we were exclusive or anything. He said monogamy was such a bourgeois concept. Also," Allie said, hesitating, "Richard was pretty limited when it came to sex, had some trouble... performing. He asked me once if I would go down on another woman while he watched. I said no way in hell. He didn't push it."

"But you stayed with him?" I asked, glad she'd reminded me about smart-ass comments or that kinky proposal would have drawn one for sure. The image was sticking with me.

"Absolutely. I loved his mind, not his body. I was in the *movement*, man, and we were going to change everything. A peaceful world! No more war. Power to the People. And this wild man said he loved me. It was very exciting."

"And you believed that was possible, a world like that?" I asked, really wanting to know the answer.

"I still do, as an aspiration. We don't have a choice. But violence was the big hang-up. I kept going back and forth on it. Most of us did. Did the ends justify the means? That kind of thing. Richard said it simply had to happen. It's the only thing that the pigs understood: raw power. He kind of dragged me toward that conclusion, but ultimately, I couldn't get there, didn't want to be just like them."

"Like me," I said. I couldn't help it.

"Not like you." She flicked hair out of her face. "Don't interrupt. This is hard. Then Asshole Nixon invaded Cambodia. I don't think I slept for three days. Our actions began at the colleges, including occupying the Administration Building at Claremont Men's College, the most conservative school. The chaplain's building next to the library was home base. It felt like an ocean of change— so many students joining us. It was so intense but also really fun, people passing joints and big jugs of cheap red wine around."

"That would have been my job," I said, "buying the booze for the cadre."

"Yeah, I bet. But when we thought it couldn't get any worse, Kent State happened. Four people, no different from me, murdered by the stupid National Guard soldiers. I couldn't believe it, so crazy—I still can't believe it. After that, it's a total blur," she said. "Benzedrine helped. We never stopped working. Within a week or so, we won a major victory. Claremont College stopped classes in May for the rest of the semester. It was fantastic!"

"Kent State affected me too," I said. "What were those guys thinking, shooting at students?"

"Pure panic is my guess," Allie said. "Anyway, even though there were no classes students here were free to engage in anti-war activity instead of their regular course work. They called it the Renaissance Program. Or they could work with the unions on social issues. It was a big deal, happening at colleges all over the country."

"I remember. What about Richard?" I asked.

"He blew it, began to lose his mind. He should have been happy, or at least excited. All these regular students were joining us, trying to end injustice, end the war. Instead, he was furious all the time, lashing out at everybody, including me. He accused all of us of selling out. He threw me out of the house, can you believe it? Out of his fucking house, for meeting with the administration on the Renaissance Program.

"There was this new outfit, the 'Guevara Brigade' they called themselves. Richard was the 'brigade commander.' He was off in his bad boy fantasy land." Allie stopped, reaching for her pack of Camels.

"That must have been hard," I said, pouring her more coffee. I remembered the energy level back then, though I was removed from it. Our band was split. Sokoloski, with his long hair, was a welder at General Dynamics in Pomona. He was working class, against the demonstrations. Still is. Our dip-shit singer, on the other hand, was all in. "Woodstock Nation." That was his thing. I stayed quiet, played my fiddle, grateful that I didn't have to bust any college kids.

Allie started in again. "I began seeing Richard as some sort of complicated fraud but was too busy to dwell on it. The college chaplain was mediating the negotiations with the administration over amnesty, course credit, reduced ROTC presence on campus, and other issues. All of it was really difficult, since some in the administration, not to mention outraged alumni—now there's some real assholes—were fighting us tooth and nail.

"It was maybe a week after Kent State when the first bombing here, the library bombing, happened. I thought it might be Richard—that he'd gone all the way. I wanted to ask him, but he'd gone underground. 'On an alternative action,' one of his 'comrades' told me. What a bunch of shit."

"Did you see him again?"

She poked at the remains of her donut, then left it on the plate. "No, not even once. I'd never go back to the house. But later I figured out where he might be, because Richard had a secret. There was this shack, north of the colleges."

"How did you find out about it?" I asked her, sensing a breakthrough.

"It was mid-April, before Cambodia, when we still lived together. A woman came to the house and handed me a package. It was wrapped in brown paper. A van was waiting for her in the street, the engine running. It was weird, like she was scared or something.

"Richard went crazy when he came home and saw it. He tore it to bits and stormed away to the garage."

"What was in the package?" I asked.

"Chocolates—they were all over the floor—and a torn birthday card signed 'LUV,'—spelled L-U-V—'Your Best Girl.'" Allie puffed on another Camel. She was chain-smoking. "Then I heard Richard starting his car."

"And I bet you followed him."

She nodded. "Yeah. I felt really sneaky, but it was kind of groovy too, like being a spy. He went north past Foothill to Baseline Road and turned right. We were near the old quarry. He made several turns, and I almost lost him. Then I saw a cloud of dust. He'd turned onto this dirt road behind a warehouse, and then stopped at this small house, a little bungalow. I parked at the warehouse, ran to the back of the house, and then snuck around to the front. He was on the porch talking to the same woman who had delivered the package. She was much older than I'd realized. When I got there, he was saying, 'Don't ever let anybody know you're here. No matter what.'

"Somebody came out of the house as they were talking, kind of a hippie girl. She handed Richard a joint, he took a puff, like he didn't really want to, and then handed it to the older lady. She took this big greedy toke, smoked the whole thing. Suddenly I felt very uncomfortable. This scene was none of my business, man. So, I split."

"Did Richard see you?" I asked.

"I don't think so." She pushed herself out of her chair. "Listen, I've got to take a break from this. Let's go for a walk or something."

"Come on, Allie. What happened next?" I asked.

"No, mister cop. That's all you get." She kissed me to soften the words.

Every instinct told me to push it. I was just about there. The witness was about to deliver the goods. But at what cost?

"Sure, babe. We can stop," I said, knowing that I'd failed. We grabbed jackets and left the tangled past behind, choosing the breezy sunshine instead. We held hands as we walked in the canyon and spent the rest of that glorious day enjoying the mountains, as if we didn't have a care in the world. The further mysteries of Richard Manning could wait, or so I tried to convince myself, being the boyfriend rather than the cop.

CHAPTER ELEVEN

THE CALL CAME IN that evening. Allie was cooking dinner, and I'd just opened a bottle of wine. It had been a great day, cozy and domestic. The call smashed the mood.

"Gunshot victim, female, alive, but in critical condition," Dispatch said. The location was Cucamonga. Fifteen minutes away if I hauled ass, running all the red lights on Baseline, using my siren.

A pair of squad cars were parked out front when I arrived at the two-story stucco office building abutting a shopping mall. I knew the building. The tenants were mostly doctors and dentists. It was empty at 7 p.m. on a Sunday night. I'd heard the wailing of an ambulance as I approached.

"What's up?" I asked a patrol guy, one of the new ones, a Pomona redneck, like I might have been except my parents raised me right.

"Woman was shot in a second-floor office. It's secure."

"Who called it in?" I asked.

"Cleaning lady." He gestured toward a woman sitting in the back of his vehicle. "She don't know nothin'," he said.

"Put her in the front seat. She's not a criminal," I said to the young officer. I went upstairs. Crime scene tape was loosely fastened around the office door with a stenciled nameplate of "Niklaus Van Kamp, M.S., Consulting Psychologist." I went in and crossed through a small waiting room. There were two offices. Van Kamp's, plush and tony with lots of books and art, was empty. The other small room told the tale. A swivel chair was knocked on its side. There was a pool of blood on the tan rug and more spatter on the blonde maple desk. A cheap name plate on the desk said, "Ellen Corby, Clinical Assistant."

A purse was hanging on another chair. I looked through it. Corby's California license was in the wallet. She was twenty-six. Makeup, a pack of Marlboro Lights, tissues, a hairbrush, and a diaphragm container were also in the purse, along with some house keys. I looked around the room and saw no slugs or shell casings. She'd either been shot while sitting in the chair or knocked from the chair and then shot. I needed to interview her ASAP, assuming she was able to speak. I also needed to talk with her boss—Van Kamp. I wanted to inform him about the shooting unless, of course, he already knew.

Crime techs were on the way from San Bernardino. "Keep the scene secure. Nobody in until the white coats do their thing," I instructed the officers. "Which hospital?" I asked and was directed to Mountain Baptist.

I headed there, calling Dispatch to get Van Kamp's address and also to patch me into his phone. There was no answer. It was a Claremont address, Carol's turf. Dispatch called her number for me. Five rings later, a sleepy-sounding woman answered. It wasn't Carol.

"Uh, is Carol Loomis there?" I asked, thinking Dispatch might have dialed the wrong number.

There was a delay, a murmuring of voices, then, "This is Carol Loomis. Can I help you?"

"It's Jimmy. I've got a shooting in Cucamonga at the office of a psychologist, Niklaus Van Kamp. He's got a Claremont home address. The victim is his assistant. She's at Mountain Baptist, hurt bad. I'm heading there now. Her name is Ellen Corby. There was no answer at Van Kamp's house. Can you check it out, but be careful, he might be the shooter." I gave her the phone number and address.

"Pepperdine Lane, yeah I know it, near Condit School. Middle-class neighborhood, low crime rate." Carol was all business now. "I'll let you know what I find," she said and hung up.

Ellen Corby was in surgery when I arrived at the hospital, no information yet on her condition. I called Sam Fuller, filled him in, and hung around the waiting room, drinking coffee and waiting for Corby to get out of surgery. I wondered who had answered Carol's phone earlier, and knew that Carol would tell me about it when she was good and ready.

Minutes later, the receptionist motioned to me, saying I had a call. It was Carol. "It's real bad at Van Kamp's house," she said. "We've got a dead body, adult female, wrapped in plastic in the swimming pool, her head beat in. I've called in the LA County Sheriff's Department to come and work the crime scene, our usual arrangement. They're not here yet, but I'm pretty sure it's Van Kamp's wife. A neighbor came over, started crying and screaming, saying it was her."

"Any sign of Van Kamp?"

"No," Carol said. We've an APB out for him: forty-five-year-old white male, five-eleven, hundred sixty pounds, brown hair and eyes, mustache and glasses, and his car, a slate-gray two-door 1970 Volvo sedan with California plates. One more thing. There's a daughter, ten years old. She's missing."

"Jesus." I closed my eyes. Could it get any worse? "Okay. I'm going to talk to Corby here at the hospital as soon as they let me. I'll call you when I know something."

The doctor came out soon after, looking for me. "She's incredibly lucky. The bullet, small caliber, lodged in her skull, missing the brain. I was able to remove it. Lots of swelling and bleeding, but she's going to be okay."

The doctor was young and excited to be part of a crime story with a happy ending. He didn't know about the wife or missing kid, and I wasn't about to tell him. "Is she conscious? Can I talk to her for no more than five minutes? We need to find the guy who did this to her."

"Okay, but make it fast," he said, sounding like a television doctor.

I was led to Ellen Corby's small recovery room away from the hustle and bustle of the ER. Her brown hair was shaved in back, and part of her skull was covered in bandages. She was fully conscious, but drugged up. A nurse hovered nearby.

"Miss Corby. I'm Sergeant Sommes, San Bernardino County Sheriff's Department. You've been badly hurt, a bullet wound. Do you feel capable of answering a few questions?"

"Okay."

"Do you know who shot you, Miss Corby?"

"I was talking to Niklaus," she said, speaking softly. The nurse was staring daggers at me, not wanting me there. "We'd been doing lots of acid lately. He said it was his sacrament. I'd come down but he was still flying and was very excited, saying he'd found the portal that would free us all. 'The psychodrama was real,' he said. His earthly vigil was concluded. I was trying to stay with him, to understand, but I couldn't, and he could tell."

"What happened tonight?" I asked, trying to get her focused.

"Niklaus was staring at me, looking sad. Then he walked behind me and started rubbing my neck. Then I heard this incredible noise and woke up here." Her eyes roved around the little cubicle. "It hurts."

"There was nobody else in the office, is that correct?" I asked. "Just the two of you?"

"Yes. But you must understand, the rules for Niklaus are different. He lives in several dimensions. I don't, and he punished me for it."

At this, the nurse shook her head and left the room.

"Miss Corby—"

"Please, Ellen." Her weak smile was making this harder for me.

"Okay. Ellen, we believe Niklaus may also have harmed his wife. Is that possible?"

"She hated his work, mocked him. Made him feel small," Ellen Corby said. She coughed. There was a trickle of blood from her nose.

The doctor came in. "Officer, she needs to rest now."

"Of course. One last question, Ellen. If Niklaus wanted or needed to get some rest, some peace and quiet, was there a special place he went?"

Her eyes were closed now. "We went together sometimes," she whispered. "Puddingstone Reservoir. 'The best spot for harmonic convergence,' he'd say." She opened her eyes again, grasped my hand, and squeezed. "We used to get so high. It was magic. Until he got too crazy."

"Thanks. Puddingstone's big. Any more details?"

"Officer, you must stop now." The doctor was raising his voice.

"No. Wait," Ellen said. "The campground near the old airport. We used to make love there, under the stars." She looked sad and bitter and dreamy, her blue eyes tearing up.

That answered one of my questions. I wanted to tell Ellen that this monster shot her and left her for dead, regardless of what fucking dimension he was in, but it wouldn't have helped her one bit. So, I squeezed her hand instead and left.

****

Things moved fast after that. I gave Carol the Puddingstone information, and she passed it on to the LASD's High Alert Team, who scrambled all hands, including a chopper and tracking dogs. After wrapping up my Cucamonga crime scene, I followed the Van Kamp pursuit from our Fontana command center since Puddingstone was LA County, off my beat. Our primary concern was the daughter. To my relief, she was found spending the night at a friend's house, unaware of all the chaos and heartbreak.

Carol called me about midnight. "It was too weird. All of us were just about to call it a night, cold as hell, when two of the deputies heard noises from under a big pepper tree near the airport fence, right where your witness said he might be. They closed in and told me the perp was sitting barefoot and cross-legged saying 'Nam myoho renge kyo' over and over again."

"That's a Buddhist chant," I said. "Our bass player does that sometimes, but he's not a killer."

"Neither are millions and millions of Buddhists," Carol said. "Anyway, this crackpot, Van Kamp, waived his right to counsel. They made him formally sign off on all Miranda rights. When asked about his wife and his assistant, get this, he said he had no interest in 'earthbound matters.' He also said the deputies could search his 'material possessions.' A bloody hammer and small-caliber revolver were found in his pack. They got sent off to the crime lab."

"Good work. I figure this dude will spend the rest of his days at Camarillo State Hospital."

"Unless he's crazy like a fox and gets a great lawyer. Josie and I, she's a youth counselor with LA County, had to break the news to the daughter about both her mother and father. It was awful. She's just a little girl. I saw her room, a David Cassidy poster on the wall and stuffed animals on her bed. She just cried and cried, wanting her mother. The wife's sister, in pretty bad shape herself, came and took the girl to her house. Josie's going to meet with them again tomorrow. What a night."

"Get some sleep, kid," I said.

"You too."

It was the middle of the night when I got home. Allie was gone. Her note said, "Feeling weird about Manning stuff... and your job. Let's leave it alone for a while. I'll call you." She was good at leaving. I poured myself a shot of bourbon and downed it, then poured myself another, trying to shake the murder and mayhem. It didn't help much, since I had this terrible feeling that I'd blown it with Allie, in more ways than I even knew.

CHAPTER TWELVE

THE FOLLOWING WEEK WAS dominated by the Van Kamp case. Although the Claremont murder of his wife took legal priority, I needed to process the Cucamonga assault as if it were the only case. Fortunately, Ellen Corby was recovering—at least physically.

Early Friday morning I found time to retrace the route Allie had taken while tailing Richard Manning that April day in 1970. I turned right on Baseline Road, near the quarry, looking for old shacks. A large retirement complex—the kind of place my mother says she'll never live in—occupied the land where the shack might have been. Nearby, a shopping center was under construction. It was hopeless. Unless Allie was mixed up on the location, the house Richard Manning had visited that day was long gone.

Still, that day had included hippies, and dope. That might be the way in. I backtracked to Fontana and paid a visit to our special county unit that worked on drug cases only. In my view, this group focused too much on little guys—keeping its arrest records high—and ignored the big-time dealers. But today that might work to my advantage.

"May or June 1970. That's a long time back, Jimmy." Sheila, the clerk, yawned and looked at her nails. I made a mental note to quit if I ever started looking that bored on the job.

"Come on, you've already picked the winners at Santa Anita this afternoon," I said, pointing to her completed racing form, "so how about helping me out."

"Okay," she said, "but I just put a hundred bucks on a fifty-to-one shot in the seventh race. If I hit it, I'm gonna quit and never help you again. I'll pull my trailer down to Ensenada, drink beer, and sit in the sun. I already bought my space by the way, near a propane tank and the women's head."

"Good for you, sweetheart," I told her. "Maybe this is your day. Meanwhile, let's look at those files. I need the dope arrests for Cucamonga and Alta Loma, anything near the Upland line."

Sheila trudged off to find them. In my experience, druggies mostly acted stupid. They needed their stuff, so they robbed stores, stole cars, hurt people in the process, and then got busted. It was the same story over and over again. I wasn't sure if that shack Manning went to back then rose to that level, but it was worth a shot. Sheila dumped a bunch of files on a nearby empty desk then picked up the paper and started in on the crossword puzzle.

After an hour of digging, I found a couple of locations that looked promising. There was this industrial base yard just above the city of Upland, next to the dry wash, where companies sold gravel and other construction materials. There was a dump nearby, operated by San Bernardino County. We'd actually found a dead body or two in there over the years.

The map showed a cluster of three old shacks halfway down a ravine, out of view from the roads. Lemon growers used them for their migrant workers in the old days. In July of 1970, the county fire department had been called in to put out a fire that burned the buildings to the ground. Nobody much cared since the fire didn't spread to the more affluent areas. It might have been arson. No follow-up was mentioned in the file. No drug busts, but the area was worth a look.

The second possibility was right on Baseline Road, near a dentist's office in a residential neighborhood between Claremont and Upland, my turf. I knew that address, it triggered a recollection, but I couldn't place it. Sheila's radio phone blared, "Code 9, possible homicide in Colton. All units respond." The research could wait. I thanked her and left, put the blue light on my roof, hit the siren, and headed for the scene.

****

Eight hours later I called it a day. It had been a gang fight, Blacks and Chicanos fighting each other for territory. No deaths but there were two serious gunshot injuries, plus plenty more from knives. I helped the gang squad process the scene, interviewing suspects and victims. San Bernardino was getting like East LA in spots. These young men were pros, dangerous as hell. I was glad to leave the rest of the work to the squad that did this full-time.

Driving west toward the setting sun, I guided my Charger through the Baseline Dips, going fast. The car held the surface until I hit fifty-five, then it went airborne for brief blissful moments, like Steve McQueen's Ford Mustang in *Bullitt*. It was a cool, stupid game I'd been playing ever since I got my first license—like hundreds of other kid drivers. Most grew out of it.

Baseline Road had been envisioned as and built to be the main drag between Pasadena and the desert. That never happened. First Route 66, and then the damn freeways, took all the traffic instead. That's why they'd never fixed the dips. The landscape was a mix of scrubby desert, pre-war wooden frame homes with citrus and avocado trees in the front yards, small grocery stores that still had gas pumps in front, and even a fruit stand or two. It was old California except in Claremont, where expensive, featureless houses had taken over the street, like an invading army.

Nearing the Upland/Claremont boundary line, I passed a wedge of unincorporated San Bernardino County, my turf. I remembered! Those records of Sheila's, that 1970 drug house—hashish, speed, and cocaine available at a drive-up window, like McDonald's—it had been our case. I'd had a partner then, senior to me and lazy as hell. But we'd shut down that house. The neighbors were happy to be rid of it, especially that dentist.

I was almost home when, on impulse, I turned left toward Claremont village instead. It was as good a time as any to take a second crack at Jason Phillips, Esq. I parked in front of the clinic, walked in, and got lucky: a kid at the desk made a mistake and told me that Mr. Phillips was in. I headed for his office. Annie Hoover, the office manager—and maybe Carol's new friend—tried to cut me off.

"Mr. Phillips is in conference," she said, the usual lawyer dodge.

I ignored her and kept moving. Since I wasn't planning to arrest the guy or seize evidence, the only risk was pissing him off, which didn't bother me. In fact, I wanted to bust his chops, maybe get him to talk. Phillips and I were passing acquaintances, having both attended Claremont High School, but we had never had a real conversation, then or since—in part because he was two years older.

I knocked on his door and then opened it without waiting. Phillips was half-reclining in a fancy swivel chair, his leather cowboy boots up on an otherwise empty desk, stereo headphones covering his ears. He stared at me, trying to focus.

"Led Zeppelin's *Whole Lotta Love*," he said, taking off the headphones with obvious reluctance and hitting a button on the desk to turn off the stereo. "I never get tired of it, especially the trippy part in the middle—somebody said it's like an orgasm on acid—and you just interrupted me. What do you want, Jimmy Sommes?"

"I'm surprised a big shot like you even knows who I am." I noticed his long hair was balding in front, detracting from his otherwise perfect, hip look.

"Yeah, right, big shot. I know who the cops are, and you were in the paper recently, shooting tin cans or something."

"It was a tear gas canister with a shotgun; my boss said it was a perfect shot." Not cool, the bragging, but I couldn't stop myself.

"Good for you." He sat up and put his feet on the floor. "Now that we've established your expertise, what can I do for you, Sergeant?"

I was in no hurry to tell him. "My buddies and I never missed your football games. Against Glendora High for the regional title, you threw that perfect pass, fifty yards right to the goal line, a game-winner. I can still see it. But the split end dropped it, a heartbreaker."

"Hank Jenkins. That was his name, and yes, he dropped it," Phillips said. "I repeat. What do you want?"

"I'm going to ask you a hypothetical question. If I was a committed student radical who bombed a college library reference room, thinking it was empty, but mistakenly injured a young woman—"

"Hypothetical, my ass." Phillips started to get up.

"Let me finish. I kept a scrapbook about you in high school, Mr. Quarterback, all your victories and statistics, so please indulge me a moment." I'd never told anybody that. It just popped out.

He sat down. "That bought you two minutes."

"Okay. Let's further assume that this same student radical, now rotting in a federal holding cell in LA, has no idea who blew up the college professor. That's a murder rap, maybe even the death penalty, not the ten years he's looking at for the library bombing. So why the hell not say so? Hypothetically speaking?"

Phillips pulled out a cigar, clipped off the end with a fancy cutting device, and lit it. It smelled good. "Cuban. I've got friends there," he said and offered me one. I took it and put it in my pocket for later.

Phillips took a deep pull on his, the lit end burning bright. "As you know, the McMasters firm in Los Angeles represents Mr. Richard Manning. I can't and won't talk about an active case."

"But you did represent Manning, for about thirty-six hours. He hasn't said a word since. You put the fear of God in him, didn't you? You shut him up good."

"Objection. No foundation and calls for speculation on the part of the witness. Objection *sustained*," Phillips said, playing lawyer and judge. "And your precious two minutes are up. Good to see you, Jimmy, but this is the second time you've shown up at the clinic with this Richard Manning bullshit. Don't bother me or Annie again."

Phillips hit an intercom button on his desk. "Sergeant Sommes is leaving now," he said, putting his headphones on, puffing on his cigar, and turning up the music so loud that I swear I could hear Led Zep playing through the top of his head.

Annie appeared and escorted me out to the street. I started to talk but her look silenced me. "That was entirely inappropriate," she said, "bursting in like that." But her eyes were telling me a different story. I saw encouragement, mixed with something else. Fear?

CHAPTER THIRTEEN

"DO YOU THINK WE should bag the whole Manning thing?" I asked Carol. "Nobody cares but us." We were walking her dog in the park, a chore she assured me was imminently necessary. Suited me. Maybe the dog would keep my mind off Annie Hoover and whatever she was to Carol.

"Funny. I was going to ask you the same thing," she said. "You first."

"No, you go first, since I asked first." Jeez, we sounded like fifth graders or something.

Carol took a deep breath. "Okay, but don't make fun of me. I can't stop thinking about the case. I'm still having the same frickin' dream, maybe once a week, walking into the Harper Hall mailroom, finding the body parts, you can't even call it a body, just blown all to hell. I can't seem to shake it. Come on, Max." Her pug was pissing on every bush in the park.

"Does working the case help you?" I took the dog's leash. Max and I were friends.

"I think so, and my psychologist thinks so too," Carol said. "Don't tell anybody that, about me seeing a shrink. I know you won't. What about you? Do you want to lay off? That would be okay with me."

"I've had this weird feeling, from the moment Acid Bill Dixon whispered in my ear, that everything's connected— Allie, Manning, the bombings, the whole business. I don't think Rebecca Meadows got a fair shake. So, no. I don't want to stop either, but no more of this part-time crap. Here's my idea. Let's each take two weeks' vacation and work this case properly. If at the end of the two weeks, we come up empty, then that's the end of it."

Carol thought about it for a moment. "That's a great idea. You're on. I need a break from the mayor and all the small-town Claremont stuff."

****

Three days later, we were sitting in a Chinese restaurant in Solana Beach, a ritzy suburb north of San Diego. The small downtown looked like Claremont, only richer. It consisted of three blocks of low-rise faux adobe buildings with red tile roofs extending down to the Pacific Ocean. Florists, restaurants, antiques stores, and a combined bookstore/coffee house/wine shop were visible outside the restaurant window.

It was fish or cut bait on the Manning investigation, and good timing for me. Allie was in New York interviewing for the *Village Voice* job—a formality since her aunt did the hiring—and I wasn't sure when she'd be back, or if she even wanted to come back. She'd clammed up about Richard Manning. I'd blown it that day, hadn't pushed her hard enough.

Since the FBI had latched on to Manning and congratulated themselves for solving the cases, Carol and I decided to start at the beginning. We planned to learn about Richard Manning's life, especially since the life of the victim, Rebecca Meadows, had been such a dead end.

Manning had told the FBI that his parents were dead. Not so. A *Los Angeles Times* reporter found them a month after his arrest, in June 1970, living in Solana Beach. Frank Manning had "no commented" to the reporter's questions.

Nobody followed up.

The Mannings lived in the Solana Beach Country Club Villas, a golf course community located within a mile of where we were sitting. We could see the country club, perched on a hill above the town, looking like a Mexican fort. The newspaper article mentioned that Mr. Manning was a San Diego insurance executive with his own company, and his wife was a former president of her Kappa Kappa Gamma sorority at the University of Southern California.

Carol had asked some questions of a San Diego Police Department friend—who happened to know a cook at the country club—so we knew a little bit more. Both Mr. and Mrs. Manning were excellent golfers and drank a lot with their Reagan Republican buddies at the club's elegant bar. Frank was semi-retired, and Olivia didn't work. "She wears the pants in the family," the cook had reported. "And the guy is a mean drunk."

The community was gated, something we should have anticipated. How the hell were we going to get in?

"We could seek the assistance of the local police department." Carol was popping open a fortune cookie.

"Too risky," I said. "The local gendarmes protect their own in towns like this, practically a private security service."

An idea took shape as we paid for our lunches. "Real estate, that's the ticket." I'd spied a Century 21 office down the street. "We're married and meeting Kara at a house for a showing. Something in there must be for sale. Let's have a look."

"Out of our price range, sweetie," Carol said. "But we can dream."

We studied the listings on the front window of the real estate office, including a handy-dandy map of the country club homes. The back of the Mannings' lot abutted the thirteenth hole of the championship golf course. Luckily, a house two blocks away from them was listed for sale at $90,000, definitely out of our range.

"I wish I'd dressed better," I said, looking at my Hawaiian shirt and jeans.

"That shirt looks cool, like you're a rich guy slumming. Just act like you belong," Carol said. "You were close, by the way. The agent's name is Karen."

I'd washed and waxed my Charger so at least the car looked good. I drove up to the guard gate and announced, "Hi, we're the Fishers. Karen of Century 21 is meeting us at the Via Aventura house."

The young man consulted his list. "I don't see your name here."

"Jesus, Karen is such dingbat," Carol said with a throaty chuckle. "Look, Jeff"—she'd read his name badge—"we drove over from Escondido and we're late. Can you cut us a little slack here, honey?"

I think she batted her eyes at the kid. "Sure, just sign here, sir," he said, "and put down your license plate number." Which I did, writing both illegibly. We were in!

"That was easy. I hope they're home," I said, driving up a tree-lined, winding road. We encountered a landscaping crew, all Chicanos, using rakes and brooms to clear away any annoying scraps of nature. They moved out of our way in slow motion with no eye contact. I felt like telling them it wasn't my fault.

We'd decided to hit the Mannings hard with the authority card. We were police officers following up on an important lead.

"Republicans respect authority," Carol said, "sometimes blindly."

"I vote Republican sometimes," I said.

"You make my point. You're an authoritarian."

I turned into a four-house cul-de-sac. The Spanish-style "villas" were identical from the outside. We were just in time. A couple, the Mannings, I assumed, were walking out their front door, rolling their golf bags. We parked, got out of the car, and approached them.

"Excuse me, Mr. and Mrs. Manning. Could we talk to you a moment? I'm Sergeant Sommes, homicide investigator for the San Bernardino County Sheriff's Department, and this is Officer Loomis, Claremont Police Department. We're following up on a lead relative to your son's case and—"

"How the hell did you get in here? Let me see some ID," Mr. Manning said, scowling at us. His face was leathery, with a pink, almost purplish hue—an advertisement for skin cancer if a heart attack didn't get him first.

"Oh, stop it, Frank. Mr. Tough Guy. I'm Olivia Manning, and we're always glad to help law enforcement," the woman said. Younger than her husband, she was very attractive, maybe fifty, with silver-blond hair cut in a short bob, a trim figure, and a killer smile—a well-preserved cheerleader some thirty years later. "We do have a two o'clock tee time, though."

Frank Manning, tall and starting to go to fat, was examining our identification, squinting at our badges. I could smell the gin. Tough to play golf when you're loaded. Unless you cheat.

"But I must tell you, Sergeant Sommes," Olivia said, "if this is about my husband's son, Richard, we have agreed to offer no comments on the matter. In fact," she looked into my eyes, acting flirty for no conceivable reason, "we haven't seen that, uh, young man, in several years. We simply appalled by the bombings. Isn't that right, Frank?"

"Yeah, right. What the hell does a San Bernardino deputy sheriff have to do with this?" Frank asked, repeatedly poking his index finger into my chest as he spoke. "It's a goddamned outrage, a man can't be left alone in his own community." He kept pushing at me.

"Easy there, buddy," I said, knocking his hand away. He rolled back on unsteady heels. I then made the rookie mistake of looking away from him to the more pleasing visage of Olivia. That's when the son-of-a-bitch nailed me with a right hook to the jaw. I tasted blood, and my tongue felt a loose tooth. More as a matter of reflex than anything else, I punched him as hard as I could in the stomach. Another mistake, since he puked all over my silky shirt as he went to the ground.

Carol pulled me away as Olivia tended to her fallen husband. Just then a Solana Beach patrol car pulled up to the curb, containing two cops. "What the hell is going on here?" a young patrolman, the driver, yelled out as he jumped from the car. "Hands in the air!" His voice cracked slightly.

"Hello, sir," Carol said. "We're police officers, here on a case. Sorry about this misunderstanding."

"Bullshit. Keep your hands up," the other patrolman said, exiting from the passenger side, hand on his holster, ready to draw down on us. He was older and meaner. I knew the type. "So you're not the Fishers from Escondido," he said in a fine sneering voice I might have appreciated in other circumstances. Instead, I was raking pieces of regurgitated crab salad off my aloha shirt. So much for the real estate ploy. That damn kid at the guard gate had ratted us out.

"Gentlemen, gentlemen, and, lady, please!" Olivia Manning said, taking control. "First of all, my husband, who's suffering from the flu, started this altercation. He's not himself today, and I'm sure he's very sorry." Frank groaned from his fetal position on the sidewalk. "Officer Sommes was merely defending himself. How about we all step around to the terrace and sort this out," Olivia said, quickly scanning the cul-de-sac for witnesses. There were none. Maybe it was all about appearances, but I was glad to have her on my team.

One of the cops helped Frank to his feet, and we all followed Olivia around the house to a handsome redwood deck surrounded by purple and red bougainvillea bushes. The sky was a bright metallic blue and contrasted nicely with the lush green, sloping fairway located just beyond the Mannings' property. The Pacific Ocean extended to the west, as far as I could see, its color a perfect combination of sky and land.

A foursome had just finished driving off the thirteenth hole, an elevated tee, and were moving down toward their golf balls in two golf carts. I could see all four balls resting some 200 yards below them on the fairway, certainly different from when my buddies and I hacked around our local municipal course, spraying balls all over hell and back. But at least we walked for the exercise.

A maid appeared from the house, carrying a large silver platter with a pitcher of iced tea, glasses, and a ceramic bowl filled to the brim with a combination of cashews and raisins. Carol caught my eye. She was choking back laughter. My tooth hurt—at least I hadn't lost it—or I might have joined her. A garden party in Solana Beach with two rich Republicans—one violent—the local cops, and us. Why not? We relaxed while the patrolmen sought guidance from higher-ups, and Olivia filled us in about her recently planted gardenias. Frank Manning had disappeared into the house.

"He wants to talk to you." Mean Cop motioned for me to come to the telephone.

"Sergeant Sommes, this is Dexter Wilcox, Chief of Police for Solana Beach. I want you to get the fuck out of my town and never come back. Is that clear enough for you?"

"Yes sir, I just want you to kn—"

"I have no interest whatsoever in why you and your partner are sneaking around Solana Beach harassing our citizens. None."

Obviously, there was no point in any continuing dialogue with Chief Wilcox, so I hung up. "Carol, we've been asked to leave. Let's go."

"You hung up on the Chief," Young Cop said to me. "That was rude."

"Frank Manning threw up on my shirt. That was even ruder."

"After you slugged him, asshole," Mean Cop said, signaling his partner. They left without even thanking Olivia for the tea and snacks.

"Speaking of rude, those fellows need a lesson in manners," Carol said. She turned to Oliva. "Thank you for the tea. But we better go too, while the coast is clear."

I finished my tea and started on my way. Olivia had given me some aspirin for my toothache, letting her hand rest in mine for a moment. Or had I just imagined that? Gazing at the sparkling ocean and the perfect golf course while bidding farewell to this Solana Beach enclave, it occurred to me that it wouldn't be the worst thing in the world to have money. "Thank you, Mrs. Man—"

"Just a moment, please," Olivia interrupted. She stood in front of the terrace gate, blocking our passage, holding a big half-empty glass of white wine. "I'd like to talk to you a moment. Frank has gone to bed. He really is fighting the flu—as well as too many gin and tonics—I should have cancelled golf."

We returned to the table. It had a pole in the middle holding up a red parasol umbrella that shielded us from the sun. Carol and I waited for Olivia to begin. I ate some more cashews—the really expensive kind that I never bought at home—separating out the raisins as best I could—and being careful to only chew on the right side of my mouth.

"Frank and I married about ten years ago, both coming away from troubles in our first marriages. We met here, at a mixed scramble—that's a golf term," she said, looking at Carol, pegging her correctly as a non-golfer. "You saw him at his worst today. Anyway, he told me that he was estranged from his son, who had chosen his mother at the time of the divorce, blaming Frank for it. After that, Frank's first wife and his son moved away. I thought we'd never hear from them again."

"Mrs. Manning, you don't need to justify anything to us," Carol said.

"I know that. But it might be relevant to your, uh, inquiries. Frank's first wife went wild in her middle age, started taking LSD, the whole hippie business. In fact, she and her son attended that crazy Monterey Pop Festival together in 1967, smoking marijuana, sleeping in the same tent, no hygiene. I know because it made the paper here, since she was a former resident. The headline was 'Hippie Mama Rocks Out,' and there was a picture of her on her son's shoulders, wearing a bikini that barely covered anything, sagging every which way. Frank took a horrible ribbing about it at the club."

"Just one big happy family," I said.

Carol's eyes told me to shut up, as Olivia continued.

"Earlier, she—Frank's first wife, Melody—had worked as an accountant here in San Diego, at his company. That's how they met. After the divorce, she took a job at a bank in some crummy desert town out east, Yucaipa, I think. That was pretty much it, until one evening near Thanksgiving time, 1969, I think it was—there was that Apollo flight going on. Frank loves moon flights. His den is full of space stuff."

"Apollo 12," I said. "My dad got excited by moon landings too. Yucaipa's not so bad, by the way."

Olivia went on, ignoring my plug. "We were watching Walter Cronkite on television—the astronauts were on their way home—when there was this hammering on the door, somebody yelling. Frank grabbed his three-iron, turned on the porch light, opened the door, and there was his son, Richard, drunk or high or something, shouting, 'You ruined my mother's life, you bastard.' He looked demented."

I noticed then that Olivia's eyes changed color, depending on the light. They were hazel now, green earlier. She caught me checking her out, which was embarrassing, but I could tell she liked it.

"Did Richard come in the house?" Carol asked.

"For a while. He must have snuck by the guard gate on foot. Frank didn't know what to do so he invited him in and gave him a beer. Richard saw the television program, started saying that all the NASA money should go to helping the poor instead. Stuff like that. He was prowling around the living room, couldn't sit down. Then he confronted Frank again, saying his mother got fired from her bank job for embezzling money because Frank cut off her alimony and child support. That infuriated Frank, who said he'd paid, and I quote, 'every dollar that hippie bitch was entitled to.'"

"Was that true?" I asked.

"I believe so. Frank is very good about money. Anyway, Richard began to sober up, or something, and his tone got very cold. He went on this political rant, saying Frank and I were part of this corrupt capitalist system that was destroying humanity. Frank yelled at him, calling him a communist."

Olivia paused, took a big swallow of wine, finishing the glass. "This is all so difficult. They kept yelling, then suddenly Richard threw his beer bottle against the wall, just missing that watercolor." She gestured toward a colorful painting of wildflowers visible in the living room. "Richard said, 'The revolution is coming, old man, and I'll do whatever it takes to bring you down.' Frank told him to get out."

"What an experience. Was that it?" Carol asked.

"Yes. Except for one last thing. Richard accused my husband of something... something to do with Melody. I couldn't really understand it. He had his face right up to Frank, something about going to hell for what he did. Then Richard departed and the two haven't spoken or seen each other since."

Olivia rubbed her eyes with a handkerchief. "Frank told me later there was nothing to it, that of course he'd never done anything harmful to his first wife. I believe my husband. But he won't talk about it, says they're all dead to him, his family."

It was time to leave. Olivia was depleted. I thanked her and gave her my card in case anything came up.

"Let's get out of this soap opera," Carol said. Feeling a little shaky I gave Carol the keys. She drove down the hill, past the same landscaping crew. They hadn't moved too far. A Solana Beach squad car, containing Mean Cop and Young Cop, was parked just outside the guard gate, waiting for us to leave. I stuck my head out the window and waved at the officers. Mean Cop gave me the finger, but the kid in the guard shack grinned and waved back. I figured he had a future in politics.

Carol gunned the engine as she merged onto I-5, heading north.

"How about we visit the underrated city of Yucaipa?" I asked. "I used to work there. My first posting with the county."

"Sure," Carol said. "As long as you change your shirt at a gas station. It stinks. Eau de puke is not your fragrance." She looked at me, a gleam in her eye.

We were on the hunt now, feeling it. Hippie Mama was, in all probability, the woman Richard had met at the Baseline Road crash pad at the time of the bombings. The "whys" of all this remained to be discovered, but at least the facts were coming together.

CHAPTER FOURTEEN

"I'LL HAVE THE BOB'S Big Boy Combo with onion rings instead of fries, blue cheese dressing on the salad, and coffee," I said to the waitress and found myself adding, "I used to eat here three or four times a week a few years back." She didn't seem too interested and left to place our orders with the fry cook, who gave her some good-natured grief about being faster picking up the orders. The cook was a dead ringer for Jimi Hendrix, including the afro. I thought of a headline for *The National Enquirer*: "Hendrix not dead! Hiding out in Yucaipa!" Except this dude was way too big to be Jimi.

Carol had ordered a tuna salad sandwich, and a Tab to drink. "You don't know what you're missing," I said. "The Big Boy Combo is the best diner food there is. You can eat tuna fish at home. Something else, these dirt-brown uniforms they make the waitresses wear. I don't think even Raquel Welch would look good in one of them."

"You take care of your own business, Mr. Opinion," Carol said. "I've got to make a call." She left the table, knocking off a fork in the process. There was a pay phone next to the bathrooms. All these restaurants were set up the same.

We'd already checked into rooms at a Motel 6 in Redlands, because the only motel I remembered in Yucaipa was a dump. I'd convinced Carol to join me for dinner at this Bob's Big Boy, off the I-10 near Yucaipa, for my special walk down memory lane. Somehow, she wasn't sharing my enthusiasm.

"I just broke a lunch date for tomorrow with Annie, you remember, the manager of that law clinic we went to in Claremont, when we were looking for Jason Phillips," Carol said when she came back. "Annie and I are seeing each other, and I don't want to hear a goddamned thing about it from you." She gave me an icy glare.

I tried to keep my expression neutral and my voice level. "Okay."

"Is that all you've got? Okay? Jesus."

"You just told me not to say anything." No way I'd get out of this unscathed.

"That doesn't mean you need to act like a smirking redneck."

Her anger wasn't working on me. It was hard not to burst out laughing. "I figured that was Annie who answered your phone that night, the Van Kamp case," I told her. "And I don't smirk."

"Caught us in the sack, did you, Mr. Detective," Carol said, louder than normal.

The waitress was hovering ten feet away, holding onto our plates, thinking she was interrupting a lovers' quarrel, especially since my left jaw was bruising black and blue, as if Carol had already whacked me one. I gestured for the young woman to bring the food, which she did, smacking the plates down and hurrying off to escape the line of fire.

"I've been looking forward to this Big Boy Combo for the last two hours, ever since my toothache went away," I said. "I don't want you to wreck it for me. I'm your best friend, and if Annie Hoover makes you happy, that's great. So, I suggest you eat your tuna sandwich, which was a mistake to begin with, and stop picking a fight with me."

"You don't really get it, but that's okay," she said, with

a hint of a smile on her face. "Gimme an onion ring."

Since Carol still seemed gloomy, I regaled her with tales of my earlier time here in Yucaipa, whether she liked it or not. "There was this crazy night my first year on the job. We were cruising the interstate and there was this big semi bearing down on Mr. Green Jeans, the latter waving a whiskey bottle and driving his John Deere tractor about twenty miles an hour. They were approaching this tight curve heading up toward County Line Road. I swear the truck was going to force this farmer off the road. My partner was an old pro. We got both of them off to the side of the road. I gave the farmer a citation for drunk driving, impounded his tractor, and called his son to drive him home. My partner cited the trucker."

"For what?" Carol asked. At least she was listening.

"That's what I wanted to know. He hadn't been speeding. My partner, Wally was his name, showed me the ticket. He'd cited the trucker 'for being a dickhead in San Bernardino County, which is a violation of the Penal Code.' The ticket was fake! On the back, Wally had printed in neat letters, 'Slow Down and Fuck You.' It was hysterical. Dickhead. Violation of the Penal Code."

"Okay, enough with the comedy act. I get it," Carol said, concentrating on her sandwich, but looking happier in spite of herself.

Toward the end of the meal, as I polished off the last morsel of my hamburger, Carol was clearly ruminating on something. At last, she pushed her plate away and said, "My, uh, situation with Annie. It's not quite that simple."

"Yeah, I'm sure—"

"I don't mean that," she interrupted me. "I'm comfortable with who I am, as long as the mayor—now there's a dickhead—doesn't find out."

"Don't worry. My lips are sealed."

She studied me for a moment and then leaned forward. "Look, it's about her boss, Jason Phillips. He's into some bad shit, maybe drug smuggling. At a minimum, he's snorting way too much cocaine. It's making him paranoid as hell. Annie and I agreed when we starting seeing each other, no shop talk at all, too complicated. But sometimes, you know, pillow talk." Carol blushed. "It's really bothering her. She wants to talk about it but can't. It may even tie into the bombings, but I'm not sure about that. It's creating some strain."

I nodded. "Kind of like Allie and me," I said. "Man, look at us, both dating people with possible knowledge of this case. Two sticky situations."

"Except mine is worse," she responded. "Annie is bound to some degree by attorney-client privilege. Plus, she's blindly loyal to this jerk."

****

Next day, I didn't see a soul I knew when we showed up at the Yucaipa's Sheriff's substation. Not too surprising, since I'd left this location six years earlier, transferring to my current Alta Loma station. We asked to speak to a detective.

"Well, look who's here, Mr. Hot Shot himself, Jimmy Sommes," an attractive female deputy piped up. Noticing my puzzled expression, she said, "Blonde hair. It does wonders."

"Wow. Shelley, it's you. How ya doing?" I remembered a shy, skinny, brunette deputy who'd started at this station just before I left. She'd always worn a coat. Now she was practically bursting out of her uniform, in a good way. None of my business, so I continued, "This is Carol Loomis of the Claremont PD. We're tracking down a lead."

"Hi, Carol. Is that the Claremont in Jimmy's neck of

woods, or that other one near San Diego?"

"The first. Can we talk someplace?" Off the ladies went with me trailing. I was better at punching people. Carol was better at talking to people. I loved it. Made my work easier. Sometimes it got lonely working solo, although I told people I preferred it. Of course, it depended very much on the partner. Carol was perfect. I'd had my share of dickheads.

The three of us sat around a beat-up old table in the station's conference room, and Carol began. "We got thrown out of Solana Beach yesterday, since we've got absolutely no jurisdiction over this cold case we're working."

"That never stopped Jimmy before." Shelley winked at me. "They still talk about his... ah... investigative techniques around here." Wow. I had no idea I was such a legend in these parts.

"Melody Manning moved here maybe ten years ago with her son," Carol continued. "Worked at a bank, likely embezzled money, got fired, went hippie. That's what we've heard."

"Hmm. Doesn't ring any bells with me, but I can ask around. Plus," Shelley gestured at the file cabinets lining one side of the wall, "you're free to check our records."

A thought struck me. "Shelley, do you like rock 'n' roll?"

She wrinkled her nose. "You don't remember, do you? You drove me and my then boyfriend to a Johnny Cash concert up in Riverside. I love country and rock."

"No, I don't remember, part of getting old, I guess. But we heard that Melody went to the Monterey Pop Festival in 1967 and got her picture in the paper."

Shelley paused, then snapped her fingers. "Wait. Yeah, that rings a bell. 'Hippie Mama.' I do remember that because I was jealous. I'd love to have gone and heard all those bands, without," she added primly, "all the dope, of course. Let me check with this guy out front who might be able to help." Shelley gave me another wink and left the room. I figured she toked up plenty off the job. Lots of younger cops did. The older guys stuck to alcohol.

Carol was checking her Manning file. "Okay, so we've got Melody here in 1967. That's a start. Richard Manning was born in 1947. He went to UC Berkeley—that figures—so he's in college by then."

"But not far from Monterey. Anyway, that concert was in summer, right?" I was studying the table, looking for the initials I was pretty sure I'd carved in the old relic.

"I think so, but come on, Jimmy, you're the musician."

Shelley returned, accompanied by a string bean of a man with a receding hairline. He kept his eyes staring down at the rug, as if he'd lost a nickel. "This is Cliff. He keeps our records and remembers everything that happens in this town."

"Melody Manning, aka 'Hippie Mama,' actually lived next door in Calimesa near the I-10," Cliff droned.

"And near Bob's Big Boy, my favorite," I added.

"Yeah, right," he continued, still not making eye contact. "It was about the time of the Monterey concert, we got a call from the Redlands PD asking about her. She worked in the mortgage loan department of the Bank of America branch there. Some money was missing, not much by that bank's standard, but enough that B of A called the police."

"What's not much?" Carol asked.

"Five thousand, I recall. They asked if she had a record or any arrests here."

"Did she?"

"No, but later the son, Richard, held some sort of sit-in at the high school." Cliff's eyes never left the carpet, like his memory was stored there and he was reading it off.

"Wow. You do have a hell of a memory, Cliff," Carol said, buttering him up. "Would you mind putting together a file for us?"

"Sure, if my boss says it's okay," he replied, looking at Shelley, who nodded yes.

"One last thing, Cliff," I said. "What happened with the bank and Hippie Mama?"

"I heard they terminated her but brought no charges. She'd denied the whole thing, saying it was a bookkeeping mix-up. Redlands PD closed the file. Melody Manning left Yucaipa after that. No idea where she went."

We thanked Cliff for the information. He looked pleased with his performance. Every station needed a Cliff. Shelley said they'd mail a Melody Manning file to me in a couple of days. She had not made the connection to Richard Manning, campus bomber, and I saw no need to bring it up.

Carol and I started to pack up.

"I feel a need for some education," I said.

"Yucaipa High School?"

"You bet."

In my experience, most high schools had a beloved teacher or two that had been there forever. He or she might teach English, or history, or biology—it didn't really matter—because the key criteria was that they loved their students, and vice versa. I'd laid out this scenario to Shelley. After thinking about it, she identified a history teacher named Emily Simpson as our best bet.

Carol, although attractive, always looked like a cop, even in civilian clothes. It wasn't that she was mannish, far from it, but there was something official about her bearing. Not me. I could pass for a cleaned-up auto mechanic, or an over-the-hill ballplayer, or maybe even a country-rock fiddle player. I almost always wore jeans, a blue work shirt, and a leather vest, except for court. Kind of a cowboy look. My boss let me get away with it as long as I did my job. I'd throw on a loose-fitting sports jacket if I was carrying my sidearm, though I usually left it in a gun case in the trunk. Safer that way

Given this difference in our appearances, we decided that I, not Carol, would brave the high school administration office and ask about Miss or Mrs. Simpson's schedule that day. Hell, I could say her car was ready.

****

Simpson was easy to find. The high school secretary was nice, not the battle-ax I'd anticipated. "Miss Simpson finishes her last class of the day, Senior Seminar on Twentieth- Century American History, at noon in Room 227. Would you like a hall pass? Then you can meet her there," she said. Didn't even ask me why I wanted to see her.

I hung around in the hall while the teacher and several students engaged in an animated after-class discussion about Roosevelt's New Deal. The door was open so I could hear them. Simpson had long straight blonde hair and looked to be in her forties. I could tell these students thought she was very cool. Finally, they drifted away, and I approached the teacher and said, "Richard Manning."

She broke into a broad smile. "Wow. I wondered if anyone was ever going to ask me about him, and here you are."

I explained who I was, established that this was an informal inquiry, and invited her to join Carol and me for lunch. She looked surprised but was willing to skip the high school cafeteria's fare.

"Say, is the Calimesa Country Club still open?" I asked. The answer was yes so we agreed to meet there.

It was a short drive through a residential neighborhood first, then orange groves, and finally up a small rock-strewn hill that overlooked the town. The old wood-shingled building looked exactly the same. The scent of pine trees greeted us.

"Nice place," Carol said.

"Yeah. This was one of my spots."

I was surprised when Emily Simpson ordered a glass of Chablis with her French dip sandwich. She saw me looking. "Friday afternoon, no classes," she said. "Also, I'm a little nervous. I don't hang out with law enforcement as a rule. No offense. Just not my scene."

We had a table overlooking the driving range. "I didn't peg you as a country club guy," Carol said to me.

"It's a public golf course with good food. They just call it a country club."

Emily agreed. "We have school functions here sometimes."

"I'll have a Budweiser," I said to the waitress, not wanting Emily to drink alone. Carol had her usual annoying Tab. *At least have a real Coke*, I thought but held my tongue.

Without the need for much prompting, Simpson started talking. "Richard and his mother moved here just before he started junior year, not a great time to be a new kid. All the groups and cliques have formed by then. I knew he'd tried out for football but hurt himself, a badly sprained ankle as I recall, so he wasn't on the team. I had him in my standard American History Survey course and could tell right away that he was very bright. We started talking some after class, just like you saw today," she said to me—Emily seemed shy relating to Carol, so she talked to me. The reverse of the usual.

"What year was this?" I asked her.

Emily grimaced. "That's an easy one, unfortunately. 1963. Richard was in my class, third period, when the news came: President Kennedy had been shot. Richard stayed around that day, even after the announcement that the president had died and the principal let school out. My fiancé—we're not together now—and Richard's mother both had to stay at work. It was a Friday. I wheeled in a television set I got from audio-visual—the clerk was so upset she didn't even ask for a requisition, 'just bring it back on Monday', she said—and we watched the news coverage. Some other kids came in and watched too."

"How did Richard take the news of the assassination?" Carol asked in a soft voice, making eye contact, breaking down Emily's reserve. She was so good at it.

After taking a sip of wine, Emily paused, as if weighing her words. "Better than me, actually. I loved JFK, thought he was going to be great, still do, Bobby too. What terrible things we do. Anyway, Richard didn't want to miss a minute of the news. He was very intense, not like a kid about it, as if he was growing up right before my eyes."

I realized that her sandwich was getting cold. "Let's break for a while," I said. "Enjoy your meal."

We all chomped away in silence, thinking back to that time, November 22, 1963. Everybody remembered where they were. I was still an MP in Germany, due to muster out in a month. We were put on high alert when the news came through in case the Russians had done it. Tensions remained high that entire month.

"I was in college," Carol said, as if reading our minds. "My roommate was in the student lounge on Sunday morning drinking coffee and actually saw Jack Ruby shoot Oswald on live TV. Can you believe it?"

I went up to the bar and ordered two more drinks for Emily and me. Normally I liked talking about the Kennedy stuff, but not today. We were going down a rabbit hole and it was a distraction. I wanted to know what Emily knew about Manning. I was not in the best of moods. The motel bed had been too soft, like trying to sleep in quicksand. Plus, I'd been tossing and turning, thinking about Allie. Around 3 a.m., I'd been jolted with a bolt of startling clarity. She was gone. It was over. Sure, like movie actors that knew their lines, we'd play out a few more scenes. But the ending was clear. And I felt like a chump, a sucker, for letting her in, for being vulnerable. Any idiot could have seen this coming...

"That'll be two dollars, sir," the bartender said, bringing me back. I paid, gave him a fifty-cent tip, and made my way back to the table, determined to learn more.

I handed Emily her glass of wine and she resumed her narrative. "Richard became more politically active his senior year, mostly in relation to the civil rights movement. Yucaipa has no Black residents to speak of, so this really was just Richard reading and talking about things, expanding his knowledge."

"I heard he led some sort of a sit-in at the high school," I offered.

"Ah, that came later." She smiled. "The Berkeley Free Speech movement started the very year that Richard started college there. Good timing. So, the next spring—it must have been sixty-six—he came back to town and decided to organize the high school's kitchen workers. They were predominately Mexican, and Richard figured they must be underpaid. The whole thing was kind of comical. Several workers reluctantly joined him in a 'stop work action'— as he called it—and the football players got mad because their lunch was late. The police showed up. It all blew over quickly, and Richard went back to Berkeley."

Emily took a big slug of Chablis, enjoying our attention. The waitress brought the check and Carol grabbed it.

"Did you see Richard after that?" I asked.

Emily nodded. "Only once. It was a little scary to tell you the truth. Richard came by to see me late one afternoon. I hardly recognized him with the long hair and red beard—the change was quite impressive. He seemed all wired up, agitated. We got into an argument about politics, and I said I was against radical action."

"How did he take that?"

"Not well. He didn't exactly push me, but the next thing I knew I was against the wall in my classroom, right next to a Lincoln Memorial poster, and he was in my face. It was quite alarming. 'You're just another liberal loser, part of the problem not the solution,' he yelled. And with that he walked out. I haven't seen him since."

"Were you surprised when you heard about the bombings?" Carol asked.

"At first, yes. It was so violent. But then I remembered the crazed look on his face that last time, when he swore at me, threatened me. So maybe not so much."

"Another thing," I asked, "did you see the 'Hippie Mama' newspaper article about Monterey Pop?"

Emily snorted. The Chablis was loosening her up. "Yeah. I saw it but didn't pay too much attention. That's about the time my wonderful fiancé decided he could do better than a lousy, underpaid high school teacher and ran off with a real estate agent."

Oops. Enough wine. Time to thank Miss Emily Simpson for her time and send her on her way. She'd been helpful though, she'd earned her lunch.

As we walked toward the car, Carol stopped, took a deep breath, and surveyed the desert town of Yucaipa. "I'm beginning to think Hippie Mama may be the key to this whole deal."

CHAPTER FIFTEEN

I WAS DRIVING TO breakfast the next day after a good night's sleep in my own bed when my radio phone blared. It was Sam Fuller's personal secretary. "He wants to see you this morning."

"Hey, I'm on vacation."

"He said right now, Jimmy, and he's not happy," she said. "Look out." Sam's temper was legendary, particularly since he rarely lost it.

There was a wreck on the I-10, so I took Route 66 to San Bernardino, which made me even later to the meeting with Sam. His office was located in the county building, an example of drab SoCal modern, right next to the courthouse. When I got there, I was motioned in without the customary small talk with the staff. Sam was shuffling papers, not really looking at them. Even his hair looked mad.

"Hi, Boss." I tried a cheery wave to lighten things up.

"Sergeant Sommes, what the hell were you doing snooping around Solana Beach on Monday?" he growled.

"Well, there's this case—"

"Richard Manning. First, it's not your case, not even close to it. Second, I can't have my officers sneaking around in other jurisdictions, telling lies, causing trouble, punching civilians. Jesus Christ! What's the matter with you?" I'd never seen Sam's face so red.

"Boss, the guy punched me first and—"

"Zip it, Sergeant. It so happens that Solana Beach Police Chief Wilcox and I started in this business together." Sam glowered at me and continued. "Rookie cops in South Pasadena after the war. He's a good man, and your little stunt embarrassed me, made it look like I can't control my officers. I convinced him not to file a complaint against you or your Claremont buddy." Sam took a slug of coffee from his Rose Bowl mug and glared at me. "But you better come clean right now."

So, I told him the whole story, including the theories that Carol and I had about the Manning case. At first, he was impatient, even looking once at his watch. But then he started taking an occasional note on his legal-size yellow pad, a good sign. Then he cancelled his next appointment to let me finish.

"Okay," he said when I finally ground to a halt, fresh out of convincing tidbits. "Your theory is that two weeks after Richard Manning, a known radical, set off that bomb at the library, a copycat criminal murdered this Claremont economics professor with a bomb to make it look like another radical act. Is that right?"

"Yes," I managed to say.

Sam continued his summary of my long-winded version. "After the murder, Manning's initial lawyer, Claremont's own Jason Phillips—who hangs out with radicals and uses drugs—then convinced him, via blackmail of some sort, to clam up and say nothing about the case—except to spout radical slogans—even if he may not have set off the second bomb. And who the hell is this 'Hippie Mama' lady?"

I had to admit that it sounded more than a little preposterous coming out of Sam's mouth.

He went on. "And why murder the college professor? Got any evidence? Any motive? Man, it's quite a theory, but that's all you've got."

"I don't know the motive," I said. "The victim, Rebecca Meadows, is a mystery, no family, no close friends. Everybody liked her, but nobody knew her. Anyway, the same person that threw a brick through Carol's car window might be the real blackmailer. None of this, as you just demonstrated, is solid. It's all rumors and whispers. But you've known me for a while now, Boss, and both my gut and my brain are telling me something's very wrong with that second bombing. It stinks, and neither the FBI nor LASD gave, or give, a shit about the discrepancies, which is why Carol and I have been freelancing this thing."

"The Feds, I get it," Sam said. "They've got their radical bomber, so Hoover's happy. At present, the FBI would trade two mafia kingpins for one long-haired radical bomber any day of the week, which is tragic." Sam rubbed his iron-gray crewcut. "But LA County, you need to work with them, no more sneaking around. That goes for your girlfriend too." Sam gave his desk globe a spin—a habit of his—closed his eyes and then checked the spot where his finger was when the world stopped. "Poland," he said. The locations didn't seem to matter.

I tried to keep a straight face. Sam was going to let me keep working on this, maybe even on the clock. "She's not my girlfriend."

"Whatever. Let me give some thought to who at LASD I might call to ease the way."

"Thanks, Boss. I appreciate it. We've been working some with Al Sevilla out of San Dimas, but he's not interested, thinks it's all crap," I said.

"It'll be someone higher up," Sam said. "Somebody who knows how fucked up the FBI can be on occasion." Sam gave me one of his looks. "You've got a week. I'm not sold on any of this yet, in fact it seems pretty nuts to me, but your instincts are usually pretty good." He stood up. The meeting was over. Then Sam added a final thought. "So far, all you're telling me is that some guy didn't murder her. Not good enough. You gotta tell me who set off that bomb, or at least develop some suspects."

I nodded and got out of there.

"Did you get fired?" Sam's secretary asked me on the way out, knowing that I didn't.

"Hell no, but I've got some work to do," I said, eager to give Carol the news.

****

It had to wait, as Carol's office in Claremont's small city hall was empty. The whole place, a one-story adobe-style building with a red tile roof, seemed deserted. I found Virgil, the police dispatcher and office clerk, out back watering a patch of marigolds.

"Carol told me to tell you she's gone to Pomona to study property records. She said you'd know what that meant," Virgil said, looking up when his watering can was empty.

"Where's the mayor?"

"Up at Marie Callender's, giving a speech to the Kiwanis Club," Virgil said. "That man eats for free way too much. He's starting to look like a bowling ball."

I left Virgil to tend his flowers, happy that Carol was on the hunt.

****

The singer and sometimes rhythm guitarist in our band was a dipshit. He could sing and play okay, but he always wore super-tight pants and muscle shirts, prancing around the stage like some kind of low-rent Mick Jagger. I ignored him as best I could and left the business to Sokoloski. I just played in the band, man.

Andy—that was the singer's name—had a new girl-friend who wanted to join the band and sing backup. Which was why I was practicing the fiddle part on *White Bird*, a song by a San Francisco outfit called It's A Beautiful Day. Andy's girlfriend loved it and wanted us to play it with her singing along. We actually did need another singer. Nobody except Andy could carry a tune, which was why we put up with him. I was working through the progressions on my fiddle. There was not a trace of country music to it, so I guess you'd call it rock violin. It was a nice tune—kind of a hippie anthem—and violin was the lead instrument. The lyrics were kind of sappy, but Sokoloski and I could trade licks, get something good going on the breaks. We needed a new jam song.

The phone rang. It was Allie, after midnight in New York. "How ya doing, Jimmy?" She sounded drunk, or high.

"I'm fine, working on a song." I filled her in on the *White Bird* thing, talking too much, knowing instantly that something was wrong.

"Uh, look, I can't talk too long," she said. "You see, I'm not coming back to Claremont. Pomona is letting me finish from here, get my diploma. Somebody will come by for my things. I started the *Village Voice* job. It's really cool, just what I want. So, that's my news."

"I guess that's it then," I said, realizing I'd been waiting for this particular hammer to fall—maybe since that first moonlight kiss. There was some background noise, Allie whispering. Did I hear a man's voice calling to her? Were they in bed?

"Where are you?" I barked, my head spinning. "Are you alone?"

"None of your business, man." A slight giggle. "Sorry, I really am sorry." She hung up.

Well, fuck.

I got out a bottle of bourbon. People shouldn't drink to escape their problems—good advice I'd given to others on occasion. But there were two clear exceptions: getting fired and getting dumped.

Three fingers of Jim Beam on the rocks, a splash of water, shake it around, letting the ice cubes jangle against the glass. The second one tasted even better than the first. My memory is hazy after that. Except that damn song kept playing on the stereo, over and over again, the needle arm set on repeat. The *White Bird* had flown from her golden cage. And the joke was on me.

CHAPTER SIXTEEN

A TERRIBLE NOISE WOKE me up; somebody was drilling my brain. It was the next morning, and Carol was calling from the Village Grill for our postponed breakfast meeting.

"I'll be there in half an hour," I told her. Thank God I was on vacation. I threw some water on my face and tried to wake up.

Carol was waiting for me. She was wearing her uniform, blue slacks and a dull green work shirt with "Claremont Police Department" stenciled on it. She almost always wore it, even on days like this, when she technically was off-duty. I'd asked her about it once.

She'd said, "Out of uniform, I'm a moderately attractive, slightly overweight thirty-year old woman that nobody pays attention to or takes seriously. The uniform gives me authority."

No argument from me. Cops do whatever they need to get an edge.

Our food arrived. Was I hungry? The Thursday breakfast special at the grill was French toast with bacon. I hoped I could keep it down. Carol had taken one look at me and figured it out.

"Allie?"

"Yup."

"Okay. How do you feel?" Carol held my gaze. "And tell the truth, no bullshit. Life's too short."

"There was this seminar last year at the Fairmont Hotel in San Francisco," I began, pausing for a bite of bacon. Carol, impatient, started to interrupt me. I put my hands up to stop her, which hurt my head. "No. Hold on. It's related. Sam made me go. It was an FBI thing on preserving a crime scene."

"Which is important."

"Yeah. But all these guys from DC, and also from the State AG's office up in Sacramento, their suits cost a fortune. Big shots and boy did they know it, circling the room like politicians, shaking hands with everybody, lots of hearty laughs. I'm sure I can work a crime scene better than most of them. I wanted to get out of there, away from them, their pretension. It wasn't about the work. It was about... power."

"You've lost me. Wouldn't Allie hate those guys?" Carol asked, a puzzled look on her face.

"Yeah, in one way. But they share a world... and she doesn't even know it. That's the thing. Allie comes from money, new money, which can be the worst. No matter how radical she thinks she is, part of her brain is waiting for the servant to clear away the dishes, the maid to make the bed. I've never had a fucking maid. Allie's a pipe dream, good stuff, and I wish her well, but I know who I am; an Okie cop from Pomona, and proud of it. Does that make any sense?"

Not sure it did. My head hurt. I should just shut up.

"Okay. I think I get it. You're also fourteen years older than her, and that matters." Carol patted my arm. "You ready to work?"

I nodded and finished my coffee, determined to fight off the Allie blues. And the French toast had tasted better than the bourbon.

Carol rubbed her hands together. "Good. Because I've

got news. Melody Manning got married again. Get this. To a Hells Angel biker half her age. The guy rode, or rides, out of Fontana, your territory."

"Wow. Hippie Mama's back in the game. When?"

"The marriage license is dated January 12, 1970, before the bombings. I did a records search. The guy's name is Anthony Harris."

"You can bet the dude's Angels' handle will be different. Let's pay a visit to the old Fontana drag strip," I said. "Give the Angels a wake-up call."

"Do we need backup?" Carol looked worried, jiggling her spoon.

"Nah. SBSD has an understanding with the Angels. 'Don't murder anybody or sell drugs to kids, and we'll leave you alone' is pretty much the deal. Each chapter is different. This Fontana group, mostly they just ride their choppers, tinker with spare parts, take pills, and drink beer. They're better than the Barstow desert rats; those guys will stick a knife in your back just for fun."

"Good to know," Carol said. "Just the same, I'm going in armed to the teeth."

"Me too." I settled the Village Grill bill.

As we walked outside, the morning sun roasted my eyeballs, damn near flattened me. I gobbled three aspirin, put on my shades. "You'd better drive," I said. "I don't want to kill us on the freeway."

I grabbed my gun case out of the Charger. It looked something like a musical instrument case, so nobody freaked out on Yale Avenue when they saw it. We walked to Carol's car, which was parked behind Claremont City Hall. The San Gabriel Mountains looked close enough to touch, framed by bright blue sky. Carol waved at Virgil, who was out watering his marigolds again. Did that man ever work? I got into her loaner Chevy Nova. It smelled better than my Charger.

It was Thursday, April 27, 1972, or Day 1 without Allie—or even the possibility of Allessandra D'Amico coming back to me.

****

Virtually shut down by the national safety board on account of too many crashes, squeezed on all sides by housing developments, and vilified by local officials, the once famous Fontana Drag City had fallen on desperate times. "All that place attracts is tricks, trouble, and trash," a San Bernardino county commissioner recently groused. Hookers had begun to frequent the area in numbers, along with assorted gearheads, drug dealers, and, ironically, the most stable group, the Fontana chapter of the Hells Angels motorcycle club. "How'd *he* know about the hookers?" Sam Fuller had mused abou the commissioner at last week's deputies meeting.

"When I was a kid, my dad used to bring me to the drag strip on Saturdays for the races. Loudest thing I ever heard," I told Carol.

It had been one of those complicated father-son deals where I wasn't sure either of us liked it but pretended to for the sake of the other. What I did love for sure was the great Orange Julius lunch we had afterwards at a little joint on Foothill Boulevard in Claremont, when the Orange Julius sign still had the devil on it. Best hot dogs in the world, with mustard and relish, plus that frothy, sweet orange drink they whipped up in a blender. Or sometimes I got the Lemon Julius, just to be adventurous. The wooden structure with picnic tables outside was long gone, torn down in the early '60s to make room for a real estate office.

Carol was a newcomer, having moved to Claremont

about five years ago after her first job as a patrol officer in Bakersfield.

"You like Orange Julius?" I asked her.

"You mean that place at Montclair Plaza? Never tried it." She was concentrating on her driving, always a good idea on the I-10. "Why?"

"No reason. I used to go there as a kid, not so much anymore."

Orange Julius just wasn't the same in that antiseptic shopping center. The little devil was off the sign, and nowadays indifferent high school kids earning the minimum wage made lousy Julius drinks and gave you lukewarm, barely cooked hot dogs. I missed the real thing.

"Okay, forget Orange Julius, how do you want to play this and what do we need from the Angels?" Carol asked, her fingers tapping the steering wheel.

"Their leader is a dude named Freeway Freddy. He has a relationship with SBSD."

"A snitch?"

"Not exactly, but he'll give us a name now and then if it strikes him as in the Angels' best interest. That type of thing. We return the favor in various ways. For today, let's find anything we can about Anthony Harris and especially Melody Manning. We find them, maybe we can figure out what's up with Richard Manning. It should be a simple, short meeting. But don't act scared."

"Yeah, right," Carol answered with a grimace. I was a little nervous myself.

We stopped at a Taco Bell in the shadow of the billowing smokestacks of the Kaiser Steel Mill, back in business after the long strike. Carol bought a box of burritos while I went next door and bought beer at a discount liquor store. Fontana was booming again, but it still was ugly as sin.

We approached the ramshackle remnants of Drag

City. The Angels had taken over the best part of the staging area, a large warehouse, complete with a skylight, filled with their glorious Harley-Davidson choppers, all shined up and ready to ride. Carol parked right in front, twenty feet from the door. Nobody was stirring at ten in the morning, so we started making noise, talking loudly, not wanting to sneak up on anybody—kind of like hikers in the woods worried about a bear.

We each were carrying our short-barreled shotguns at our sides, slightly behind our backs. Better safe than sorry.

"Hello, we brought breakfast," I yelled, as we walked through the door.

"Is it that goddamn Jimmy Sommes, redneck cop?" a voice called out from behind us, right where we'd entered. He'd completely surprised us.

Freeway Freddy was grinning at us, not a pretty sight as he was missing a lot of teeth. "When I bring breakfast to somebody, I generally leave my shotgun at home," Freddy said, nodding toward our weapons.

He was big, smart, and borderline crazy. No sudden moves was always the rule.

"Sorry, Freddy, we knew it was early for you guys and didn't want to spook anybody."

"I don't spook, man."

"Yeah, whatever." 'Spook' may not have been the best choice of words. The Angels often worked with the notorious Aryan Brotherhood, a white racist outfit that was especially big in the prisons.

Carol put the box of burritos on a table, clearing away assorted debris. "Hi, Freddy, I'm Carol, from the Claremont PD. We're looking for somebody we heard rode with you, Anthony Harris. He's not in any trouble. We just want to talk to him."

"Not much for small talk, are you, lady cop." Freddy turned to me. "Did you bring beer?"

I put a cardboard carrier with six longneck Budweisers on the table. "So, here's your breakfast of champions. Do you know anything about Anthony Harris? It's not a hard question."

"You mean Tony the Tiger. Kind of a little guy, but he sure could ride. Anyway, him and his old lady, and, man, she really was an *old lady*, went north. That's all I know."

"What's his old lady's name?" Carol asked.

Just then a woman in tiny pink hot pants, a bikini top, and bedroom slippers decorated with Peanuts cartoon characters shuffled out of the back room, a cigarette dangling from her lips. Her outfit left nothing to the imagination. Parts of her were hanging out every which way. A rose tattoo decorated her left breast, just above the nipple. She took a bottle of Bud and a burrito and left without saying anything. I looked at Freddy and raised an eyebrow.

"Don't worry. She's over eighteen," he said.

She'd looked over thrity to me. Hard living in Fontana will do that.

"Anyway, to answer your question, Tony's old lady's name was Melody. I remember it because I thought the name was cool, like music," Freddy said.

I couldn't get the image of the hot pants woman out of my mind. Not sexy, just weird, especially the slippers.

"People always misunderstand the Angels." Freddy was talking louder, getting warmed up. "All we want to do is ride the open road, man, feel the wind in our faces, and be left the fuck alone."

"You said up north. That's real general. Can you do better than that?" I asked.

"Maybe," Freddy said, helping himself to a burrito. It disappeared in two bites. "Bring Mr. Taco next time. Better than Taco Bell. I heard Tony might have ended up in San Luis Obispo, riding Highway 101."

"Last question," Carol said. "We really appreciate your help. Did Tony and Melody leave the chapter before or after the Claremont bombings?"

Most people in SoCal remembered the bombings and what they were doing during that time. Freddy scratched his beard, downed a Budweiser in one long gulp, unleashed a titanic burp, and thought about it.

"It was just after. Tony the Tiger, him and his old lady just up and split. He said he needed some fresh air. I remember the timing," Freeway Freddy's tone hardened, "because some of your buddies from the sheriff's office came barreling in here after that first bombing asking us questions about it, like we did it or something. How fucking stupid was that? Lots of Angels have served this country with honor, man. We've got no truck with radicals."

"Sorry, man. We've got a few desk jockeys in San Bernardino who can barely find their dicks," I said, trying to cool Freddy down. No luck.

"You shoulda given us that guy after you arrested him, the bomber. We'd have tied his ass to one of our Harleys and dragged him through the desert. Saved you some time and trouble. Goddamn commie prick." Spit flew out of Freddy's mouth along with words.

Time to go. I motioned to Carol, and we headed for the open warehouse door. "Thanks, Freddy. See ya." He just stared right through me, lost somewhere, maybe back in Vietnam, out on patrol. "I'll bring Mr. Taco next time."

He came out of his trance. "And Dos Equis beer. It goes better with Mex food." He smiled at Carol. "Don't be a stranger, little lady."

Carol went over and shook his hand. The biker pulled her into a hug and I tensed, but she had the situation in hand and quickly disentangled herself. "Bye, Freddy," she said, pulling away.

"You'll need to fumigate that uniform," I muttered as we walked out the door, starting to relax.

Too soon. We were blocked. Four Hells Angels were standing in our path as we made daylight, about ten feet in front of Carol's car.

"Don't stop walking," I whispered.

The men peeled away just as we passed, but one of them stomped on the back of my right ankle with his heavy boot, and I felt something sharp. It hurt like hell, and I could feel blood flowing out. Carol jiggled her keys, trying to keep me focused.

"What a pussy. Does the chick need to drive you, pig?" the stomping Angel said, a young one who didn't know any better.

I turned and made a slight motion of if to raise my shotgun, testing him. He had a sidearm in his hand, looked like a Colt. It was a *High Noon* moment on a dusty western street. I liked my odds.

"Have a *great* day, Jimmy," Freddy yelled. Quick as a cat he'd gotten himself outside, between us and his men. He motioned them to back off, and they retreated into the warehouse, the young punk the last to drift away. I memorized his face.

Freeway Freddy gave me a "you owe me one," look, a mock salute, and spun off toward the door, the spurs on his boots shining in the sun.

One problem remained: the rattlesnake coiled on the ground directly in front of the passenger car door, head reared and ready to strike, its rattles quivering. A coincidence? No. They must have put it there.

No matter. I blew its head off, in no mood to negotiate.

Carol drove us out of there in a cloud of Fontana dust,

her Chevy fishtailing as we hauled ass away from the old drag strip, me with my head out the window, shotgun at the ready, checking for pursuing bikers. Nobody followed us.

"So that's your idea of a simple meeting," Carol said when we were back on the main access road, shaking her head. "Take the rest of the day off, Jimmy. For both our sakes."

CHAPTER SEVENTEEN

THE ASSHOLE BIKER HAD just missed my Achilles tendon with his razor boot, his spurs, or whatever the hell it was. Three stitches and an ace bandage did the trick, but the doctor told me to take it easy. I was limping around my cabin, at loose ends—Lefty Frizzell on the stereo—when a friend of Allie's called, wanting to come by and pick up her stuff.

Christ, she'd wasted no time. I told the friend to come on over and get it. There wasn't much and it was neatly packed in a box and ready to go. Did she already know? Wait, I forgot the bathroom. I gathered her toothbrush and shampoo, the woodsy smell of the latter giving me a Allie flashback—her naked, soapy body, firm breasts, the way she arched her back when I touched her. I slammed the bathroom door.

I stood in the bedroom, trying to stop the flow of memories. Then I noticed a book, *The French Lieutenant's Woman*, which she'd left on the bedside table. It was bookmarked at page 166. I read the page, hoping it would provide a clue to her departure—or possible return? Nothing jumped out at me, it was a scene at the English seaside. But then I looked more closely at the bookmark. It was from the Hundley Book Store at the colleges and decorated with a printed psychedelic flower pattern on the front. The back was blank except for the notation, "Jason, 624-8626." There was an artistic doodle next to the number, a big mushroom growing in a valley with the sun shining.

Local number, I called it. An answering machine, a metallic voice said I'd reached the home of Jason Phillips and to please leave a message. I checked the phone book. No listing for it. What the hell? She had his private number.

I'd ask Allie why, except, if memory served, she'd dumped me over the phone from New York two nights ago while likely screwing some guy. She wouldn't welcome the question. The answer might be simple. Perhaps she'd bought her coke from him.

We'd never talked about it, the mirror I'd found in the bathroom. Allie and I never talked about much, especially since her Richard Manning revelations, such as they were.

The doorbell rang, interrupting my thoughts. I pocketed the bookmark, put the book and the bathroom stuff in the box, and handed it to the young woman at the door. I'd seen her once or twice with Allie. "Have a nice day," she said and departed. Yeah, sure.

I had to get out of my house. Ghosts were prowling. Carol was busy, searching real estate records of the old drug houses I'd identified earlier. No sense bothering her. I drove to a diner in Pomona and ate lunch at the counter, thinking about Allie, the bookmark, and especially Jason Phillips. The dude was all over this case, initial lawyer for Richard Manning, likely cocaine dealer, and current tormentor of Annie Hoover.

A quick stop at the Claremont PD where Virgil let me look at a file. We were beginning to be friends. The file gave me Jason Phillips's home address, plus some other juicy details. It was a fancy address, up in Padua Hills above Claremont. I decided to do a drive-by, nothing dramatic.

The wind had stopped blowing and it was smoggy as hell as I drove up Mountain Avenue. Every local school kid, me included, had made the pilgrimage up to the Padua

Hills Theater on a field trip. It specialized in a hokey and idealized version of Spanish life in early Southern California, mostly designed for tourists. But the grounds were gorgeous, as was the theater, which looked like a large residential rancho straight from a Zorro movie, only real. The houses up the mountain from the theater had fabulous views, but not today. Muddy, brown smog fouled the air and obscured everything. It reminded me that all of us living down in the flatlands were breathing poison. Hell, and it wasn't even summer yet.

I meandered up Padua Hills Drive and found Phillips's house. Not a soul on the streets this Friday afternoon, which was typical for Southern California. Phillips's white-washed two-story adobe-style home rose sharply from the curb behind a polished black wrought-iron fence. I parked in front. Unlike his neighbors, there was no front yard. But I knew there would be a big swimming pool in back, and an elegant pool house.

According to the police report, the pool house was where Phillips had found the television actress, Beverly Edwards, babbling incoherently with blood coming out of her nose, a spilled glass of champagne on the floor, and a pile of cocaine on the table. Thanks to good medical work, she'd survived the overdose, and was still riding the range on Saturday nights, breaking the cowboys' hearts. A quiet felony probation rested lightly on her record.

As for Phillips, he'd pulled off the helpful and concerned friend routine. He had "no idea" where the cocaine came from, the actress had been "depressed lately," worried her show might be cancelled. The patrol officers— Carol was off-duty—the goofball Claremont mayor, even the DA, they all bought it.

Thus, Jason remained a model citizen in the eyes of the locals, a fair-haired boy, and a reliable patron of civic and liberal causes. Except that a few of us, suspicious by nature, knew better. Jason Phillips, my high school idol, the star quarterback, was a rat.

There wasn't a whole lot for me to do up in Padua Hills, and my presence, even just sitting in the car, was starting to draw attention. A maid taking out the trash at a house across the street had already checked me out. Time to go. As I started the engine, my eyes were drawn to an upstairs bedroom window at the Phillips house, a quick movement. A curtain closing? Good. My visit was not a secret. We needed to ramp up the pressure and then see which way the rat scurried.

****

"Fuck!" Mark Collins threw his Dodgers hat to the ground, then quickly glanced around. It was a quiet Saturday morning, only two other golfers on the driving range, and neither seemed to have noticed his temper tantrum. He pulled back his blond hair into a short ponytail, secured it with a tie, and retrieved his hat from the adjoining Astroturf mat.

His inability to control the distance of his five-iron shots was driving him nuts. He was hitting it 160 yards, with a lower trajectory than normal. It had to be something with his backswing. Maybe he should try a six-iron instead for most of his approach shots, keeping the distance to no more than 150 yards. Otherwise, he risked going long, playing for pars and bogies instead of birdies—which meant losing, and Collins hated to lose. But the six-iron brought the front sand traps into play. It was a vexing dilemma.

The club championship started in two weeks. His goal was to finish second, like last year. The champion got noticed too much, had his name etched on the trophy.

Valuing his privacy, Collins knew how to tank a shot, or miss a putt, at just the right moment to fall into anonymous second place, knowing full well that he'd really won the championship. It was a game within a game, and made the entire contest even more exciting.

First, though, there was a job. He'd picked up the file yesterday at his North Las Vegas post office box and called the contact telephone number for additional particulars. It was to be staged as an accident, but time was of the essence, one week—so it could be straight elimination if necessary. He had all the intel he needed on the subject and the variables.

However, there was a problem. In fact, Collins had told the client no at first. He had a rule against repeat assignments in the same location. He'd done Claremont back in May of 1970. Rebecca Meadows. A sweet job, one he was proud of. Normally that would be it. His territory covered the western United States, and he could afford to be picky. But the client was persistent, loaded with money, and less volatile to work for than the mob guys. He didn't have to worry about some goombah shooting him in the back for no reason at all. Collins also recognized that he needed a new challenge, something to keep him from throwing his hat at the driving range, and the Claremont client was offering double his normal fee.

Collins had said yes to the job, provided the client gave him complete control. He'd pack his weapons, a .44 Magnum and a .270 Winchester rifle, in case the accident scenario didn't come together quickly. He'd made a reservation at an airport Holiday Inn near Claremont, checking in two days from now, using his William (Bill) Hanson chemical engineer identity. Bill lived in San Diego, was an avid sportsman, and possessed all the requisite California licenses for the weapons.

The client had asked for one more item in addition to the hit, namely that Collins toss a woman's apartment and photograph every document she had. The concern was that she was playing a double game of some sort. Collins agreed since the job—too easy, really—would provide additional information on the prime target.

Collins loved information, thrived on it. The planning was the fun part. There was no shortage of men, and even some women, who killed, who got off on the violence. Not him. Formulating the plan, implementing the plan, and then getting away clean with no blood on his hands. That was the thrill.

Collins stretched his back muscles, which were too tight. He realized that he'd broken the rules for this client, treated him differently than the others, maybe on account of how they met in that Godforsaken jungle. The doc had fixed up his busted teeth, stopped the bleeding. Collins was still grateful for his help but knew he needed to keep to the rules that had kept him alive in this business.

He rotated his arms, trying to loosen his shoulders. It was time for a steam at the Dunes. He'd take a cab. It was too hot to hit any more balls. The Las Vegas strip was visible in the western sky, an Oz-like mirage. He loved the casual viciousness of the desert. Five miles from a cushy resort, it could kill you in three hours, turn you into jerky.

Collins collected his clubs and headed out, still thinking about the upcoming job in Claremont. He hadn't been back there since 1970. No reason to go. But she'd gotten to him, that economics professor, unusually so. Still, that was the past. He'd made his choices. The Corvette was at Augie's getting a tune-up, ready on Monday morning. He'd drive it to Ontario Airport, park there, and then rent whatever vehicles he needed for the job.

Figuring out his damn five-iron would have to wait.

****

I played a smoking *White Bird* that night at our LaVerne gig, prepared for dramatic thoughts about Allie, with me in the role of tortured artist. No way. The song worked as my rock violin hit the high notes while Sokoloski came in underneath me with some funky guitar riffs. Andy's girlfriend provided a strong vocal, and the crowd loved it, rock 'n' roll energy filling the hall. We'd found a new singer and a reliable new song.

I felt free, unburdened, when I played the song, the reverse of what I'd anticipated. Maybe I was destined to be a loner, drifting in the desert wind with no permanent attachments, doing my job, catching the bad guys, and playing my fiddle. Not all bad, when you think about it. Still, when the bass player asked me where my "old lady" was—the band liked Allie—I said she was traveling, not about to update the guys on my love life. We were taking a break soon anyway, no gigs until June. Sokoloski, divorced, was going to take his two kids on a trip back east.

****

I slept late the next morning, awakened when an excited Carol rang the doorbell and then barged in, donuts in hand. I met her in the living room in my bathrobe.

"Bingo!" she exclaimed. "Blue Sky Enterprises, the corporation that owns that Baseline Road property, the old drug house, is in turn wholly owned by a John Green and Jason Phillips. And they've owned it since 1969, before the bombings. It was their goddamn drug house. I had to drive all the way to the San Bernardino Courthouse to find out. It's in your county, man." She gave me a "why didn't you know that" look, couldn't help herself.

It took a minute to sink in, then I didn't blame her for the look. "Jesus, I missed the boat on that one. My partner and I screwed up. He was so damn lazy. We busted the tenant, got him evicted, working with the owner's 'agent.' That was stupid. Anyway, who's John Green?"

Carol had gotten an orange from my fridge, smelled it, and was peeling it. "I asked Annie that question. Have you heard of the Brotherhood of Eternal Love, in Laguna Beach? John "Jack" Green is a big mucky-muck in the Brotherhood, and, according to Annie, a world-class jerk."

I'd heard of the Brotherhood. They were surfers, some championship level, who also were international drug smugglers; they sold hashish from Afghanistan, cocaine from Peru, and their own brand of manufactured LSD, "Orange Sunshine." *Rolling Stone* magazine had labeled it the acid of choice.

I grabbed the box of donuts and we headed for the deck. "You know the Brotherhood's being investigated, right? Orange County has a big task force going, wants to bust them up."

"Yeah, I heard. They hate hippies almost as much as commies in Orange County." Carol, ignoring the orange she had just peeled, was licking donut glaze off her fingers. "Me, I love donuts. Tell me never to buy them again." She threw her last bite to a squawking scrub jay who'd descended from a pine tree to my deck railing, looking for a handout.

"So is Jason Phillips in the Brotherhood?" I asked.

"I don't know," Carol said, "but you'll hear about it tonight from Annie. I made dinner reservations at the Sycamore Inn. It's time. She's ready to talk. But go easy on her. She's confused and scared."

"I'll be cool, but listen, we've got a problem." Sam's final words at our last meeting still were bugging me. "We don't have any idea who killed Rebecca Meadows."

Carol nodded. "Annie knows stuff, maybe a lot."

CHAPTER EIGHTEEN

SUNDAY NIGHT DINNER AT the Sycamore Inn on Route 66 was a tradition. People came from all over for their prime rib and steak dinners. At least they used to, before more modern, "swinging" joints began to cut into its business. I arrived early and was sitting in a plush red booth waiting for Carol and Annie Hoover to arrive. I'd put on a blue blazer for the occasion, feeling like I was about to meet up with my kid sister who was bringing a date, who just happened to be a woman.

The ladies arrived. Both were dressed up; Annie wore a long dress and had put on some lipstick. It softened her face. She was taller than I remembered. We were by far the youngest people in the room. Carol, in particular, seemed nervous as she and Annie slid in across from me.

"How about gin and tonics for the table?" I asked. It wasn't a pitcher of margaritas type of place, but this meeting cried out for some lubrication.

I placed the order, adding shrimp cocktails on a whim. "My mom and dad brought our family here for Easter dinner a couple of times," I said, trying to keep up the patter.

"When was that?" Annie asked, doing her part to pretend this was a normal social dinner.

"Late fifties sometime," I said. "Cucamonga was still country, and the winery across the street was going strong. According to my dad, it specialized in rot-gut red."

"Still does," Carol chimed in.

The gin and tonics arrived, and Carol practically gulped her first drink and asked for another from the buxom red-haired cocktail waitress, who was wearing some sort of black corset-like thing with mesh stockings up to her butt. She looked completely out of place among the white-haired senior citizen diners, but some of the old folks were getting an eyeful. Me too.

After squeezing a wedge of lemon over the peeled shrimp swimming in red cocktail sauce—the whole conglomeration resting in an iced glass—I dug in with the tiny fork. This had been the height of luxury for my sister and me when we were kids. An ancient waiter approached us—he might have served my family in the fifties—wearing a tuxedo with a crisp white napkin draped over his right shoulder. He recommended the prime rib dinner, and all of us ordered it. At least Annie wasn't a vegetarian. Carol ordered a bottle of red wine for the table.

"Who's driving?" I asked.

"Not your problem," Carol said, too sharply for my taste.

Okay. Sounding like a cop, and not caring, I plunged in. "Annie, I know you can't and won't say anything about the confidential workings of your law clinic, or Jason Phillips's role. But—"

"That's correct," she interrupted me.

"But I'm concerned that Mr. Phillips, wholly apart from your professional relationship, might be mixed up in some pretty serious activities pertaining to drugs." I sounded like Jack Webb or some other bonehead lawman. This wasn't going great.

I caught Annie and Carol exchanging a glance, like I was a narc or something. It pissed me off. They were already ganging up on me. I took a sip of wine, not my favorite drink, to settle down, and signaled the waiter for more rolls.

"It *is* 1972, Sergeant Sommes—"

"Call me Jimmy, please."

"Okay, Jimmy, as I was saying, many professionals these days, not just hippie types, engage in occasional recreational drug use. It's not my thing, but I'm not going to judge Jason too harshly for it."

It sounded stiff, silly, stupid, and rehearsed.

"Me neither," I said. "I don't care about his *recreational drug use*, but we're talking about felony dealing of a Schedule 1 narcotic, and the possible sponsoring of a drug house. Those are 'go to prison' type offenses. Christ, you know that. You're a lawyer."

"But you don't know if Jason is involved in any of that." She looked wary. Carol had told me that Annie was still defensive, trying to talk herself out of this mess.

"No, I don't know entirely about Jason, but, and pardon my French, we sure as shit know that Jason's buddy, Jack Green, Mr. Eternal Brotherhood, was and is knee deep in dealing coke, speed, grass, LSD, you name it. And you know it too."

On that happy note, the meal arrived, the plates steaming and sending off wonderful aromas. "How about we enjoy this fine prime rib and Yorkshire pudding before it goes stone cold," Carol said, "and pick up the conversation later."

Protecting her girlfriend. It was okay with me. Nobody ever had to ask me twice to eat.

During dinner, Annie told us about her clinic's efforts to get Chicano citizens registered to vote, a much safer topic for us to discuss. Agreed, the roadblocks erected by local government to prevent voter registration were downright shameful. But I was getting bored with the earnest talk.

Finally, Annie, perhaps fortified by the gin and the wine, put down her fork, looked at me, and told the truth. "I'm scared to death and need your help." Carol quickly patted her hand and then moved her hand away, wanting to be discreet.

"Okay. Tell this any way you want to," I said, trying not to sound too eager.

"This is going to sound corny, but there are two Jasons," Annie began. "I still see the smart, funny, passionate man who founded the clinic and cares deeply about social justice—the Jason who hired me—but he's not around very often these days. The other guy, wired, secretive, paranoid, and bad-tempered, is showing up more and more. And he's messing with the Clinic's money."

"Embezzling?"

"Even worse. He's the owner of the non-profit, so obviously he's got the right to run the show. But I'm in charge of the operating budget. Too *much* money is showing up. I think it's drug money, and money laundering."

Annie paused to drink some water. She was drinking less alcohol than either Carol or me. "The money comes in and then disappears. Jason says it's all anonymous donations for *capital projects*, or some such bullshit. The clinic doesn't have capital projects, except the data processing system that we need for our voting rights work."

"How much mystery money in total?"

"More than a hundred thousand in the last year."

"Wow. Your accountant must be going nuts."

"Jason changed accountants. When I asked why, he said 'Leave it to me.' That was about the time he bought a BMW sedan and a van out of the same company account. He said they were business expenses, and the new accountant cleared the purchases. I've never seen either one at the clinic." Annie paused. "Sorry, this is really freaking me out." Carol handed her a Kleenex. "You said 'scared to death' earlier. Has Jason threatened you?" I asked.

"Jason and I had a big blow-up about two weeks ago. Another large deposit of money had come in. The clinic's board of directors is comprised of community members, union and business reps, politicians, and college people. When he wouldn't tell where this new money came from, I got angry and told him I was going to the board and tell them about the money."

"How did he react to that?"

"He ordered me not to say a word to them, saying he'd already briefed 'leadership,' and that he'd fire me if I disobeyed him. I chickened out and agreed. I need my job. But then things got worse. I called his house last week—he doesn't spend much time at the clinic anymore—with a routine legal question. Jack Green answered. He's been hanging around the clinic more and more, yelling at people, rifling through Jason's stuff. Anyway, it was the middle of the afternoon, and I could hear a party going on. Green said, 'You're the chick who asks way too many questions' before giving the phone to Jason, who was too stoned to make much sense. I gave up on my question and was about to end the call when Green came back on the phone and said, 'Annie, don't fuck with our operation, or you'll regret it, maybe *permanently*,' and hung up. Maybe nothing more than macho nonsense, but it gave me chills."

The waiter brought coffee. We were shutting down the dining room, the old folks having finished their meals and shuffling off for home. The bar action, however, was picking up.

"Bring some California brandies, will you?" I asked George, our waiter.

He went over to the corseted cocktail waitress, who

was looking better and better to me as the night wore on, talked to her, and then gave me a thumbs-up. The snifters of brandy arrived soon after, borne by the red-headed beauty.

"Here you are, sweetie," she said to me, her breasts in my face. I didn't mind, but cautioned myself to keep my mind on Annie. Her information was a gold mine, and the other monkey business could wait.

"Annie, were you the office manager at the time of the Claremont bombings?" I asked, collecting myself.

"Yeah, I'd just gotten promoted. Things were really good then. I never met Richard Manning, by the way. Jason handled him as a personal client."

I swirled the brandy around in my glass, pretending I knew what I was doing. "Manning has a mother who may have lived up here then. Does that ring any bells?"

"You know, Carol and I were talking about that earlier today. I've got a random recollection of a woman waiting for Jason outside the clinic around that time, looking very upset. He'd been real jovial as we locked up that day, then he saw her, said, 'Oh shit,' and walked away from me without another word. I didn't think that much about it at the time. We get all sorts of agitated clients at the clinic. It goes with the territory. But now that image resonates. That woman was really angry, yelling at him. It wasn't a normal interaction. So, like I told Carol, it might have been her. Sorry, best I can do."

The lights dimmed in the dining room. George asked us if he could seat us at a table in the bar, saying, "Lisa will take care of you," and gesturing toward the cocktail waitress, whose answering smile gave me another buzz. We carried our drinks to a table in the bar where a Dodgers game was on the television, a rare Sunday night game because of a rain-out. Don Sutton was pitching, and the

Dodgers were ahead in the late innings.

"God, I just remembered something." Annie actually shuddered as she spoke. "Back during those Kent State protests two years ago, just before the grad school bombing, Jason was talking on the phone in his office, really angry at someone. 'I can't do that,' he said. 'There's got to be another way.' Then it got really quiet. After a while Jason opened his door, looking sick and pale."

Annie gave a rueful smile. "I was such a suck-up back then. I asked him if everything was okay. He recovered pretty quickly, said this contractor wanted to cut corners on a building job at his house, not use union workers."

"You don't think that was it?" Carol asked, picking at a bowl of peanuts on the table.

"I did at the time. Representing unions is a big deal for our clinic. But now... his reaction was too intense, too personal. My God, do you think he actually knew what was going to happen to that woman?" Carol moved closer and gave Annie a quick, sisterly hug, the best she could do in public.

"We don't know that yet, but none of this is your fault," I said, feeling her guilt. "Thanks for talking to me tonight, and," I hesitated, feeling a wave of emotion, "and for making my best friend so happy." Getting sentimental. Must be loaded. Even Carol teared up at that.

We drank some more brandy and moved on to easier subjects. The Dodgers won, and announcer Vin Scully said, "Goodnight, everybody" in that special voice of his, like he knew every single one of us as his good friend. The bartender turned off the set. The evening was winding down, just another Cucamonga night, until I noticed that Lisa, the barmaid, had written her phone number and address on a cocktail napkin and put it in front of me while nobody was looking.

I'd made a deal with Carol: she paid for the food, I paid for the booze. I figured it was about even, or I might be ahead now. Carol and Annie left around midnight and I walked them to their car. We agreed I would come over to Carol's the next day and help Annie figure out what to do next. She'd already decided to call in sick for tomorrow.

"And don't get pulled over, for God's sake," were my parting words to Carol.

"Take care of yourself, Romeo," she replied. How did she know?

I went back to the bar and ordered a beer. Lisa left at one o'clock, the same time as the manager. "Good," the bartender said and put a Jethro Tull tape, *Stand Up*, on the sound system, loud. Perfect for my state of mind. Maybe our singer was right about something for a change, I thought, him saying that we should rock harder. Tull sure sounded good.

Anyway, I left about 1:30. Lisa's building was easy to find, one of those eight-plex jobs in Upland with the apartments surrounding a swimming pool. I knocked on her ground-floor door. She opened it, wearing only a towel, her red hair wet from the shower. "I wondered where you were, handsome."

She looked older, and better, without all the eye make-up. The towel fell away as she pulled me through the door. Oh, man. Her body was California golden, even her freckled breasts, and she smelled like ripe peaches. I couldn't get enough of her, a lovely lady who knew the score.

CHAPTER NINETEEN

IT WAS NOT QUITE one in the afternoon when I got to Carol's bungalow the next day. Annie opened the door and waved me in.

"How'd you sleep, Jimmy?" Carol called out from the kitchen.

"Like a baby. Didn't wake up until almost noon, a record for me." I'd left Lisa's apartment at dawn, both of us knowing I'd be back.

Carol came out into the living room, barely room for the three of us, with sandwiches—their lunch and my breakfast. Carol was full of energy for someone who'd put away so much booze last night. I was impressed as she briefed me on her work.

"So, I called the Orange County DA's office this morning, identified myself as a Claremont police detective, and asked for information about the Brotherhood of Eternal Love Task Force. First, they put me on hold for fifteen minutes, then some pompous SOB came on the line and told me, in so many words, to buzz off and mind my own business. Do they teach that in law school?"

That got a smile out of Annie. "Not at Stanford," she said, then turned to me. "I called in sick today, said I had the flu, was throwing up like crazy. It's almost true, after those gin and tonics last night. Do you think I have to stay away from the office? There's so much work to do. With Jason all messed up, I pretty much run the place."

Carol shook her head. "Annie, Jack Green threatened you last week. My friend on the Laguna force said he's a psycho, maybe the worst of the bunch. So, yeah, you need to stay very sick this week while we figure things out. The clinic can survive until then. You've told me your staff is great. Let them carry the ball for a change."

"I wonder, does anybody at your office know about Carol, about your relationship with her?" I asked.

Annie bristled at the question. "I keep my personal life to myself. Why does that matter?"

I looked at Carol, who saw where I was headed. "It matters, Annie, because I'm a cop," she said softly, "and we're dealing with criminals. When they find out about me and you, and they will, it will be that much more dangerous for you."

I had an idea. "I've got a DA friend who represents San Bernardino on the Brotherhood Task Force. I want him to take your deposition, get everything on the record. Will you agree to that, Annie? It's for your protection."

"That's going to implicate Jason, right?" Annie frowned. "You know he never lets his, uh, difficulties interfere with the clinic's work." She was still hesitant, and so naïve.

"Maybe so, but *you* might get in big trouble," I said. "You've been loyal to a fault. It's time to protect yourself, get ahead of the Task Force, ahead of the arrests."

It took a while, with me being reasonable and Carol cajoling, but at last Annie agreed, and I got on the line with my friend.

My friend did one better. He persuaded one of the Orange County Assistant DAs to come up and take her statement. Two hours later, the tape was rolling. The lawyer homed in on the money laundering angle. And Annie, as office manager, authorized the Task Force to examine the clinic's banking records. She also, in my cop view, effectively covered her ass. Better late than never.

Annie was quiet afterwards, probably sensing that her life had taken a turn that couldn't be undone. Carol cooked some chili. We ate it and went to bed early. I stayed over, sleeping on the couch, feeling a need to protect both of them, sensing a lurking evil that was beyond my experience, and hoping I was up to the task of taking it on.

****

The next day we turned Carol's den into a war room. Sheets of paper were taped to the walls, with dates, victims, suspects. Jason Phillips was the focus, since he connected back to the May 1970 bombing, as did the mysterious Jack Green. Added, in bold letters, were the names of Melody Manning and Anthony Harris, aka Tony the Tiger. I badly wanted to journey to San Luis Obispo and find them, believing that Melody might be able to unlock her son's secrets.

The phone rang mid-morning. It was for Annie. She listened for a minute. "No, I didn't call an electrician. Is he still there?" She put her hand over the phone. "Jane, my neighbor, I gave her this number. We look out for each other at the building. There've been some break-ins."

An *electrician*... man, I wasn't sure about that. It seemed to confirm my forebodings of the previous evening. I asked for the phone. "Hi, Jane, this is Sergeant Sommes of the San Bernardino Sheriff's Office. I'm afraid you may have stumbled into an active investigation. Tell me what you saw."

Jane was a hospital nurse and had come home from her overnight shift. Climbing the front stairs, she'd noticed a van parked in front with "Jensen's Electric" on the side panels. She then saw a curtain move in Annie's apartment.

Knowing Annie was gone, she peeked in the living room window. The curtain was drawn, but she could see movement through a small slit. She thought about calling the police but decided to call Annie first.

"You did exactly right," I told her. "The man you saw may or may not be an electrician. Please lock your door, and don't open it for anyone. I'll be there in about twenty minutes. I'll check on Annie's unit first, then come talk to you. I'll give the door three loud knocks to let you know it's me. So just take it easy until then."

"Okay." She sounded breathless, uneasy.

"Give me your keys," I said to Annie, who'd been listening. She handed them over.

I asked Carol for some paper and a pencil and gave them to Annie, saying, "Draw a quick layout of your apartment for me." She did as I asked and handed it over.

"You're unit thirteen and Jane's unit fourteen, is that right?" I asked. She nodded.

I grabbed my hat and gun. "I'm going over there. Gotta check this out." The bad guys were coming for Annie. I could just feel it.

"I don't want you to go over there. It's too dangerous." Annie had wrapped her arms around herself and was biting her lower lip.

"It's my job."

"But it's *my* apartment. I forbid it."

I glanced at Carol. This was getting weird.

"Annie, we're going to lose an opportunity if Jimmy doesn't go over there," Carol said. "We need to find out what's going on. Believe it or not, he's good at this."

I saw calculation in Annie's eyes; something more complex than worry about me was going on. Screw it. I left and Annie didn't stop me.

Carol walked me to my car. "Do you want backup?"

I told her no, and that I'd call Sam Fuller from the road.

"Are you okay?" she asked, clearly thinking that I wasn't.

"Yeah, but everything about this feels different. I better be on my A game." I gave her a quick hug.

Once in the car I called Sam Fuller's special line on my radio phone. "I need to talk to him *now*," I told his secretary.

Sam came on the phone. "What's up, Jimmy?"

"I got a situation in Upland, a man in Annie Hoover's apartment, the woman who works for our friend Jason Phillips."

"Him again," Sam grunted.

"The address is 2440 West Arrow Highway. It may be nothing, an electrician doing his job, but I'm going to find out."

"Okay. What do you need from me?" Sam asked.

I thought about it. There probably was an innocent explanation to all this. "How about two squad cars on Arrow Highway, one at Mountain to the east, and one at Monte Vista to the west. And give me a special frequency to reach the cars, code name 'Jumping Jack Flash,' in case the guy has a scanner. I'll contact the squad cars from the property in about ten minutes."

"You got it." Sam signed off.

I drove on. A dump truck blocked my way near the arroyo separating Claremont and Upland. I was tempted to blast him with my siren but held off, staying cool—not knowing what I'd find at Annie's place.

The sixteen-unit apartment complex where Annie lived was old but well-maintained. I recalled attending a party there some years before. Resident and guest parking was in the rear. There was no security personnel or swimming pool. Not a place for swinging singles. Turning right off Arrow Highway, I drove to the front of the building.

The Ford Econoline with "Jensen's Electric" stenciled on the side panels was parked in a striped service area directly beneath Annie's apartment. The license plate was smeared with mud and unreadable. I established contact with the squad cars, gave them the info, and told them to stay alert. Then I parked next to the van.

The complex was quiet, folks at work or at school. Looking around to get my bearings, I saw towering date palms that bookended the property, clearly older than the building. As I approached it, I noticed the groundcover was ivy, with small ornamental fruit trees spaced every ten feet. Everything was tidy.

Units 13 and 14 were located on the second floor, each with a small balcony facing the mountains. A cat strolled by, oblivious to me. A blues song flashed in my mind... "black cat crossed my path." At least this cat wasn't black.

I climbed the exterior stairs and started along the outdoor walkway toward Annie's apartment. My mouth was dry, and I felt like a rookie. Adrenaline usually kicked in for me in these situations. Not today. Fear was clinging to me like a bad dream.

I knocked on the door. There was no answer. I knocked again.

"Who's there?" A male voice.

"Jimmy Sommes, a friend of Annie's," I said, not wanting to identify myself yet as a police officer. "She asked me to pick up a file for her."

The door opened and a bushy-mustached man of medium height and build, wearing white overalls and a Dodgers baseball hat, greeted me. "How ya doin', man. I'm Edward from Jensen's Electric. Come on in. Landlord has us checking all the fuse boxes in the complex, seeing if they're still good." He pointed to the open fuse box panel in the kitchen. "Just about done here."

I noticed his expensive-looking gloves, odd for your everyday electrician.

I glanced into the living room. Papers were scattered all over a small desk and several had fallen onto the rug. Annie struck me as too neat to leave such a mess. The man followed my gaze, not missing a thing.

He handed me a business card. "I'm not sure why it's your business, man, but call the landlord if you want. His number's on the back." The smile stayed on his face as he pulled out a cigarette and lit it, but his cobalt blue eyes were the coldest I'd ever seen.

I made a mistake, I looked down at the card...

Next thing I knew I was breathing shag carpet, my face was in it and my head hurt. How long had I been out? I heard an engine starting outside. I rose and staggered dizzily toward the front door and made it outside just in time to see the electrician van pulling away. I reached for my Colt revolver. It was gone.

Then the damnedest thing happened. The van slowed and turned slightly. The man faced me from the driver's seat window, maybe thirty yards away. Huge sunglasses covered his face, along with the bushy mustache. For some reason, the man was staring up at me, making contact. He then tipped his blue baseball cap, flashed a quick smile, and gunned the van toward Arrow Highway. It chilled me, and suddenly I felt grateful to be alive.

Shaking off his spell, I ran down the stairs to my car. The front tires were hissing where he'd slashed them. My radio antenna lay twisted on the ground, with my Colt revolver placed right next to it. Well, shit.

Back upstairs, I called Sam on Annie's phone—wasting at least two minutes getting through—and explained to him that the suspect had knocked me out and disabled my car. Could he alert the squad cars that the electrician's van was on the move?

"Roger that. You need medical attention?"

"No, just a crime scene tech who can check Annie's unit for prints. And better call the Upland PD. It's their burglary."

Remembering Jane, the nurse, I knocked three times on her door. She took one look at me and sat me in a chair, fed me three aspirin, and gave me a wet towel for the bump on the back of my head. I told her the intruder was gone.

How had Mr. Dodger Hat moved so fast? I was facing him when I'd glanced down at the card and somehow, he hit me in the back of the head. Maybe a fast punch to the stomach first? My gut literally told me that was a no. I'd never come against anyone like him before.

I sat there, trying my best not to puke. It definitely was a concussion, but I'd had worse. The dude knew just how hard to hit me. He'd taken my weapon, which was humiliating, and returned it, which was almost worse. I'd have to tell the Upland cops all about it. Word would get around. Maybe Sommes is losing his touch, they'd say at the donut shop. Screw it.

I called Sam again from a phone in Jane's kitchen. One of the squad cars had found the Jensen's Electric van abandoned behind a gas station on Central Avenue, its engine still warm. The man had gotten away clean. No surprise. We could put out a BOLO—Be On The Look Out—alerting other cops to his existence. What existence? A white male with medium-length hair and a bushy brown mustache wearing large sunglasses and a baseball cap—it sounded like half the crowd at a Dodgers game. There would be no prints or other evidence in Annie's apartment, since he was obviously a pro. And had those gloves.

I needed to call Carol. "You guys better get over here,

pronto," I told her. "It was an intruder. I interrupted him, and he cold-cocked me. And look out. He's dangerous. Maybe Annie should drive, and you ride shotgun."

Carol sighed loudly, letting me know she hated it when I told her how to do her job, and hung up.

Dizzy again and feeling faint, I went back and sat in the chair. My heart was beating too fast. I took a deep breath, closed my eyes, and thought about The Beatles performing *I Want to Hold Your Hand* on *The Ed Sullivan Show*, with Lennon and McCartney singing at different mics, and Harrison standing between them whaling on that big, shiny, Gretsch guitar of his. It was a relaxation trick of mine that worked every time.

The cops came, and I gave a statement, swallowing my pride.

Carol and Annie arrived and waited with me until the crime scene tech finished his work. I filled them in.

Annie remained something of a mystery to me. She was less frightened than I'd anticipated. Carol fussed some and said I should go to the hospital for treatment. I declined, just wanting to sleep, so she gave me a ride home.

"Let's go to Paso Robles tomorrow, get the hell out of here," I suggested. "We need to find Melody Manning."

"What about Annie?" she asked.

"Bring her along. She'll be safer with us. Something funny's going on. The man who hit me, he's some sort of special ops guy. Regular crooks can't do that to me."

****

Twelve hours of sleep did wonders for my head. I ate bacon and eggs on the deck in the glorious California sunshine, reflecting on the events of yesterday—a close call. Mr. Dodger Hat was out there somewhere. He was no garden-variety burglar, and Annie had offered no clue about why he'd been there. I realized that I didn't trust her, but there was no reason for it other than my stubborn cop intuition. Maybe I was jealous. She was taking my best friend away from me.

At noon, I threw some clothes and bathroom stuff together, locked up, and took my pack down the wooden steps, along with my gun bag. Waiting for the ladies, I turned and took a long look back at my squat, brown cabin—not elegant, but solid. My dad had built it when I was stationed in Germany. I wanted to see it again, soon. It was my refuge, a place where I didn't have to be tough or brave, where I was just Jimmy Sommes. Which reminded me that I'd better call my mother from Paso Robles, since I was going to miss our monthly Walter's Café brunch.

At last, I heard the welcome sound of Carol's loaner car coming up the canyon road, not exactly her Bel Air, but good enough. It was time for us to find Tony the Tiger and see if that led us to Hippie Mama.

Carol gave a quick wave and beckoned for me to take the front passenger seat that Annie was vacating. They were both wearing floppy hats and shades. Annie hugged me and thanked me, for the first time, for stopping the intruder, then climbed in back. She made some comment about the bang on my head and Carol laughed.

"It's about time Jimmy used his head for something productive." Smart-ass Carol.

Normally I'd be all jacked-up, since I loved road trips, but Mr. Dodger Hat stayed in my thoughts. He was after Annie, whether she realized it or not. An Upland police detective had offered a half-assed theory that I'd simply interrupted a robbery, like the guy was going to steal a television or something. It was nonsense, but I'd let them chase that rabbit. It kept them out of my way.

No. This was different. This guy was special ops, like in the movies, and so fucking fast. I wanted him to wander back to Hollywood, where Steve McQueen or Clint Eastwood could deal with him. Not me. And why the smile, the contact, the tip of the hat? What did he want from me? My performance reports had often criticized me for over-confidence. One supervisor even branded me a "real hot dog." That desk jockey would be happy to see me now, "All Shook Up," as Elvis might say. I realized I wasn't just hustling Carol and Annie out of town. I was escaping from Mr. Dodger Hat too.

****

Mark Collins drove his gray Toyota west on Foothill Boulevard. He was pissed off. The intel on this job had been ridiculous. What had that cop been doing at Annie Hoover's apartment? That fuckup had put him one step away from aborting the entire operation and returning to Las Vegas, before he'd changed his mind after talking to the client, who'd pleaded with him to stay with it. They were going to meet soon in Pasadena, a neutral site, to discuss the next steps and ways to avoid any more screwups. The big job lay ahead.

The recent mess kept replaying in his head. Nobody should have been at the apartment. Normally, he would have confirmed this through his own surveillance, but time was short, and he hadn't. Was he losing his step?

He'd heard the souped-up Dodge Charger pull in next to his van. He'd looked out the window and seen this lanky dude in jeans, a black Stetson, and an oversize beige sports jacket get out and eyeball the van. The dude had then radioed somebody from his car. Backup? Everything about him screamed cop. Then, as if to confirm it, the cowboy took out his revolver, flipped open the cylinder, checked it, and then clicked it back. The cop was staring directly up at the apartment. There was no doubt about his destination.

Collins had flung open the electrical panel in the kitchen. Should he kill the cop? That would be messy as hell and would complicate the planned hit. No, he needed to get out as fast as he could, after disabling the cop. Which he had done, no problem, taking the man's weapon and splitting, leaving him unconscious on the floor.

It had been common sense to slash the cop's tires and tear off the radio antenna. But why had he left the cowboy's gun where he could find it? And why the fuck had he slowed the van and looked up at the cowboy? He could have taken him out then and there, but for some reason he'd tipped his hat to the dude, as if to acknowledge "game on." Somehow, he'd felt a need to recognize his adversary, which was atypical.

The rest had been easy. It took him three minutes to ditch the van, jump in his little gray rental car, and lose himself in the vast morass of southern California traffic. Driving toward Pasadena, his anger at the lousy intel fading, Collins felt something entirely different and unfamiliar. Doubt.

CHAPTER TWENTY

PASO ROBLES, TWENTY MILES north of San Luis Obispo and about midway between Los Angeles and San Francisco, had a nice, lazy feel to it, with restaurants and shops framing a large downtown park. The trip from Claremont up Highway 101 had been uneventful, but it was brutally hot. The oak-dotted brown hills surrounding the town were baking in the dry heat. We'd all been mostly quiet during the drive. We listened to a cassette of one of my favorite fiddlers, Bob Wills, playing western swing music with his band, The Texas Playboys. It was a live recording of a Houston show from back in the '50s. Man, I wished I could get his tone on my fiddle.

Somewhere north of Santa Barbara, Carol turned off the tape machine. "Sorry, country boy, I need a break from all this ancient stuff." She found the Yardbirds' *Heart Full of Soul* on an FM radio station, cranked up the volume, and started singing along. Even solemn Annie finally joined in. Me too, feeling better and better the further I got from LA.

We rented two rooms at an old-style motel and then Carol and I walked three blocks along Highway 101, which temporarily turned into Paso Robles' main drag. Annie, uncharacteristically subdued and passive since the break-in at her apartment, stayed behind, locked down and out of view. We told her to use the pool if she got bored but under no circumstances to call her office. She was locked down, whether she liked it or not. The realization that a strange, dangerous man had entered her apartment for no good reason had clearly sobered her.

Since Sam Fuller knew the Paso Robles police chief, we had decided to make the town our base for the trip, and Carol and I had an appointment with the chief in thirty minutes.

"You're gloomy. What's up?" Carol asked. I was drinking beer—she her Tab—at a nearby bar to kill time before the meeting. The building the bar fronted had a turret and looked like it was from the 1920s or earlier. Families were picnicking in the park across the street, kids running around in the sprinklers to keep cool.

I told her the truth. "This guy, the one at Annie's, he's some kind of hitter, and he's better than me. I'm out of my league against him." Carol was the only person in the world to whom I would confess this. I downed half my Coors, waiting for her response.

"Men amaze me, always thinking about who has the 'bigger you know what,'" she said. "Maybe he *is* better. I don't know, but you and I, we're a team. He's probably a lone wolf, from your description. Let's use that macho stuff against him. If he thinks it's mano a mano with you, then maybe little old me can sneak up and get him. Although, that's kind of awful."

"Why awful?"

"Because it will be dangerous for you, exposing yourself."

I couldn't resist. "You mean exposing myself to see who has the bigger—"

She laughed, almost choking on her Tab. "Exposing yourself to danger, you weirdo. Let's go see the chief."

The Paso Robles City Hall, on the other side of the park, was modern, ugly, and completely out of character with its surroundings. One of those going-to-the-lowest-bidder jobs that local governments specialize in. The flags outside were at half-mast and I wondered who'd died. The chief's office was on the second floor. He had the regulation gunmetal-gray crewcut and looked bone tired. We were likely his last appointment of the day. After we introduced ourselves, the chief held forth.

"Yeah, Sam told me what you were after. Now, we're a nice little city. Money comes mostly from ranching and other agriculture. Some vineyards moving in, rich folks from San Francisco. Most of the big city crap, drugs and whatnot, has missed us, at least so far. Cowboys getting drunk and busting stuff up is still a Saturday night event," he said, leaning back in his chair. "Like I said, a nice little city." Almost like we were disturbing his peace.

"What about the Hells Angels?" I asked.

The chief's face darkened. "Bad news. They ride out of San Luis Obispo, but from time to time come roaring through here on 101, especially on their runs up to Soledad Prison. Word is most of the dope and the weapons that show up at the prison are delivered by the Angels, especially to the Aryan Brotherhood." He shook his head. "Stay clear of the Angels."

"We want to, Chief, believe us," Carol said, "but there's this one guy, Anthony Harris, aka Tony the Tiger. We need to find him."

"Your boss mentioned that," the chief said, handing me a piece of paper. "We've got an address in Atascadero. Harris got busted for drunk and disorderly last year, pleaded out, got probation. Check with Alvin Rhyne, he's the Atascadero police chief. I'll give him a call, so he'll be expecting you tomorrow." The tired man stood up. "So, if there's nothing else…"

"One last question, sir. Why are the flags at half-mast?" I asked.

"J. Edgar Hoover died this morning," he said, "and Nixon ordered all the flags lowered."

"Sam told me once that Nixon hated Hoover," I said to Carol as we walked down the stairs.

"It's politics," she said, "nothing more."

We went back to join Annie at the motel, bringing pizza and salad from one of the restaurants fronting the park. We could see her out by the pool, getting the last rays of sun.

"I didn't realize how exhausted she was by the whole Jason Phillips deal," Carol said as we walked toward the pool. "I'm pretty new at this relationship thing."

"Just treat her like you treat me," I advised.

"Why? I like her."

Good old Carol. She knew that busting my chops was the best way to get me going again.

****

Tony the Tiger lived in a dilapidated old cottage at the end of a dirt road in the wrong part of Atascadero. The brown house dead-ended against a rusted-out chain-link fence with railroad tracks directly behind, maybe the Union Pacific line. A freight train rolled by its noise deafening. Trash decorated the house's front yard. The three of us—Annie insisted on coming—were conducting a quick drive-by before our meeting with the Atascadero police chief.

"What a dump," Carol sniffed as she wheeled her Chevy around.

The house did have the advantage of security, I noticed. Nobody could sneak up on it. But neither could somebody get away easily. A mixed bag. There was a closed garage. Tony's chopper probably was in there. But there was little more to be learned.

After our reconnaissance, we headed for our 11:30 meeting with Alvin Rhyne. Once out of Tony's neighborhood, the rest of Atascadero was nice. In fact, the police department was located in an amazing circular building that looked straight out of ancient Rome or something.

Annie pointed to it. "Wow. Looks like Frank Lloyd Wright or some other hotshot came through town."

"Or maybe Julius Caesar," Carol replied. We found a parking place and headed in.

Alvin Rhyne was a kick. He insisted on telling us war stories, most of them humorous, about life along the Central Coast, for half an hour before getting down to business. Then he brought in his biker team to brief us. "Ralph, Bill, and Delores," he rattled off. No way would I remember the names.

There was nothing glamorous or interesting about this violent Central California Chapter of the Hells Angels, they told us. "But it's our worst criminal element," Alvin said. We did learn something important. Tony the Tiger was not in the chapter anymore; he had drifted away after last year's arrest. The police biker team—they seemed like a strong unit—did some occasional surveillance on him, as they did on all the local Angels, past and present.

"He mostly stays in that crummy little house of his," Delores said.

"Anybody else live there?" Carol asked in a neutral voice, not wanting it to seem like our key question.

"That's a funny thing. We used to see a lady with him, older looking, but not since he broke off from the Angels. We figure she split town or something."

We began to discuss an operation. The biker team wanted in. It would have to be tomorrow night, so we agreed to meet the next morning to go over the details.

As we left city hall, I saw an old-fashioned A&W Root

Beer drive-in down the block. "Let's have lunch," I suggested, thinking about a frosty ice-cold mug of root beer. The ladies agreed. After lunch, a quiet afternoon by the pool appealed to me. Annie and Carol were talking about going for a hike. We also made a pact, no calls to anybody's office today. I didn't even check for messages, something I later regretted.

We went to a movie that night, some dumb-ass comedy. I fell asleep. So far Paso Robles was serving as a brief and safe respite from our troubles at home. I could feel the tension coming out of my back and neck. Annie was looking happier too.

The next day dawned crystal clear and cooler. The scent of the pine trees was glorious. Although it was twenty miles to the west, I could sense the presence of the Pacific Ocean. There was no smog. Maybe I'd retire here. While Carol went out for a box of donuts to take to the morning meeting with the Atascadero biker squad, Annie and I waited for her by the pool, drinking motel coffee. The silence was awkward.

"Carol's a wonderful person," I finally said to Annie. It came out weird, almost like I was confronting Annie. I couldn't help myself.

"Don't you worry, I feel the same," Annie said. "Maybe someday..." Annie looked up, saw Carol, and stopped talking.

No donuts. Carol was holding out a copy of the morning *LA Times*. She was ashen, mute, as she handed the Metro Section to Annie. I could see the headline: "Prominent Public Interest Attorney Dies in Car Accident." Jason Phillips was dead. The brakes on his BMW had failed and he'd driven into a ditch off Baseline Road in Alta Loma. A one-car accident, no foul play involved according to the San Bernardino Sheriff's Department. "We are deeply saddened by the loss of this fine man," Undersheriff Sam Fuller was quoted in the article. Others chimed in, including Claremont's mayor.

"Son-of-a bitch got him," I said, feeling sick, angry, and badly outmaneuvered.

Annie got up and looked at me, cold as ice. "You don't know that. You don't know anything." She took a deep breath, barely holding it together, and went on. "I'm a lawyer. I should have been there, doing my job, serving our clients, trying to help Jason with his difficulties, not running and hiding with you. I feel like a traitor to my friend." Her voice broke and she walked away.

Her words made no sense—Jason had crossed to the dark side of things, a drug smuggler—but the emotion rang true. Carol followed her to their room. I had a feeling she was going to have to make a choice. And I knew they'd be leaving soon.

I called Alvin Rhyne and pushed our meeting to the afternoon. I told him my partners needed to return to Southern California to attend to other business, and I asked if his biker team could pick me up. Alvin said sure and told me to be outside the motel at 2 p.m. With time to kill, I went for a walk through town, needing to clear my head, and ended up at the park.

I found a bench facing a statue of some guy in an army uniform and reviewed the situation. The hit made sense. It was Jason Phillips, the cokehead, who likely posed a greater danger to whoever was pulling all the strings. Was it this Jack Green character? Somebody else? Did they kill Rebecca Meadows? I didn't know the answers but remained convinced that we still needed to know why Richard Manning kept silent. He was a key. Which was why I was planning to stay to roust Tony the Tiger and, hopefully, to find Manning's mother.

Something about Annie Hoover kept nagging at me. Most burglary victims felt violated, needed to talk about it. She was stoic, solemn—and she didn't like me one bit.

What about now? If Carol and Annie left—and I knew they would—were they heading straight back toward the killer? Should I try and stop them? My instincts, usually good, were telling me that the women were safe for now, especially since Carol was a professional. I still believed in my gut that we'd gotten away from Claremont clean. Maybe too clean. The killer had a clear run at Jason Phillips while we'd enjoyed our brief vacation, and he'd made the most of it.

Carol and Annie were packing when I returned. No stopping them. I called Sam Fuller from my room.

"Where the hell were you yesterday?" he demanded. "I called twice."

"Sorry, we were taking a day off. My fault. Was this really an accident?"

Sam barked out a mirthless laugh. "Hardly. It was murder. His brakes were tampered with, but we put out that no foul play statement trying to show the killer or killers that we're pretty stupid out here in San Bernardino. Probably won't work, but worth a try. What about you? Any progress?"

I filled him in, including the fact that Annie and Carol were likely heading right back on account of Phillips's death. "We'll give Annie some protection whether she likes it or not," Sam said. "Good luck rousting that biker," he added before hanging up.

Carol came over to my room, a rueful look on her face. "I feel like a grown-up for the first time in my life, responsible for somebody else. Annie called her office and said she'll be there on Monday, but she didn't tell them where she was." Carol's face showed her conflicting emotions and she let out a deep sigh. "It's not easy. Annie's almost as mad at me as she is at you."

"She'd be—"

"I know, Jimmy. She's lucky to be here with us, but it's going to take some time for her to process all that." Carol paused. "There's one other thing, and it's big. A month or so ago, Phillips called Annie into his office. He was morose, but lucid. He told her that if anything happened to him, there was a letter addressed to her in a safe deposit box at the Claremont branch of the Bank of America. He gave her the key and a letter authorizing her to access the box. She was flattered, thinking it was a will or trust document naming her as executor. Now she's wondering if it might be different. A confession? Maybe he named names."

I felt my heart lift. This *was* big. "Maybe so. Where are the key and the letter?"

"In her safe deposit box at the same bank. Annie's very organized."

It was my bank too, everybody and his uncle used it. My mind was processing the information. "It's Thursday. Please stay clear until Monday. Go visit Hearst Castle or something. I'm going to try and get back by then. But I need to follow through on this thing up here."

"I know," Carol said. "I want to stay, to help you, but I've got to keep Annie safe."

"Understood. Sam's going to have some people watching you two. Is that okay?"

"No problem," Carol said. "You know me. I'm no hero."

Then I lied to Carol, something I couldn't recall doing before, at least about anything important. "You know, Sam and the investigative team really do believe Jason's death was accidental. They're still looking at the car but can't find anything."

"Maybe the hitman is too smart for them." Carol lifted

an eyebrow.

"Yeah, I'm not sure either. I think you should stay at a hotel and not go near your house. My lawyer friend, the one who took Annie's statement, can help with that."

Carol gave me a look. "Not my first rodeo, pardner." I held up my hands in mock surrender. "Be careful yourself up here," she said, her glare softening.

"Don't worry. I'm meeting Alvin and the biker squad this afternoon, and hopefully we can stake out Tony's house tonight."

There was one more surprise for Carol and Annie. As they prepared to leave, Delores Figueroa of the biker squad showed up in a black Ford Thunderbird sedan. She handed the keys to Carol. "This is a loaner. Get it back to us in one piece when you can. And don't inhale too deeply, or you might get a contact high. We got it in a bust near San Simeon."

Carol and Annie moved their bags to the T-Bird. Annie wouldn't make eye contact or talk to me. As if all this was somehow my fault. They drove off, and I shook my head. I couldn't help worrying, though I knew Carol would keep her safe. The T-Bird was a nice touch. Every little bit helped when it came to keeping them invisible. Until Monday, it would be best if Carol and Annie didn't exist. I'd drive the Chevy back.

Watching them go, I hoped I hadn't wrecked my friendship with Carol by lying to her. I'd have to let Sam know about my subterfuge too. Tangled webs never work. But my instincts were guiding me. It wasn't Carol I was concerned about. It was Annie. The less she knew the better.

CHAPTER TWENTY-ONE

DRESSED IN ALL BLACK, I crouched under a wooden picnic table behind Tony the Tiger's shack. It was close to midnight, and Bill, one of the biker squad, and I had cut through the railroad fence and crawled to the table, taking advantage of Tony's noisy departure earlier. The other two members of the team had remained in a battered old orange Volkswagen van parked in front of the house. The VW fit in well with the other cars in the funky old neighborhood. Tony had gone out once during the early evening for groceries. Then, an hour ago, he'd left again on his Harley, the engine roaring. Everything in the neighborhood was drab and scruffy except that bike, which gleamed silver and black, Oakland Raiders colors.

The Volkswagen van followed him to a biker bar off Highway 101 and then came back to take up position in front of the shack again. We didn't know how long we had, and it was an illegal entry if we just barged in since we had no probable cause. Then we caught a break. As we circled the house, we found a door to a cellar down about ten concrete steps. Mud had collected at the bottom of the steps. A rat scurried away as I shined my flashlight down and descended. I could hear something else, not a rat, a different scratching sound. There was a small, filthy window in the padlocked door with metal bars across it on the inside. That's when I saw her face, framed by scraggly gray hair and pressed against the bars. She was mouthing the words "Help me."

Jesus... my heart skipped a beat. It was like a horror movie. Now we needed to go in and rescue her. Bill used the fence cutter to cut the padlock off the door. It also was locked from the inside, so I kicked through the rotting wood to find a scene of unimaginable squalor.

The dirt floor basement stank to high heaven. There was one flickering lightbulb hanging from the ceiling by a frayed wire. It illuminated an overflowing bucket of human waste. The emaciated woman, dressed in rags, hugged me. I did my level best not to recoil. God knows when she'd last bathed. Even after twelve-plus years as a cop, this horrific scene challenged me. I needed to focus on helping her.

The woman was chained to a high-backed chair by leg irons that gave her about ten feet to stand up and drag the chair behind her. Her hands, however, were free. "I slipped the cuffs," she said proudly. "The bastard doesn't even check 'em anymore. When I saw your flashlight, I pushed the chair toward the window so I could look out. Lucky I did."

Lucky indeed. I had a canteen full of water in my backpack and gave it to her. "Are you Melody Manning?" I asked as she guzzled the contents. This brought tears to her eyes. "God, I used to be Melody. Maybe I still am. Get me out of here, please."

We waited in silence as Bill ran out to get the rest of the team. I gave her my coat to wear and a candy bar to eat. There were interior stairs leading up, probably to the kitchen. I walked over and tried the door. It was locked. Another rat ran past my feet.

"Does anybody else live in the house?" I asked.

"I don't think so. Just the little creep and me." She was rubbing her arms. There were welts.

"How long have you been down in this basement?"

"I don't know," she answered. "It feels like forever."

Looking around the filthy, stinking room, I could only imagine what it had been like.

Sergeant Figueroa arrived with a blanket and some coffee. "Come on, sweetie," she said to Melody. "How about a shower and a hot meal?" She turned to me. "We'll take her to the emergency room, a separate room. I'll keep her safe." Her hand drifted down to her gun belt. I didn't doubt her.

"You can talk to her in the morning, if she's up to it," Figueroa added. She used a skeleton key to open the leg irons and gently extricated Melody's bruised legs. Then she helped the woman, all eighty pounds of her from the looks of it, up the stairs and out the door, practically carrying her.

As Melody limped off, she turned and faced me. "Thank you, sir." She shook her head in bewilderment. Then a hint of a smile played across her face. "What a long, strange trip it's been, man."

Even after such an ordeal, she had spirit.

A crime scene tech arrived. "Not yet," I said to him. "We've got to get the guy who did this when he comes home."

"Already done," a booming voice answered. "I arrested the son-of-a-bitch myself in the parking lot of the Lovelady Lounge." Alvin Rhyne came through the door. "Might have used a little too much force. No little prick's gonna imprison a woman in my town and get away with it," he added, hitching his belt up over his belly. "Man, it felt good to be out in the field again."

****

Anthony "Tony the Tiger" Harris was not intimidated by his surroundings. It wasn't his first time in a police station interview room. He'd already lawyered up before Alvin and I got there; his only comment before his attorney arrived was the cryptic, "I do what I'm told." There was a one-way mirror into his interview room so I could see him. His right eye was bruised where Alvin must have given him some extra help getting into the squad car.

George of the biker team was leading the interview. He came out, looking frustrated. It appeared that Tony had clammed up for good. I asked if I could take a shot at him. When Alvin agreed, I went in and sat down at the battered old wooden table covered in cigarette burns. The metal chairs were chained to the floor, and the room smelled of fear and hopelessness. I introduced myself, said hello to Tony, and then just sat there, looking at him. In my experience, sometimes this really shakes a guy up, gets him talking no matter what his lawyer says. Two or three minutes must have gone by. Sure enough, Tony was getting antsy, his chair scraping the linoleum floor. The young attorney was bored, popping his gum.

"Why, Tony?" I finally asked him, a blank look on my face. "Why'd you do that to Melody? She's your old lady, man."

"Don't answer," the lawyer barked. Tony obeyed him.

I stared at him some more, then said, "I talked to Freeway Freddy down in Fontana. He said you were a punk, a pussy. That you only beat up women. He said he threw you out of his chapter for being a fucking disgrace."

Tony growled, "That's bullshit. I left cuz Jack told me to split." The lawyer rolled his eyes.

Bingo. "Jack Green, there's another piece of work," I said. "You do whatever he tells you to, punk?"

"He could kick your ass, pig," Tony sputtered at me, and then stared at the floor.

I thanked them and left the interview room, having gotten what I needed.

****

Mark Collins figured that Jason Phillips had about thirty seconds of terror before his car plummeted down a dusty hillside into a field of boulders scattered among tumbleweeds and creosote bushes. His body, unrestrained by a seatbelt, had flown out the front of his BMW convertible into one of the boulders, to lie there contorted and motionless, a broken rag doll.

The key when cutting a BMW's brakes was to leave a sliver of the metal filament. It gave Phillips the illusion of safety before he hit the downhill stretch of Mills Avenue north of Baseline. Then the brakes gave out. Collins watched through binoculars as the panicked lawyer pulled hard on his emergency brake. Nothing happened, not surprising since Collins had disabled it.

The only remaining variable had been the crash site. Collins had driven it several times in his Toyota rental, his foot off the brakes until the very last second. He hoped for the boulder field since it lessened the chances of collateral damage. Perched on a hiking trail a couple hundred yards away—decked out in birdwatching gear—he'd been prepared to race down the hill and finish the job if necessary. Looking down at the lifeless body, Collins knew his work was done and continued up the trail instead, his bird book in hand. Thirty minutes later, an ambulance came and picked up the body, not using its siren. Then the cops blocked the road.

Collins returned to his hotel, using a different route, and watched game shows on television. He liked to give himself a day to unwind after a job, assuming there was no heat.

That night, drinking a scotch and soda in the hotel's soulless cocktail bar, Collins experienced an epiphany. He was done killing for money. This was his last assignment. Long ago his mentor had told him, "Ten years max for this line of work. After that, go to Maui, drink mai tais, buy a cat, and put your feet in the sand. Otherwise, all you'll think about the rest of your life is killing people."

Collins was in year nine—he'd gone private in '63, after Dallas—but he had plenty of money. There was, however, some unfinished business. Munching on cocktail peanuts, he made another decision. He was about to violate operational protocol, and he realized he didn't give a damn about that. He paid his bill, went to his room, and called Doc Green, using the emergency phone number.

They planned a meet for that same night at a bowling alley bar south of the freeway—actually for the next day at two in the morning. Collins got there early and ordered a beer. Doc Green never seemed to sleep, and he didn't even seem surprised that Collins had called. Green was a creepy guy, but also brilliant in his way. Like the hit on Rebecca Meadows—who else could have come up with that radical bombing ploy? Certainly not his mob clients. But still, Doc Green was too personal, too enamored of vendettas for Collins's taste. Having a woman killed because she wouldn't fuck him? That violated Collins' sense of professionalism. But business was business.

Doc Green arrived, grunted a hello, and ordered bourbon. Collins put aside any misgivings about the man and pitched a business proposition to him, something he'd been toying with for a while. Collins had contacts in Sinaloa; contacts who sold cocaine, weed, and heroin. He offered to set up a meeting between Green and those guys, someplace neutral, like Phoenix, to see if they wanted to do business. If so, Collins would get a cut of the profits, the percentage to be determined. Collins sweetened his offer by saying he'd do the two cops, Sommes and Loomis, for free. Doc Green was cagey, saying he'd think about it.

"What about Annie Hoover? Friend or foe?" the Doc asked.

"I don't know," Collins answered. "I got interrupted at her place, in case you forgot. But I saw her bank records, no pay-offs. She's not getting rich. No smoking guns at her place. I'll leave that to you to figure out." Collins got up to leave. He also made a point of not telling Green he was planning on retiring from the murder for hire business, not wanting the man to get too comfortable in his presence.

Driving back to Vegas the next day, Collins wound the Vette up over 100 mph over the El Cajon Pass. The machine held the road perfectly as he zoomed past startled drivers laboring up the mountain. Collins knew he had to get rid of the Corvette. Even though it was owned by a fictitious person, it was a possession capable of being tracked. The registration was good for another three months. He'd make a decision before then.

He slowed down later, enjoying the emptiness of the desert road. The tape machine provided his soundtrack: Chet Baker blowing his trumpet like a man possessed. That made Collins think of Paris in the rain, a place he loved and had never worked. Maybe he'd move there one day.

In the distance, a large turkey vulture was feasting on some sort of roadkill in the median strip in the midday glare. The road was empty. Collins downshifted and slowed his Corvette to fifty, pulled out his handgun, and pretended to blast the carrion bird, thinking all the while of Jimmy Sommes.

CHAPTER TWENTY-TWO

I WOKE UP AT the Paso Robles motel, needing a minute to remember where I was. I thought of Allie as I shaved and showered, mostly thinking about that beautiful body but also that laugh that came from deep down in her belly. She didn't laugh often, so when it happened you felt especially rewarded. But recently a dark idea about Allie had taken root in my memories. Had our entire relationship—such as it was—been a sham? She'd had Jason Phillips's phone number tucked in that novel. How come? Of course, she'd been involved earlier with Richard Manning. She was a radical, like him. So, it made sense she might know his lawyer. And another thing: I was pretty good with the ladies, but not that good. Was she keeping tabs on me for Jason? Was I even more of a chump than I knew?

Wanting to shake these negative thoughts, I called Alvin Rhyne. "Where's the best breakfast in your town?"

"Giuliano's Diner, next to city hall. I'll meet you there in thirty. And Jimmy, great work last night."

Damn, I really liked the guy. He'd cheered me up already. Rather than retire here, maybe Alvin would hire me and I could relocate right away. The violence and gangs in Southern California were only going to get worse, and I liked the whole setup here in sunny Atascadero. And it was only four hours from my mom's place in Pomona. Close enough. Or she could move up here too, just not the same town.

175

Alvin was drinking coffee and chatting with the waitress when I showed up. "Jenny, this is the top gunslinger in San Bernardino County. At least that's what his boss says."

"That so." She smiled at me through tired eyes. I ordered bacon, eggs, hash browns, toast, and coffee. Jenny approved. "I like a man that eats," she said. Jenny was pushing forty by my reckoning and wore a wedding ring, but that smile was worth waking up for. Every truck stop and diner in the country needed its "Jenny," a lady who kept a motley cast of characters—cops, truckers, drifters, night owls, and even criminals—halfway sane as they traversed America's dark corners, often at 3 a.m. when all the civilians were asleep.

Alvin was only drinking coffee. He patted his ample stomach. "My wife has me on yogurt and oatmeal, says she won't abide me dying on her." That accounted for his wistful look as I'd made my order. "By the way"—he was dumping two packets of sugar into his refilled coffee—"your partner Carol called, saying she just missed you at the motel. I filled her in on finding Melody and busting Tony. She was thrilled, said to tell you that she has Annie safe and squared away."

Good for Carol. She was doing the right thing. "What about Melody Manning?" I asked.

"She's getting a full physical today. The initial reports were okay, no broken bones or other major injuries, but she was half-starved to death. Jesus, that Tony dude is a creep. I'm not sorry I popped him one, even though his lawyer is raising hell about it."

"Yeah, I know what you mean. The perps that hurt women and children are the hardest to handle. Listen, I'm going to need to get back down to SoCal soon," I told him. "When can I talk to Melody?"

"Maybe tonight. I'll check with the doctors."

****

The hospital doctor was clear. I had a maximum of thirty minutes to question Melody Manning. "One thing we've learned is that she's addicted to some sort of opiate, my best guess morphine. She'll need to be detoxed once she's stronger."

I frowned. "Was it by injection? I didn't see needle marks last night."

"No. She said the man used suppositories. Once a day, and he was rough with her. There's some tearing. I hope you've got the jerk locked up."

I said yes, not wanting to complicate things, and went into Melody's room. The hospital bed swallowed up her tiny frame. She was forty-six years old according to the chart on the wall but looked much older. Her hair was gray and thinning, her face haggard. IVs were going in both arms.

I sat in a chair by her bed. "Hi, Melody, I'm Jimmy Sommes. I saw you last night. You feeling okay?"

She gave me a wry look. "As compared to what? Being run over by a herd of buffalo?"

I laughed out loud. "Well, that's a start. Hey, last night, you mentioned 'long strange trip.' You like the Grateful Dead?"

Her face brightened. "Oh yeah, I love the Dead, like family, man. Tony and me, before he turned into a complete prick, used to take his chopper to their shows, especially when they played Bakersfield, Fresno, towns like that. He made me promise not to run away. Hell, I was so high I wasn't going anywhere." She looked down at her emaciated body. "That's back when I looked different."

"When did all this start? Tony messing with you?"

She motioned for me to hand her a plastic water glass. She sucked noisily on the straw. "I believe in the revolution, just like my son, Richard. But his thing is external, mine's internal. Gotta start with yourself, man. Otherwise, it's all bullshit." She was getting excited, and not answering my questions. I was trying to get the conversation back where I wanted it when she nodded off. I left, realizing this was going to take some time.

"What's your favorite Dead album?" I asked upon returning an hour later. The doctor hadn't said my thirty minutes had to be consecutive, and he wasn't there anyway. Melody had fresh IVs in her arms. The nurses didn't seem to care if I hung around.

"It depends." Melody chewed her lower lip as she thought about it. "If I'm tripping, it's got to be *Anthem of the Sun.* If I'm doing my hippie mama thing, either *Workingman's Dead* or *American Beauty.* What about you?"

"*American Beauty.* I play fiddle and mandolin in a county rock band, so I love good songs. That record has great songs. Listen, sorry, I gotta ask. When did you decide to leave Claremont? Was Richard there?"

Her eyes glazed over as she retreated into herself. We took another break. Resuming, I asked again, "Richard?" Just talking about the Grateful Dead wasn't going to cut it.

She answered this time. "They told me they'd take care of him, keep him safe, even in the Federal jail. All Richard had to do was shut up about the bombings and all I had to do was write him once a week saying I was okay. It was Jason's plan, and I trusted him."

"That's Jason Phillips, the lawyer?"

"Yeah, he's a smart dude, way smarter than Tony. I used to be smart too, before the drugs." Her eyes wandered off and I was afraid she was falling asleep again but then she continued. "For a while everything worked okay. I rode with Tony, wrote my letters. But then the devil, Jack

Green, showed up, and he and Tony, they got mean, locked me up. Jack Green, he started doing weird stuff to me..." She hesitated. "I told the doctor about the suppositories. Jack, he got off on it, sexually. Pervert. Then Tony kept it up after the devil left, always apologizing. But he liked it too."

Carol had supplied me with a photo of Jack Green, standing beside a surfboard, looking straight at the camera, his smile edging toward a sneer. I showed it to Melody and she recoiled.

"I'm sorry, but that's him, right, Jack Green?"

She looked at me, her eyes focusing for the first time. "What's your name, man? You helped me, didn't you?" She pointed at the picture. "Helped me get away from that monster. Are you a Virgo?"

"Jimmy Sommes. I'm a Taurus, and I want to help Richard now. I think he's innocent."

Her voice turned dreamy. "Innocent. That's a strange word. I used to be Catholic, and, according to them, I was never innocent. She looked back to me, focused again. "Don't worry. Richard's cool with his trip. He had to wake up Nixon and the other pigs, there was no choice. But he's sorry about that secretary, the one who lost a finger. She wasn't supposed to be there. Richard's a Taurus too. My baby."

The doctor came to the door, tapping his watch and motioning to me. I'd overstayed my welcome. "But that second bombing, Melody. Richard didn't do it, right?"

"No... he didn't." She turned away from me and curled into a ball, almost pulling out one of her IVs. "Jason said he would fix it, that it was part of his plan to make the world a better place." She sobbed into her pillow. "But it's not better, man, it's just dark, like that fucking basement."

I reached over and patted her arm, needing to do

something. "Thanks, Melody. It's going to get better. I truly believe that. I'm going to let you rest now."

She turned back toward me, smiled, and said in a soft voice, "Keep on truckin', Jimmy."

I thought she was very brave... and I wanted to find Jack Green and tear him apart.

****

At ten that night, Alvin Rhyne and Delores moved Melody to a small nursing home in Paso Robles. I'd explained to them that a hitman was wreaking havoc down south relative to the Manning case, and that Melody was also in danger. A rotating twenty-four-hour guard was posted at her door. Meanwhile, I found myself looking over my shoulder more and reacting to any loud noise. Mr. Dodger Hat was in my head.

I stopped to visit Melody the next day, but she was sleeping. The guard nodded to me as I left. "You know the drill, son," I said. "Nobody comes in except me, your chief, Delores Figueroa, and the nurses." He didn't need me to say that, but it made me feel better. I figured Jack Green already knew about Tony's arrest and Melody's rescue. Which meant Green's whole house of cards was liable to come crashing down. Which meant we needed to keep Melody safe. My plan was to get her down to SoCal pronto and under my watch, but that required Sam's okay. Until then, I needed to trust Alvin and his crew.

Driving south on Highway 101, I took one last lingering look at Atascadero as I passed through; a part of me didn't want to leave.

****

Carol and Annie got back to Claremont on Sunday night. They'd spent Saturday night "somewhere" was all I learned. Under tight security on Monday, Annie went to her office to meet with her staff and help finalize plans for Jason Phillips's "Celebration of Life" funeral service. It was scheduled for Wednesday night at Garrison Theater at the Claremont Colleges. A large crowd was expected for Claremont's favorite son.

Carol and I also returned to our jobs. First off, I met Sam in San Bernardino and filled him in. Just as our meeting was concluding, Sam got a call. He put it on his new speakerphone. The sound was tinny, but it was easy to understand the guy on the other end. It was the Orange County District Attorney. "Sam, let me be perfectly clear, neither you nor your men are to question, harass, or arrest Mr. Jack Green under any circumstances. Do you understand that?"

"Yes, sir, you've—"

"Good. I've got to run, but one more thing. Keep that hot dog deputy of yours, Sommes, away from this case. Two years of work have gone into our investigation of the Brotherhood of Eternal Love and we're about to round up these hippie miscreants. Don't let him, or anybody else, screw this up." The DA disconnected.

"What an asshole," I groaned.

"Indeed he is." Sam nodded. "Politician as lawman, the worst kind. But he has a point. I hear from other sources that the Brotherhood Task Force is about three days away from making the arrests. The warrants are being prepared, and the lawyers are paranoid about leaks." Sam looked up to make sure I was paying attention. "So, in this instance I agree with Mr. Asshole DA. Stay clear of Jack Green."

"Okay, I got it," I said.

"And remember, the party line for now on Jason Phillips is tragic accidental death," Sam pointed a finger at me, "but stay on the case full-time until we get some resolution. I'll make sure your station knows you're on special assignment."

"Thanks, Boss." I grabbed my hat and hit the road.

****

My next stop was the Bank of America in Claremont; I was meeting Carol and Annie to examine the papers that Jason Phillips had left behind. The results were ambiguous. Phillips had prepared a will and named Annie as his executor. He'd left his house to his sister, his artworks to a local gallery, his sports trophies to Claremont High School, his now wrecked BMW to Annie, and the remaining cash and furniture to the Justice for All Clinic. It turned out that a trust controlled by his Board of Directors, not Jason, owned the clinic. Importantly, he'd strongly urged the Board to promote Annie Hoover to general manager of the clinic for a term entirely of her choosing.

There also was a sealed envelope with "Annie Hoover" written on it. Annie opened it and read the short, typed letter, muttering, "Don't we all," then handed it to Carol and me. In it, Phillips apologized for letting people down and for "engaging in some questionable conduct that was and is inconsistent with my ideals. I deeply regret some of my actions." We were silent for a moment, then Annie left to deal with the bank people.

"This could mean anything," Carol waved the letter, "like cheating on his bowling score."

"Or helping murder somebody," I suggested.

"Or anything in between." Carol grimaced and put the letter back in the envelope

I noticed something on the back of the envelope. We'd all missed it at first. I told Carol to check the back and she turned it over. There was one sentence scrawled in pencil, perhaps as an afterthought: "Regarding Rebecca, I couldn't change his mind."

"Quick, put that in your purse," I whispered to Carol, "before Annie comes back." Carol nodded, gave me a sad look, and stuffed the envelope away.

Annie returned with a bank officer, who placed the box back into its niche in the wall and locked it. We all left the bank.

"So do you geniuses know why Jason drove off the road?" Annie snapped when we reached the street, her first words to me since we'd met that morning. She turned away, not expecting an answer, and told Carol, "I've got to go back to work and finalize Jason's service." Annie walked off without another word.

"Welcome to my world." Carol fiddled with a ring on her finger. "Annie's a different person now, cold, distant. I don't know what to do." She retrieved the envelope from her purse and stared at it. "And what the hell does this mean?"

I was thinking details, evidence. "I know the bank manager here. We played on the same Little League team. I'm going to ask him to make some copies of the letter and envelope, sign an affidavit as to their authenticity, and then put the original back in the box."

"It's still ambiguous," Carol noted, "but not innocent." She handed the envelope to me. "I've got to get back to work too. Let's do Los Amigos soon, drink some serious tequila after we get through this fucking funeral."

Normally, Carol would be jumping up and down with glee. She loved clues. But not today. I noticed her slow distracted gait as she meandered down the street. I'd never seen my friend so glum, and I blamed Annie.

I looked down at Jason's slanted handwriting, and my mood brightened. Finally, we had some evidence, albeit sketchy, to back our theory that Rebecca Meadows had been murdered.

CHAPTER TWENTY-THREE

IT WAS JUST AFTER seven on a clear and cooling May evening when I stood on the Garrison Theater's broad outdoor patio watching the crowd file in for Jason Phillips's Celebration of Life. Carol was scanning the attendees from the opposite side of the entrance. FBI experts believe that murderers like to attend the funerals of their victims. As a result, homicide investigators go to lots of funerals. I'd never seen a murderer at a funeral yet, but looking for one gave me something to do.

The theater was in the heart of the exclusive and pricey Claremont Colleges. Glancing to the west, I could see Harper Hall, its façade long since repaired from the bomb blast that killed Rebecca Meadows almost two years before. I was now convinced that Jason Phillips had been knee-deep in the cover-up of that murder ever since. I couldn't prove it yet, but it had finished him, as Meadows' killer or killers were seeking to eliminate all the loose ends. This thought led me to reach inside my sports coat to make sure my service revolver was in the holster, since I most definitely was another loose end.

The smog had lifted, and the Chino Hills were visible in the distance. This was perfect sandlot baseball weather. It triggered childhood memories of the ball cracking off the bat, followed by a gang of boys, me among them, chasing after it. Pulling myself reluctantly back to the present, I went inside the almost-full theater.

Three musicians were on the stage providing the muted music: piano, harp, and acoustic guitar. A young-ish minister kept nervously shaking long hair out of his face as he busied himself at the podium. Roses and garde-nias hung from wooden arbors. Politicians, lefty radicals, and celebrity entertainment types occupied the best seats and were engaged in respectfully earnest conversation. Sam Fuller was caught up in that mess somewhere. Annie Hoover too. Plenty of locals filled out the rest of the crowd, wanting to pay their respects to a hometown hero best remembered for his high school football heroics.

Carol and I stayed in back, looking for outliers. The service started, but I tuned it out, knowing that the sin-cere expressions of admiration for Phillips told, at best, only half the story. I knew too much.

A balding folk singer sang a ballad. I'd heard he had something to do with the Peter Paul and Mary folk group. Then he gestured for a dark-haired man sitting in the front row to join him. This tall skinny guy in a white tuxe-do and red sneakers leaped up on to the stage. He carried an electric guitar, which he plugged into an amp. Soon the hall was filled with slow, razor-edged blues riffs. The oth-er musicians remained silent as the guitar's sad, aching notes told the tale. After a while he stopped and the man I now recognized as Frank Zappa, of Mothers of Invention fame, moved to the podium.

"Jason and I used to fix bicycles down on First Street, at Bud's Bike Shop. And smoke cigarettes in the alley behind the store, and drink beer at dives in Pomona, and chase girls, unsuccessfully, at the drive-ins up on Foothill. He was a good friend when I needed one, when I was this weird geek with zits, and he was this campus hero. Jason and I lost touch. He did his thing. I did mine. I wrote this for him last night with the help of these other cats."

Zappa signaled to the other musicians, and they all proceeded to play something wonderful and complicated. It sounded like a mix of Bach and Segovia. I listened, transported to a better place. Somehow the music summoned the Jason Phillips that I'd idolized many years before, and for the first time that night I felt sad for the man, and maybe for all of the rest of us who'd lost our innocence somewhere along the line.

The moment of magic ended with the song, and Zappa split without another word. The "celebration" droned on. Then Carol appeared on my right and whispered in my ear, "Allie."

I saw her, twenty feet away from me, sitting with some Pomona College girls. Her black hair was cut shorter and styled like a movie star's. I'd never seen her wear so much makeup. It made her look ten years older. She turned and our eyes met. As usual, she knocked me out, and any notion that she'd mistreated me fell away like a forgotten dream. Only the present mattered.

I motioned to the back of the hall and walked to the exit, hoping she'd follow me. She did.

She was wearing a long black skirt, a silky white blouse, and high heels, probably D'Amico's made by her daddy's company. I noticed because the Allie I'd known just weeks before had long straight hair and her Mona Lisa eyes had never needed mascara. *My* Allie wore blue jeans, bikini panties, and peasant blouses with no bra. I guessed expensive lingerie was now part of the package. But it all worked, the new Allie. She gave me a quick perfumed hug.

"Who are you?" I asked, trying to sound clever and failing.

She shrugged. "I'm a New Yorker now. Gotta look the part. It brings out my true Italian spirit."

"How long are you here for?" Back inside, the folkie

was singing another sappy song.

"I leave tonight on a red-eye. We're on deadline at the *Village Voice*, a piece on the ownership of the restaurant where Crazy Joey Gallo got gunned down last month. My part's done, some of the research, but I want to be there when we publish tomorrow."

Allie writing about gangsters in New York? She displayed no sense of irony about this fact. Still, I had to ask, knowing it was my only chance. "The whole thing, me and you. Was it just bullshit, meaningless?"

Allie sighed. "It was enough to scare me and make me run away, but also goddamn impossible. You knew that too. Different worlds, and all that trite stuff." Allie fingered a simple gold chain that hung around her neck and showed me its pendant, a solid gold violin. "This reminds me of you every day, fiddler, since I never take it off. It's from Florence, made in the fifteenth century. Is that real enough for you? Now I've got to go."

"Allie, wait. Jason Phillips, were you and he...?"

Sadness filled her eyes. "He was my friend, and sometimes my dealer. I'm trying to give that shit up, hard to do in Manhattan, since everybody's snorting it, morning, noon, and night. Jason was a good soul but a lost man. Plus, his weird thing with Richard."

"You mean his threats about Manning's mother?"

"Whatever, I don't know," she said, running a nervous hand through her hair.

She knew more but that's all I was going to get. Allie turned to leave. I memorized her profile, never wanting to forget any detail of her face. She stopped. "Jimmy, one last thing. You better watch out for Annie Hoover. She's not exactly Little Miss Goody Two-shoes."

Allie smoothed her blouse over her breasts, smiled like she'd just heard a good joke, and started to say something else. Then her friend appeared. Allie shrugged, awkward for a moment, and said, "My ride's here." She left, walking down the outside steps of Garrison Theater into the California twilight, never looking back. My eyes followed her, trying to figure out what I'd lost, or more likely what I'd never had.

Her exit from my life was just like her entrance: an incandescent jolt of pure energy that rendered everything else drab and ordinary.

Carol came up to me and put her arm around my shoulder. "Let's get the hell out of here and go to Los Amigos."

"What about Annie?"

"She's invited to a special second gathering for the bigshots up at Jason's place. I'm not. There'll be plenty of security, and Sam said he'll drive her home afterwards. Come on, Jimmy, I've got to get out of here. I'll be in the bar." She started down the steps, not waiting for an answer. My world was getting smaller by the minute.

It took less than ten minutes to drive from Garrison to the Los Amigos Bar and Grill up on Towne Avenue in Pomona in my still damaged Charger—new tires but no radio. But it gave me time to think about Allie. At least the ending was better than that fucked-up phone call from New York City last month. I realized, for the first time, that the Allie I'd known just weeks before, the college senior, had been immature. Now she was changing lightning fast. There was nothing phony about the elegant New York sophisticate who'd just walked away from me. She had evolved, or maybe become more of what she always was. My Oklahoma mother no doubt would offer a tart answer for this, probably something like "the apple never falls far from the tree."

CHAPTER TWENTY-FOUR

CAROL WAS WAITING FOR me at a corner table in the Los Amigos cocktail lounge. She already had a large, frosted margarita glass in front of her. I walked to the bar and nodded to Dan the bartender. "Bring me the usual."

"Sure," he said. "Hey, somebody came in and said Zappa showed up at Garrison tonight. That's far-out, wish I'd been there."

"Yeah, he played some blues and then a kind of classical piece. It was cool." I laid a twenty-dollar bill on the bar. "Another margarita for the lady too."

Carol was smoking her usual Marlboros and had drained her glass. I took a seat and told her another was on the way.

"Good. I might need a ride home tonight. Jimmy, I think Annie is setting me up, playing me for some reason," she said, with no preamble. "I don't know why, but I've looked back on how we got together—nothing makes any sense—it's mostly been good, but why me?"

It reminded me of some of my paranoia about Allie, which I hoped had been misplaced. Maybe Carol's was too. "Tell me why you're worried," I asked, just as our drinks arrived. The cocktail waitress gave Carol her margarita and then placed two shots of Cuervo Gold, a bottle of Modelo dark beer, a small dish of limes, and a saltshaker in front of me.

"Okay," Carol said, after a sip of her new drink, "I

dropped by her law clinic maybe two weeks after you and I first visited, just to follow up. Jason wasn't there and Annie and I got to talking. I told her I admired the clinic's work, then we agreed to have lunch sometime. After that, the lunches turned into dinners. We became lovers. You know that I never talk about this stuff, right?"

"Yeah, I know. Take your time," I said soothingly.

That got an amused look from Carol. "Don't treat me like a perp. I know that tone. Anyway, the passion has been real as our relationship progressed, and she sure as hell is needy. But something's missing in her, deep down, and I can't figure it out."

Carol got quiet. Both of us stopped talking and did some drinking.

"What next?" I asked, chasing down the tequila with some beer. Who was going to drive me home?

"I like living alone," Carol said. "You're about my only real friend. Annie was trying to reach me, break through my defenses. Since I was lonely, I let her in." Carol lit another smoke. She was going through the pack quickly. "I missed it until our Sycamore Inn dinner; that's when I realized Annie was performing for us, playing the role of Jason's worried friend. Actually, she was ratting him out. Same thing up at Paso Robles. My cop radar may not be as good as yours, but it's pretty good. I think she was in on it with Jason. A few nights ago, I saw her going through my notes."

I signaled the bartender for more of everything. "Did you stop her, call her on it?"

"No, she didn't see me, and I chickened out, went back to bed. I'm beginning to think she's a psycho, living more than one life. And I'm getting scared, don't want her to slit my throat during the night."

"Jesus. You want to sleep at my house tonight?" She

was rattled, it was obvious. And now so was I.

"Not yet. So far, I've fooled her. I spoke to her at Garrison. She thinks we're here talking about Allie and your pathetic love life, not her."

I winced. "Thanks for that." The cocktail waitress brought our round of drinks, and I pulled out the Cuban cigar that Phillips had given me last month and fired it up. "But is she really in on it, the bad stuff?"

She waved away my cigar smoke. "I have no idea. One thing though, Annie doesn't like Jack Green. She thinks he's an idiot."

Something clicked in my mind, a flash, buried until now. "There was this guy—a dentist who was one of the people complaining about the drug house—I remember he was really strange... that cop radar thing. He was *too* interested. What was his name? Oh, fuck me! Was it..."

I went up and asked the bartender for his phone book. After some hesitation, he reached under the phone and handed it to me. "I want this back, or they'll take it out of my pay." He was being a smart ass, which I didn't need at the moment.

Carol was watching this, a ghost of a smile on her face, as I made my way back to the table. "Whatcha doing, man?"

I ignored her. A Gordon Lightfoot song, *If You Could Read My Mind*, was playing on the stereo system, except some guy was singing it in Spanish. I lost my train of thought. Allie and I used to listen to Lightfoot's records in bed sometimes. And this song was so sad, even in Spanish.

I slammed down the phone book—banishing Allie from my mind—and began leafing through the yellow pages for dentists. "It was somewhere in the 9000 numbers on Baseline, near Alta Loma High School... Christ, here he is. 'Dr. John Green, General Dentistry.' It's his home address too."

Carol was with me now, her eyes bright. "The owners of the Blue Sky Enterprises, the corporation that owned the drug house, were Jason Phillips and John Green. Jeez, I just assumed it was the surfer." Carol took another gulp of her margarita. "But this dentist can't be Jack Green, our Brotherhood of Eternal Love guy."

"Agreed. We've seen pictures of Jack Green, the surfer asshole. This dentist, John Green, is old, doesn't look like him. But maybe he's in on the whole deal." Now the tequila was kicking in. I downed another, saying, "Here's to Allessandra D'Amico, crime writer." Which had nothing to do with anything but made me laugh out loud, which also made me a little dizzy. Dan the bartender was looking at me, pointing at the phone book.

"You're pretty loaded, Jimmy." Carol's smile was lopsided. "And we've got that meeting tomorrow morning with Sam and those LA guys to reopen the cases. Kind of a big deal."

"Yeah I know, but I've got superpowers, and maybe just figured this thing out. How about we haul ass up to Baseline Road and roust this weirdo dentist. I might be developing a raging toothache."

"Nope." Carol shook her head. "We're going to drink some coffee, maybe eat something, and then figure out our next move. Suddenly, I'm sober and getting hungry. We've got work to do, man."

****

It was close to midnight when Carol and I cruised by Dr. Green's office. I'd prevailed upon her to conduct some non-contact reconnaissance of the dentist. We'd left my car at the Los Amigos parking lot, and she was driving, claiming to be less impaired. We'd eaten chicken burritos and drunk the restaurant's lousy coffee. She'd called home, no Annie, so she was free and clear for a while. Not trusting the coffee, I'd also taken one of the Benzedrine tablets I kept in my wallet, figuring it might be a long night.

"We still don't know anything," Carol said, "just driving around like nitwits." She was grumpy now that the margaritas had worn off.

"You want a bennie? I took one." I reached for my wallet.

"Nope. I've got to show up for work bright and early tomorrow or His Honor will be on my case."

I doubted that. Claremont's mayor had been one of the speakers at Jason's "celebration," and I figured he'd still be all jacked up about his starring role.

"Turn here," I told Carol. We parked at the Alta Loma High School parking lot and made the short walk over to Baseline Road. Green's office and home shared the same lot, with the office in front and the house down a driveway. It was pitch dark. A dog, or maybe a coyote, was yipping nearby.

A small park fronted the street just across the road from Green's office. Oak trees shielded us from view as we gently rocked in the swings, watching the lot. "Tell me about this guy," Carol said.

"Well, there was this group of concerned citizens pissed off about the drug house in their neighborhood, which was certainly reasonable. We met here at the dentist's house. The group harangued my partner and me about it, saying the house attracted all sorts of undesirables at all hours of the night. The dentist, our host, really gave me the creeps, acted like we were buddies. He apologized for the other neighbors after they left, said they were a bunch of wimps, stuff like that."

"Doesn't sound so bad to me," Carol said.

"I agree, but you know in those old movies there's always a guy, a real smooth talker, that ends up being the murderer. That was this dentist." It did sound lame.

"Plus, he assumed you wouldn't connect the dots and find out that his corporation owned the house," Carol said. "That's pretty brazen, like he was hiding in plain sight."

"I guess so, but the owner's representative, a young straight-arrow Realtor type, helped us get rid of the problem tenants, the druggies, without a legal eviction. Also, my partner was lead on the case and nowhere near as smart as you are." Carol glanced at me to see if I was being sarcastic. I wasn't.

"Okay," Carol mused, "now we've a dentist in the picture. What if Rebecca Meadows was a patient of his? You said he was creepy, and Rebecca was complaining about an older man bothering her." I considered this. "That's a goddamn good idea." And maybe our first glimpse of a motive.

Our attention shifted to a car moving west slowly on Baseline Road, the light from its headlights just missing us. It turned into the dentist's driveway. Carol gasped. "Jesus Christ, that's Annie's VW. She's driving and there's a passenger."

As the car disappeared down the driveway toward the house, we ran across Baseline and hid behind a hedge just to the left of the dentist's lot. I got that familiar little kid thrill of playing hide and seek in the darkness. I don't know, maybe that's why I became a cop. The hedge provided cover and a viewing angle. Peering over it, I saw the VW parked in the lot reserved for patients, illuminated by a twenty-foot light pole. Two people stood beneath it, arguing. One was Annie and the other was a slim man, about Annie's height, with long blond hair.

"Jack Green," Carol whispered. "Jesus. What does this

mean for Annie?"

I'd seen photos of Green, but this was my first look at the man. I'd expected him to be bigger, more imposing. "Kind of a wienie. I could take him with one hand," I whispered back, "and really hope I get to very soon." I remembered what he'd done to Melody Manning. And the Benzedrine was making me chatty.

"Yeah, maybe," Carol said, "but he can shoot the curl at the Huntington Beach pier. He's famous for it. So maybe not such a wienie. Bet you can't." She was sketching the scene in the small notepad she always carried.

Mr. Stoner/Surfer/Wienie was yelling at Annie by this time, but we were too far away to hear any words. A porch light came on from the house, and a man appeared. He had silver hair and was wearing khaki pants and a blue blazer, a walking advertisement for the Chamber of Commerce. It was my *old friend*, Dr. Green. He scanned the area for witnesses. We were well hidden. Seeing no one, the dentist made a sweeping motion to the squabbling pair, clearly telling them to come into the house. They immediately stopped talking, put their heads down, and trooped inside. After one more look around, Dr. Green slammed the door behind them. Good to know who the boss was.

I was exhilarated to see the three of them together, to see our work and hunches coming together. Not Carol. "I want to go in there and arrest all three of them," she muttered, "for seriously fucking up my life."

"I've got a better idea," I said, willing to be patient for once. "Let's get the hell out of here before they see us." We slipped away along the hedge.

I expected to walk back to the car and drive off. Instead, Carol headed back to the same swing in the park. I couldn't believe her. "We should ge—"

"Don't talk," Carol said. We sat there, me perched on a

wall, twitchy from the speed, her silent and unmoving on the swing, a thousand miles away. I jumped at the sound of a sudden fast movement to my left in the oak trees, then relaxed, figuring it was probably a possum. The Big Dipper was visible in the sky, no moon.

"Okay," Carol broke the silence, "one choice is to fall apart, disappear, and not go anywhere near my apartment until she's gone; for the crap pay I get from the Claremont PD, this course of action makes sense. Or, sharing your obvious and gleeful enthusiasm for all this mayhem, I can muster my courage, go undercover, continue to live with Annie, and help bust these criminals." She got up.

"And?" I checked behind me for action at the dentist's lot. There was none.

"Come on. You know what I'm going to do," Carol said, with a trace of bitterness. "The job wins for me. It always does. It's all I've got, along with you and my dog. That's it. I was foolish to hope for more. You drive." She threw me the keys. Very upset.

I got us back to Los Amigos, a silent Carol looking out the window. "It won't be easy, spending time with Annie now," she said as we pulled into the dark lot. "It freaks me out. No reason for her to be hanging out with them, except bad reasons. I've got to fool her, simple as that."

I killed the engine and put my arm around her shoulders. "Listen, I worked undercover down in Yucaipa years ago, pretending to be a buyer of stolen motorcycles. I had to hang out with these dirtbags for about two weeks. All I can tell you is try to get into character and live it."

"Yeah, but—"

"No buts. You're a wonderful police officer, better than you think. And it won't last long. They're starting to panic. You saw it up there. Melody Manning can hang Jack Green out to dry right now, and he knows it."

"You better make sure she's safe," Carol said.

"Yeah, I know. I'm going up tomorrow to see her, maybe bring her back down here."

Two scrawny cats prowled for scraps of food in the trash area behind the restaurant. The twenty-four-hour liquor store across Towne Avenue was still doing brisk business. "Tell Annie I'm a basket case after seeing Allie; that it took you most of the night to talk me down," I said, getting out of the car and handing her the keys. "See ya tomorrow."

She nodded and drove off. In truth, I hadn't thought about Allie at all. At least not then. It wasn't until later when I drifted into a light, speedy sleep out on my deck. That was happening more and more, staying out of my bedroom. Too many memories?

I was riding on a merry-go-round—chasing Mr. Dodger Hat, the shooter—but I wasn't armed. He was. Allie was with me, going up and down on a gleaming wooden palomino, wearing the same clothes she'd had on at the funeral. The shooter's eyes were fixed on me—the same skeletal grimace/grin I'd seen before—clearly enjoying the moment because I couldn't gain any ground on him. Fear glued me to my wooden mount, an ugly gray donkey. We went round and round as Merle Haggard's "Okie from Muskogee" blasted through the loudspeakers. Then Allie smiled back at the shooter, gave a slight nod... He pointed a monster .44 Magnum at my head, but then, at the last moment, turned it toward Allie. There was a deafening noise.

I woke up drenched in sweat, immediately freezing cold in the chilly night. Trying to shake the memory of the nightmare, I went in and took a hot shower. After toweling off, I wandered into the kitchen and grabbed a bottle of bourbon. I held it for a minute, staring at the Jim Beam label while my mind traveled up and down Baseline Road. Then I put it down, unopened. I felt a sense of shared destiny with the killer. Dodger Hat had murdered Rebecca Meadows and later Jason Phillips. I couldn't prove it yet, and that probably didn't matter. I had a sense, maybe a premonition, that this likely will be settled in a dark alley beyond the reach of justice. Only one thing was certain. I'd better be stone cold sober to even stand a chance.

CHAPTER TWENTY-FIVE

I SAT ALONE IN Sam Fuller's conference room at 11 a.m. the next morning, waiting for the meeting to start. Carol came in shortly afterward and took a seat next to me. I poured her some coffee from a pot on the table. "How ya doing?"

"Not great. Annie came home in the middle of the night, all charged up, and wanted to have sex. It was the weirdest experience of my life. My nerves can't take much more."

"Just hang on a little longer," I said, realizing my words sounded empty.

Sam Fuller entered the room along with two men from LASD. They all sat across from us. I recognized Al Sevilla and knew the other guy was Al's supervisor, although I couldn't recall his name. Sam gestured to him. "This is Grant Williams, Chief Homicide Investigator for eastern Los Angeles County, based in Pasadena. He'll represent LASD on this confidential task force along with Detective Sevilla, whom you know."

Now it clicked. Williams, an elegantly dressed man, looked like a television cop, and had the attitude to match. He gave us a chilly greeting. Sevilla was silent, easy to read. He didn't want to be in the room because it meant he'd screwed up the case in the first place.

"Okay, folks," Sam said, "we're now reopening the homicide investigation into the death of Rebecca

Meadows, age thirty-three, who was killed by a bomb on May twenty-fifth, 1970, at the Claremont Graduate School. This will be handled in conjunction with the recent murder of attorney Jason Phillips."

Sam looked at Carol. "Your boss has cleared your participation in this investigation, Carol."

Carol raised an eyebrow. "He talks a lot, you know."

Sam nodded. "I know, but I swore him to secrecy. He thinks it has something to do with drugs in Orange County, which it does, in a way, but our focus will be on the two murders. And Grant and Al, for your information that was a cover story about Phillips dying in a traffic accident. Somebody cut the brakes on his BMW." Neither looked surprised. They probably knew already via the cop grapevine.

Sam continued. "So far, Jimmy and Carol, rightly or wrongly, have been working the Meadows murder like a couple of Hollywood gumshoes, much of it on their own time. Fortunately for them, it looks like they were right. From now on, however, it's by the book." He pointed to the large binders on the table in front of each of us. "Everything must be documented."

"What about the Feds?" Williams asked. "Technically, it still belongs to them and the suspect, Richard Manning, is incarcerated for the crime awaiting trial." It sounded like he was already covering his ass.

"Not our concern," Sam said. "We've got the Meadows murder in Claremont—your county—and the recent Phillips murder in San Bernardino County, which happened on Sergeant Sommes's turf. I'll notify the FBI when I see fit and will also take the abuse if they get cranky about it. Clear?" A look passed between Williams and Sevilla, but they didn't say anything.

"Okay, Sergeant Sommes." Sam leaned back in his

chair and pointed a ballpoint pen at me. "Give us an overview, and *please* separate fact from conjecture."

I started in. "A dentist named John Green, his *son* Jack Green—I confirmed that relationship earlier today—and the recently deceased Jason Phillips are and were involved to varying degrees in felony drug smuggling and distribution. Jack Green in particular is implicated in the ongoing Orange County investigation of the Brotherhood of Eternal Love."

"Yeah, we know about the Brotherhood." Williams made a note on his legal pad. "Long Beach Harbor is their favorite port of entry for the Afghan hashish."

"The role of the woman, Annie Hoover, is less clear," I said, "but she's in communication with both Greens and also is the office manager of the public interest law firm that Phillips ran. The drug money was laundered through the law clinic. My partner in this investigation," I nodded at Carol, "is working undercover to gain more information about Hoover's involvement." The pun was inadvertent. Sam already knew that Carol was romantically involved with Annie, but I wasn't going to tell the LASD guys about it, ever.

"Last week," I said, continuing the narrative and watching Williams's impassive face, "I interrupted a man who had entered Annie Hoover's apartment in Upland, pretending to be an electrician. He cold-cocked me and got away. I worked with our SBSD sketch artist, who prepared a rendering of the guy. You've got copies of his report in the binder."

"What was he doing there?" Sevilla asked.

"Looking through her papers, maybe taking photos. He wasn't an electrician. And he had no trouble taking me down." Sevilla seemed to enjoy that part, giving Williams a theatrical look obviously designed to piss me off.

Instead, I soldiered on, discussing the trip Carol and I just took up north in part to shield Annie Hoover from harm and also to find Melody Manning. "We did find Melody Manning and got her out of a virtual prison in a basement. However, it was during our time in Central California that Jason Phillips was murdered."

"You think by the guy in the Dodgers hat?" Williams asked me, reading from the written summary in the binder.

"Yeah, but I can't prove it. Plus, I don't know who that guy is yet."

"Let's go back to the 1970 bombing," Williams said, pausing and looking at Sam, "and don't take this wrong, but it's sketchy as hell. You've got a radical bomber sitting in jail, who you say set off the first bomb two weeks before but not the second one, and who won't talk about it because his initial lawyer, Phillips, told him not to. Is that right?"

"And because Phillips and Jack Green kidnapped the bomber's hippie mother and threatened to kill her unless Manning continued his silence," Carol said. "The first part is fact, the second part, the threat, is conjecture."

"My initial reaction was the same as yours, Grant," Sam said, noting Williams's obvious skepticism, "but it all fits. But now for the hardest part." He stopped and looked at me.

"We don't know why Green, Green, Phillips, and Hoover, or some combination thereof, murdered Rebecca Meadows in the first place," I said. "Except that the note Phillips left, 'Regarding Rebecca, I couldn't change his mind,' reflects, at a minimum, guilty knowledge on his part. Plus, we've got solid information on the cover-ups, including the murder of Phillips. Again, we lack motive for the murder of Rebecca Meadows," I admitted in closing.

"Green, Green, Phillips, and Hoover," Williams mused.

"Sounds like a fancy law firm. You've got no real link to who killed Phillips. That note might be referring to his client, Richard Manning. I see why you're not taking this crap to the Feds."

"You don't want in, man, there's the door," I said to Williams, tired of his tone.

"Hold on," Sam said with a sharp tone. "That's why it's called police work. We've got to tie the evidence together. What's next?"

"We need to find a connection between Rebecca Meadows and somebody in the drug gang," Carol said. "She might have been a patient of John Green, the dentist. I'd love to see his records. There's also a secretary at the graduate school who Rebecca confided in on occasion. I want to talk to her again."

"And I want to convince Melody Manning to request a meeting with her son at the Federal Detention Facility in LA and take me with her," I said.

"You think she's up to it?" Sam asked.

"I'll find out."

"What do you want from us?" Williams asked, looking at his watch.

What good were these guys? It was time to test it. "Actually, I have an idea. Assuming Melody Manning will help us, I need to get her down here and stash her at a secure location with medical facilities."

"And?" Sevilla chimed in.

"I'm thinking of Pacific State Hospital, the mental hospital. It's in LA County, and out of the way. We could provide a nurse to monitor her physical condition, and there's security. She'll be safe and easy to babysit."

"Is she loony?" Sevilla asked.

"She's detoxing and has been through some dark times. That's why it's a good spot, one of those small cottages on the hospital's grounds," I said.

"Sounds like you've spent some time there, pal," Sevilla said. "Did you get committed?"

I chose to ignore the stupid joke, if that's what it was. "Actually, I went to college next door to Pacific State, at Cal Poly."

"Jimmy, Carol, could you excuse us for a moment," Sam said. It wasn't a question and he had that "Marine ready to storm Iwo Jima" look on his face.

While we waited in the outer office, Sam's secretary asked me what was going on. "Sam's gonna let them have it," I replied. "I've been on the other end of that. It's no fun."

Five minutes later we were ushered back in. "Let me summarize," Sam said. "Our small group here is trying to solve two murders, including the notorious Claremont bombing. If successful, it will make national news and all our friends at the FBI will owe us a debt of gratitude. If we fail, no harm done. These drug peddlers will be rounded up one way or another." Sam paused for theatrical effect and drank some coffee from his Rose Bowl mug.

"Accordingly, I have invited Chief Detective Williams and Detective Sevilla to get on board, share in the glory, and stop acting like LA assholes. I believe that they have accepted this proposal. Is that correct, gentlemen?" Both nodded yes. "Good. I'll leave you to it." Sam left the room.

Sevilla and Williams glanced at each other, looking like two boys who'd survived a trip to the principal's office. "Your boss and my boss go fishing together once a year up at Big Bear," Williams said, lighting up a cigarette. "Without ever quite saying so, Sam made it clear that he was prepared to make my life a living hell if I didn't play ball. So, let's catch these murderers, so I can get him off my back."

****

I called Chief Rhyne in Atascadero to check on Melody. So far so good. I told him I was driving up that night, and he informed me he'd assigned Delores Figueroa from his unit to help me transport Melody down south, which was welcome news. This was assuming Melody would go with us, but I felt pretty confident about that. She had some scores to settle.

Sevilla was making phone calls, figuring out the details of using Pacific State as a stash site for Melody. Carol was in Claremont working on a mountain of unrelated paperwork that had accumulated during her vacation. It was good cover to keep her apart from Annie.

My main concern was protecting Melody. Mr. Dodger Hat was lurking out there; I could feel him. I had to assume that either Tony the Tiger or his lawyer had talked to Jack Green about Melody. The court had denied bail for Tony, but the word would still be out. Fortunately, the Orange County DA was closing in on Jack Green for the Brotherhood stuff. But that left Dr. Green... and Annie? Jason Phillips made a convenient fall guy. They could try and pin the original murder on him. It might work.

I went home to pack for my quick run up Highway 101, expecting to spend only one night in Paso Robles. Mostly I packed guns. I called my mother to say I'd see her next Sunday for our Walter's brunch. I called Sokoloski to check on our next gig. He was back from taking his two kids east to tour Civil War battle sites. Salton Sea had been off for nearly a month. We were booked at The Corral in two weeks, early June. I looked forward to playing again, even to seeing our dipshit singer and his girlfriend.

I was also tempted to call Lisa, the cocktail waitress from the Sycamore Inn, to make a date but decided to hold off until I got home, *if* I got home. That was the dark thought dogging me, maybe from the dream. My father was a religious man, in his own way. One thing he taught me was to confront evil head on, because the devil wasn't ever going to let up. I needed my weapons, sure enough, but mostly I needed my nerve to take on this gang, especially that killer.

That's why my last call before leaving town was to Carol, my partner in all this. Without saying anything much, we fortified each other for what lay ahead. I felt ready to do battle.

****

He'd finished fourth in the club golf tournament, which Mark Collins took as a further sign that it was time to retire. The following Monday he disappeared from Las Vegas, closing his bank accounts, cancelling his utilities, donating his minimal furniture to the American Legion, and turning in the key to his apartment. His last stop was his North Las Vegas PO box. He cancelled that too after picking up several files from Doc Green, the last marked "URGENT." He checked. They were proposed jobs. Green still had not accepted Collins's business proposal. Until he did, Collins was going to ignore the requests.

He left Las Vegas, his home for the past six years, and headed north on US 95. His destination was Bend, Oregon, where a certain Douglas Prescott owned a beautiful riverside condo. Nobody, not even his bankers, knew anything about Prescott. Collins planned to keep it that way. The main difficulty with his planned retirement was that former clients might try to kill him, since he knew dangerous things and was of no further use to them. That's why Prescott was a critical identity, and why he would conduct no business in Bend. Portland was not that far away; he could set up his accounts there.

There was still the matter of the car, his little problem. The Vette's engine was growling, wanting to go faster. Collins tamed the beast and stayed within the speed limit. At 6 p.m. the temperature outside still hovered near a hundred. He'd drive three hours, then spend the night at a Best Western in Tonopah, near Area 51. CIA and Air Force spooks sometimes frequented the place. Collins could spot them. But everybody kept their heads down, a community of ghosts.

In any case, these agents wouldn't know him. Even back when he was the fair-haired boy at the Agency, his handlers had kept him hidden away, like fine wine too good to drink. That's one of the reasons Collins knew Paris so well. It was a considerable distance from the prying eyes at headquarters in Langley. Early on, Jonas, the closest thing he'd had to a friend back then, once said to him, "Luther, you're a perfect killer. The best I've ever seen—so good it's scary." That was before the Congo, before Saigon, before some other assignments best left unsaid, even to himself.

Jonas had meant it as the ultimate compliment, but it had chilled Collins then, and it chilled him now, driving through the Nevada heat. Who wants such a legacy, a perfect killer? But it defined him. Even as a kid in the dirt-poor Kentucky Appalachians, his family counted on him for meat. "Give Luther a rifle and a knife in the morning, and we'll have venison on the table by supper time," Pa used to brag to his drinking buddies. He left out the part about the beatings if Luther failed, or sometimes even if he succeeded, on dark nights when Pa was crazy mean drunk.

Collins sighed, remembering. It had happened in the late fall of 1958, in the forty-eight hours between his last high school football game and his Army enlistment. He'd never forgotten the look on Pa's face just before Luther had shot him between the eyes. The look had been a mixture of fear, surprise, and something strange, like pride. Luther dumped the old man's body into an abandoned well in a forest high on Pine Mountain. Nobody would look too hard for him anyway, since Pa was hated, or feared, or both by everybody in town. His mother already had taken up with somebody else, a salesman, so Luther figured she'd be okay.

He'd never been back to Kentucky, and rarely thought about it.

Collins put a tape in the machine of John Coltrane playing *My Favorite Things* live at the Olympic Theater in Paris. Collins liked to imagine that he'd been there, close to the stage, watching Coltrane work his magic on the alto sax. It cheered him up.

CHAPTER TWENTY-SIX

MELODY MANNING, SERGEANT DELORES Figueroa
of the Atascadero Police Department, and I approached
the gates of Pacific State Hospital at four on Friday afternoon. I hadn't slept much the last several nights and was
running on fumes. We all showed ID to the guard, who
checked the sheet on his clipboard, gave us a sticker for
the car, and waved us on. I noticed that the guard was
armed, which was good. We drove through the pleasant
grounds of Pacific State, passing a large administration
building, various residential halls, an auditorium, an infir-
mary, and a dining hall. All were well-marked in this small,
self-contained city.

I'd worked as a handyman at Pacific State one summer before going into the Army. It had cured me of my
heebie-jeebies about the place. As a kid, if I dropped a
football pass or let a baseball go through my legs in one of
our many pick-up games, the likely taunt from my friends
was, "Come on, Sommes, you retard, make that play or
we'll send you to *Spadra*." That was the name we used
for the mysterious insane asylum on the hill. Spadra, the
town, had been swallowed up by a stack of freeways just
west of Pomona. I'd heard that Pacific State also was on
the way out, too expensive to run. I wondered what would
happen to the patients.

Near the southern boundary of the grounds, I pulled
up in front of an adobe bungalow, one of several on the

residential street. Al Sevilla of LASD was waiting for us, along with a woman in a nurse's uniform, whom he introduced. I handled the introductions at our end and Sevilla left.

Despite my misgivings, the transfer of Melody Manning and our journey down south had gone smoothly. Melody and Delores already knew each other from that dark basement on the night we rescued her. Now they were buddies; the two of them had chattered like girls at a slumber party during our drive down Highway 101.

Melody had signed paperwork agreeing to being held as a material witness in the ongoing kidnapping case against Jack Green and the already jailed Anthony Harris. Since Sergeant Figueroa was with her, she technically was still within the jurisdiction of the Atascadero PD. That might change in the future, but I wasn't pushing Melody yet. She'd sent another "I'm okay" postcard to her son in the Federal lock-up before we'd left Paso Robles, hopefully buying us a little more time. I wanted her to get more rest before we confronted Richard Manning. The methadone replacement for the morphine she'd been addicted to had her sleeping eighteen hours a day.

The couch was comfortable at the cottage, and I drifted off for a while. Then I called Carol to let her know that Melody and the team were settled. "Good, cuz I might have something, something *big*," she said, her excitement coming through the telephone line. "I got all my town busywork done last night, so today, for no particular reason, I checked on parking tickets issued on May 25, 1970, the day of the bombing. There were sixteen in total, a typical day: fourteen paid, one contested, and one little sucker just sitting there, waiting for me to find it."

"Who's the lucky motorist?" I asked, giving Carol a chance to breathe.

"Don't know, but get this. It's a 1969 Nevada plate number CF8175, on a 1968 blue Chevy Corvette convertible. Cited at 807 Dartmouth Avenue at 3:30 p.m. for exceeding the two-hour parking limit. That's a block from the bombing site and half an hour before it went off."

"No meters there, right?"

"No. Just a posted sign. Our patrol guys chalked the car tires on that street that day, doing extra duty on account of that first campus bombing. Our lucky break."

"Carol, that's incredible. Tell me what you think." Pretty sure I knew the answer.

"Okay," Carol said, "we're assuming that Green, et cetera, hired Mr. Dodger Hat to kill Jason Phillips and to burgle Annie's apartment, correct?"

"Yeah, okay."

"Then let's further assume that Green, et cetera, hired the same hitman to kill Rebecca Meadows back in 1970."

"Possible," I said. "And your final assumption, Miss Sherlock Holmes, is that Mr. Dodger Hat drives a Corvette with Nevada plates. If so, the license plate is probably phony."

"Yeah, I figure that too, but the car, that fancy Corvette convertible, is real."

I stopped for a moment and considered her point. "You know, I've been making a mistake with this guy, assuming he's perfect. That's crazy. I've been in this business long enough to know that all crooks make mistakes. So, I'm going to add an assumption to yours, namely that Mr. Dodger Hat loves his blue Corvette."

"I've got a call in to the Nevada DMV to check on the license," Carol said. "Gotta go. The mayor wants me to brief him on Claremont's stray cat problem. He wants to poison them, which has pissed off lots of people, especially the old ladies at Pilgrim Place. Call me in the morning."

She hung up.

Stray cats? It reminded me that "normal" life went on. Regarding the car, I knew some guys at the Las Vegas PD. They might be able to help us find the Corvette. Probably a thousand of them in Vegas alone. But it was a lead. I could see the sun setting out the side window and a palm tree was swaying in the breeze. I'd picked a good place for Melody.

The nurse cooked too, and she asked me if I wanted a burger. I said yes, realizing how hungry I was. I fell asleep, again, in an armchair after dinner, watching an old Burt Lancaster gangster movie on Channel 5.

Sergeant Figueroa gave me a nudge. The TV was off. It was ten o'clock. "Somebody's outside, watching us, he's dressed in all black, a sweatshirt with a hood," she whispered. "Twenty yards out, behind the tree."

I shook myself awake and looked out the window. I could make out the shadowy figure. What the hell? He was small, maybe a patient, but maybe not. "I'll go out front, you go out back," I told Figueroa. "Be careful."

I waited thirty seconds, then opened the front door, slipped out, and shined a flashlight in the intruder's direction, my gun below it in the other hand. "Stop, police," I yelled. The figure took off running to his right toward a soccer field—not seeing Sergeant Figueroa, who flattened him with a perfect tackle. I jumped him, pulled his arms behind him, and put on the cuffs. "Wow, did you play football?" I asked Figueroa.

"Only with my brothers. I used to kick their asses."

"Could you get the hell off me while you continue your conversation?" a familiar voice asked.

I pulled the hood off the captive's head, and Annie Hoover's profile greeted me. Anger surged. Here was Carol's tormentor in the flesh, stalking Melody Manning. I

214

pushed her face into the dirt, wanting to hurt her.

"Take it easy," Figueroa said. "You know her?"

"Yeah, take it easy, you son-of-a bitch," Annie sputtered, spitting out dirt.

"Why should I?"

"Because we're on the same fucking team. That's why. Let me up."

****

Annie and I sat at the dining table in the cottage. Figueroa had joined Melody and the nurse in the other room. I'd taken off the cuffs. "Okay, talk," I said, "starting with how you got in here."

"The clinic has two active cases here, representing patients. I've got a pass. I was at Carol's and overheard a phone call you had with her, talking about stashing Melody Manning at Pacific State. I came over this evening, met with one of my clients, then decided to look for the cottage. I found it, thanks to your car. You better work on your security."

"So, why'd you run? If we're on 'same fucking team,' as you put it."

"Because I wasn't ready for this yet, being interrogated by you. Or Carol knowing. Plus, they wanted a report. Could I please get some water?"

I got up and poured her a glass. Annie took a big gulp, rubbed her wrists. "You hurt me, you know. You and that hard-ass lady."

"Get over it and talk. *Who* wanted a report?"

"You're really mad, aren't you? Okay, Sergeant Sommes, I'm an informant for the California Bureau of Investigation based in Sacramento. Happy now? They work—"

"I know who they are."

"Don't interrupt me and let me tell the story." She lit a cigarette—I didn't know she smoked. Evidently there was a lot I didn't know about this woman. "About a year ago I contacted an old law school friend who worked for the CBI. I told him I was in trouble, that my boss and others were dealing large quantities of drugs and were trying to drag me into it. I was looking for a way out. Instead of getting me out, my *friend* decided I was a perfect candidate to serve as a confidential informant. I said no." Annie shook her head. "They threatened me with criminal charges, saying I'd waited too long to come away clean. They had me over a barrel. I really don't like you people, cops. It's a dirty world."

"The only thing worse are the criminals," I said. "Spare me that bullshit." The story was ringing true because I didn't think she could make it up. Most civilians had never heard of the Sacramento outfit. It kept a very low profile. Cops mostly hated them because they often investigated police departments for corruption. "So, you went to work for them."

"Sort of. It turned out that the Bureau, that's what they call themselves, was particularly interested in a certain lone-wolf hitman. A judge in Stockton got assassinated two years ago, a prosecutor in San Diego more recently. The Bureau knows there's a contract killer out there, and they can't find him. But somehow, they traced him to Doc Green."

"How?"

"I don't know for sure. Apparently, Doc Green met this assassin back in some jungle war and fixed his smashed-up teeth."

"What's your deal, what do you do?" I sensed that Annie was telling the truth. Call it instinct, intuition, whatever. And it accounted for her odd moods in the midst of all this. I got up and got bottles of beer for both of us. Both of us paused to drink.

"I'm an informant, not some sort of junior G-man," Annie said. "My mother lives in a nursing home in Oxnard. I visit her once a month, the good daughter. That's been going on ever since I started at the clinic. And that's when I meet with the Sacramento guys and tell them what I know—mostly about the money laundering because that's what Jason had me doing when he got too messed up to do it himself."

"Do you have any idea who killed Rebecca Meadows?"

"No." She stubbed out her cigarette and lit another, wide, pleading eyes fixed on me. "I really care about Carol, by the way. That wasn't planned."

"Who killed Rebecca?"

"I just *said* I don't know. Jack Green mentioned once, out of the blue when he was flying on coke, that Rebecca had been a patient of his father's. I don't know; it could be true, but Jack lies about lots of things. But maybe Doc Green took a fancy to Rebecca."

It was about the oldest reason for murder, I thought. "How well do you know the father?"

"Well enough to know he's really strange. He doesn't use drugs, doesn't need the money, and seems to hate his son. But he wants to control everybody, even me."

"One night Jason took me to Doc Green's house for dinner, just the three of us. After several bottles of burgundy, Doc Green let his guard down and bragged that he'd had the last laugh on a lady who'd disappointed him and that he had a very good friend who excelled at, 'initiating corrective measures.' It was chilling to hear him talk. I think he was testing me, trying to bring me into his world."

Figueroa opened the door to check on us. I motioned her away. Annie had her eyes closed, didn't notice, and kept talking. "The next day at work, Jason made a special point of telling me not to believe all that nonsense from the night before. That Doc Green got carried away sometimes, liked to make things up."

"Must have been good wine," I said. Our theory that Rebecca was a patient of Doc Green's who'd rejected him in some fashion was looking better all the time.

"It was. Something from France I could never afford. Of course, Jason saying that just made it more real to me, and it got me scared. That's when I contacted my friend in Sacramento. Sometimes I wish I hadn't."

"Then you'd really be up the creek," I said. She was silent, looking down. Annie's energy was flagging, as was mine. The walls were closing in on us. "Let's get out of here. There's a coffee shop nearby. I'll drive."

She nodded. I notified Figueroa, and Annie and I took off. We made our way through Pacific State and Cal Poly, and then across the freeway to the coffee shop of the very funky Lemon Tree Motel. There was no talking. I was giving both Annie and me time to gather our thoughts.

"Tell me about Jason Phillips," I said after we ordered our coffee and pie.

Annie got emotional, like she was going to cry. "I loved Jason. He was my hero at first. But then he got hooked on drugs—cocaine and pain pills, up and down all the time, never straight—and ended up doing whatever the Greens told him to do. I can't defend him. Life doesn't always make sense, right? But I didn't know they were going to," she put her head in her hands, "to... kill him. Jesus, it terrified me."

"Do you think the guy at your apartment, the one I interrupted, was the killer?"

She looked out the window, thinking. "I don't know. Maybe. That's why the Bureau's keeping me in this, to get proof. I want out. Screw them." Annie paused. "But that's not completely true. They've got me hooked too, the Bureau, hooked into this game. I want to get the Greens… They killed Jason. I'm sure of that."

"Why your apartment?"

"It was the night after you, me, and Carol ate at the Sycamore Inn. I called in sick. Jason—Jesus, it was the last time I talked to him—told me to stay clear of my apartment, something vague about surveillance."

"You believed him?"

"By then I didn't care. By then, I just wanted to be with Carol, away from all this crazy shit."

"How can they still trust you, the Greens?" I asked. "With me showing up at your apartment, you going up to Paso Robles with us? I wouldn't."

Annie lit another cigarette. "Jack Green doesn't, but his daddy does, and that's what counts. He likes the idea that I'm sleeping with the enemy. It fits his perverse nature. Also, I've told them I'm spying on Carol and you, that you're dumb as a post, and that you don't know anything. Then," she hesitated, "after Jason died, I said you guys think it was him behind the murder, nobody else. I felt bad about saying that, but it worked."

"Thanks for the dumb part. One last question, do you know who threw that brick through Carol's car window?"

That got a chuckle out of Annie. "Jack Green and Jason did it. They were drunk, and boys will be boys. I'd told Jason about your first visit to the clinic, you and Carol, it was on a night after that."

"Have you told Carol?" I asked.

"No. I'm scared to. She might throw me out. She loves that car." It was nice to see traces of humor in Annie's voice. "I'll tell you one thing, though, it infuriated Doc Green. He called at the office and just screamed at Jason."

"Doc Green was right to be pissed off," I said. "Carol

and I might have dropped the investigation but for that little escapade. Thanks, Annie. That helps me."

As the night drifted along, we talked about other things—how much we both had liked Atascadero, how much she disliked my taste in music. I told her that Stanford was only good for rich snobs and liberal do-gooders. Somehow the trading of gentle, and not completely sincere, insults softened the edge between us, provided us some respite. Two lives had been taken, one innocent and one tormented. We were caught up in it, looking to stop these particular villains. For Annie, it was a one-off. For me, it was what I did. At what cost? I wondered.

It was getting late. The only other people in the coffee shop were truckers and various creatures of the night. Hookers and pimps prowled outside, drawing attention to themselves. One of the pimps was dressed like Sly Stone at Woodstock. I paid the bill and we left, ignoring catcalls from the ladies. One of them seemed to know me from some long-ago brush with the law.

"You haven't asked about Carol. How come?" Annie asked, as I made the turn toward Pacific State.

"I don't even know what to ask," I said. "She's my best friend."

"Me too, but I figure she's going to hate me forever now. Nobody, not the Greens, not the frickin' Bureau, wanted me to get involved with Carol. It was my rebellion against everybody. She made me happy, still does. Now I've blown that." Annie shivered and it wasn't cold.

"Don't know if that's true, but I have a suggestion. Let's check in with Figueroa and then drive over to Carol's house. I'll wait outside while you talk to her." I felt like a high school kid arranging a date for two friends. I figured I could sleep in the car. It had been that kind of night.

****

Something was screwy. A big black Lincoln Town Car was parked in front of the Pacific State bungalow. Two men stood outside waiting for us. They raised their hands in the air, indicating no weapons.

"The Bureau," Annie said under her breath. One had short cop hair and wore a blue windbreaker. The other looked like the drummer for the Eagles, the long frizzy hair, the flannel shirt, the whole deal.

I got out of the car very slowly, trying to figure this out. Figueroa was on the porch watching. "Sergeant Sommes, I'm Nichols, this is Wilcox," the windbreaker man said. "We're CBI. Annie Hoover is our asset."

"Fuck you," Annie said.

That drew a thin smile from Windbreaker. "Like it or not," he said.

"You undercover?" I asked the Drummer.

"Sometimes," he said. Nothing more.

Everybody was tense. It reminded me of most of my interactions with the FBI, and these "Bureau" guys clearly thought of themselves as roughly the same thing. Another car was approaching. The engine gave it away. It was Sam Fuller's ancient Jaguar coupe. "We took the liberty," Windbreaker said.

Ah Christ. I was tired. Annie was tired. Somewhere Carol was tired, and she didn't even know it. Too many lawmen. The Bureau was going to pat us on the head and assert control. If we resisted, the State Attorney General or some other bigshot was going to lean on Sam Fuller's boss—the politician pretending to be the San Bernardino County Sheriff, the guy nobody saw except at the Christmas party—and get us to back off. Forget it. I wasn't going to play.

Sam looked gray, and old. He shook hands with the Bureau guys. "What's the story?" he asked.

"Let's go inside, sir," Windbreaker said, and turned toward the door, as did Drummer. They were used to people following their orders.

"Annie and I are going to Carol Loomis's house in Claremont," I said to anybody who cared to listen. "Have a good meeting and call us in the morning."

Drummer was fast, and in my face. "I don't th—"

I grabbed his flannel shirt with two hands. "I don't give a flying fuck what you think." We stood there frozen— he smelled of spearmint gum—then I let him go with a push and started to walk away. It was a calculated risk. Sam Fuller was my protection. Drummer wasn't going to hit me over the head or shoot me, not with my boss standing there. I looked at Annie. She nodded.

We got in my Charger and drove away. The next challenge was the guard gate. They might call him. No problem. He waved us through. I got us to the I-10 and turned east. Annie started to laugh, quietly at first, then louder. I started in. By the Indian Hill exit, we sounded like a couple of wild hyenas, pretty much hysterical.

The lights were on as we pulled up in front of Carol's College Avenue bungalow. Our laughter had stopped. Annie walked in, shoulders straight, confronting her fate. I stayed in the car and waved at the Bureau guy in the Oldsmobile parked across the street; obviously he'd been assigned to nursemaid us. They'd moved fast. He watched me and I watched the house, while most of the good citizens of Claremont slept, oblivious to our games.

An hour later I was awakened by a gentle knock on my car window. Carol was standing outside with her pug dog, Max. "Annie and I are talking. It's good, but Max is bothering me. Can you take him for a walk?"

I said sure and got out of the car, stretching my aching back. So far, I'd slept on a couch, in a chair, and a car tonight. Carol went back inside, and the leashed-up pug began snuffling in the ivy. Every dark green leaf seemed to be telling him an important story. We crossed the street. The CBI guy in the Olds ignored us. What was he gonna say? Max stopped at his right front passenger side tire and gave it a long sniff. He then unleashed an impressive stream of urine, soaking the hubcap and tire. I was half-way tempted to join him in this activity but held off. Max had effectively conveyed my opinion.

CHAPTER TWENTY-SEVEN

CAROL AND I DROVE north on Las Vegas Boulevard toward the Riviera Hotel where the big marquee sign out front said "DEAN MARTIN." She pulled the Nova into the porte-cochère and a frowning valet drove it away. Maybe the car wasn't up to his standards. The two rooms were free, courtesy of Danny Sofos, my buddy at the Clark County Sheriff's Office. Just about every lawman in Vegas moonlighted doing security work for the big hotels. It created hopeless conflicts of interest, but this town played by its own rules.

"All I want to do is sleep," Carol said. She and Annie had talked all night, while Sam negotiated with the California Bureau. This morning Sam had told Carol and me to get out of town, follow the Vegas lead on the hitter, and keep away from the Bureau guys, who still were pissed at me. Meanwhile, the Bureau reclaimed a reluctant Annie as its informant but pledged to protect her from the Greens. Nobody was happy, but an exhausted Sam reminded me that the SBSD task force still was primary on the murder investigations. He'd done wonders. Carol and Annie were bruised but still together, relieved to be on the same team.

It was noon when we arrived at the hotel. Carol and I agreed to meet at ten o'clock that night in the lobby. Danny was going to take us to dinner at some steak joint. I went to my room and crashed for eight hours, didn't even move. Then I looked at the file.

The California Bureau, at Sam's urging, had given me a copy of a heavily lined-out FBI file on a retired CIA assassin. His name was Luther Simmons, and he hailed from Kentucky. He was about my age, and there was a old, grainy photo, blown up in size. The young man in the photo had fair hair, no prominent features, and blue eyes. From the photo everything looked average to me, including his height and weight. I compared it to the rendering of Mr. Dodger Hat done by the SBSD sketch artist based on my description. It could be the same man, but the lack of prominent features made an identification difficult.

Simmons had first enlisted in the Army, been stationed in Germany like me, and then had moved to what was termed "government service." There were trips to the Congo, Cuba, and the Middle East, all the details of which were blacked out. He'd fallen off the face of the earth in 1963. Despite an official request from the FBI two years ago, the CIA wasn't talking. Jesus, what a crummy way to run the government. A researcher at the CBI had put two and two together. Simmons was their current best guess for the lone-wolf assassin. The problem was, he didn't seem to exist, and the Feds were no help.

****

The steak was perfect, and the wine flowed at dinner that night. Danny Sofos was a big, handsome guy with dark hair who dressed like a 1940s movie star. He was Greek rather than Italian but could easily pass as a wise guy. He'd tipped the maître d' twenty bucks to get us a good table with a panoramic view of the strip and the spectacular new Caesar's Palace hotel. Danny and I were happily telling Carol about a case we'd worked together several years before. A mafia soldier on the outs with his crime family had relocated to San Bernardino and started to spread counterfeit money all over town. I was about to arrest him when somebody in our main office screwed up and he got wind of it. The man did a runner back to Las Vegas, but his taste for cocaine and strip clubs made him easy to find.

Danny and I had busted him in the front row of the Heavenly Babes Club in downtown Vegas as he was stuffing bills into the tiny G-string of a dancer gyrating to the pulsating sounds of "Proud Mary." Danny continued the story with obvious relish. "Since I'm a thorough detective, it was my job to carefully remove each counterfeit bill from the dancer's body, one by one, to preserve the evidence," Danny recalled, "but she kept dancing, even off-stage, and her boobs kept getting in my face. I was tempted to arrest them for hindering an investigation."

"Okay, boys, we gonna do any work tonight? Or just bullshit about the good old days?" Carol asked. "Either way is okay with me." She was smoking one of Danny's Cuban cigars and had drunk more wine than either of us.

"All right, all right," Danny said, holding up his hands. "I pulled some strings at the DMV—they can be really slow—but I'm sorry to tell you that Nevada license plate number you gave me was a dead end, literally. The blue Corvette in question was registered to a doctor in Reno who died last year. I called the widow today. She told me he'd never owned a Vette."

"So, we've got nothing," I said, beginning to think it was a wasted trip.

"Oh, ye of little faith." Danny laid a hand on my shoulder. "My ex-brother-in-law—now there's a story—loves fast cars. He owns a 1970 Corvette Sting Ray, a really hot set of wheels. He told me, before my sister said I could never talk to him again, that the Chevy dealerships were crap when it came to servicing sports cars." Danny paused to order cognac for the table.

"And..." I said.

"Everybody goes to Augie's European Service instead, a joint out near the airport. We're meeting Mr. Augie Donatello tomorrow morning at nine, which is early for me, but I know you guys want results. Excuse me now, I've got to take a leak."

Carol took a sip of cognac. "You know Danny's gotta to be dirty, right? No straight cop can live like this," she said. "But tonight, I just don't care. He's lots of fun."

Dirty or just par for the course in Vegas I wondered, taking a big slug of brandy. She got no argument from me.

****

Augie was short, fiftyish, and uncomfortable in his shop's small office. "My wife, she does the books, keeps the records, but she's at church since it's Sunday." Carol and I were squeezed into the office with him. Danny was waiting outside in the car, looking at race sheets, the Belmont, I think.

"Thanks for coming in," Carol said. "We appreciate it."

"No problem. A week away from the priest won't send me to hell." He was rummaging through the files in a battered old black cabinet. I'd shown him the Mr. Dodger Hat rendering. He didn't recognize him. We'd switched gears, so to speak. He was trying to find the car first.

"1969 blue Corvette convertible," Augie said to himself. "Not that common a color, usually black or red." Through the open door I could see a tech was working on a Porsche in the cleanest car garage I'd ever seen. "Okay, got one." He pulled out a slim file. "We had to special order a new alternator for it last year. Lemme see that picture again."

I handed him Mr. Dodger Hat again and also the older

Bureau file photo of Luther Simmons, assassin.

"Look at both of them side by side on your desk. Maybe a fifteen-year age difference between them," I said.

Augie snapped his fingers. "Yeah, I know this guy. Mark Collins is his name. No mustache, though. That's what threw me. Excuse me for a moment." The tech working on the Porsche had a question.

I reached for the file. Carol slapped my hand, like I was a schoolkid. "Patience."

Augie was back with us. "Okay, Mr. Collins is a quiet guy, always pays in cash, and keeps his machine in perfect working order. His address in 5770 Northeast Paradise Drive, Unit 26. No phone number. There's a note, in my wife's writing, that says to leave a message for him at the Sahara-Nevada Golf Club pro shop if we need to reach him."

"Thanks, Augie, this is great," Carol said. "When did you last see Mr. Collins?"

"I didn't see him, but he dropped his car off two weeks ago for a routine tune-up. We had it for two days."

"Could we get the exact dates?" I asked.

"Sure." Augie checked his file again. "Yeah, car came in evening of April twenty-eighth, picked up Monday morning May first early in the morning."

"But you didn't see him?" Carol asked.

"Nope. We have an after-hours system for some guys. They park their car in front, put the keys in the lock box. When the car's ready, we park it outside and call them with a code for the lock box. We put the keys inside the box, and they put in the money. It only works with cash."

I couldn't resist. "What if they stiff you for the money, Augie?"

He grinned. "Then their car never gets serviced again. Forgive me for blowing my own horn, but nobody services

these cars like us. Nobody's gonna stiff me for the work."
I believed him.

"Do you have any credit card receipts, work orders, or
other documents with his writing or signature?" I asked.

Augie nodded and showed me a copy of the work
order for the alternator. The signature was a sprawling
mess, but it was something.

"Can we borrow this long enough to make copies?" I
asked. Augie said sure and handed it to me.

"One last question," Carol said. "I assume you left a
message on April thirtieth at the golf pro shop that Mr.
Collins's car was ready. "Is that right?"

Augie confirmed this fact and we left him to enjoy the
rest of his Sunday.

****

Danny put a team together, calling in four of his top
men. "Look, if this guy's as dangerous as you think he is,
we can't just wander around looking for him." One team
was assigned to Palm Villas, a townhouse complex with
two-story units where Mark Collins lived in apartment
number 26. A good address according to Danny. The surveillance van had a clear view of his townhouse from
Paradise Road.

Two other men dressed in golf clothes headed for the
Sahara-Nevada Golf Club. Their specific job was to watch
the pro shop while hitting balls on the driving range. They
had walkie-talkies and sidearms in their golf bags. We
decided to approach Palm Villas first. The rental office
was close to the street and not visible from Collins's apartment. A bored-looking man was sitting behind the desk at
the rental office watching television. He didn't get up to
greet us.

"Need your help, dude," Danny said, flashing his

badge. "How about some service?"

The man got up. He had a mustard stain on his shirt. "We don't show units on the weekends," he said. "If you come back—"

"Do I look like I want to rent a unit, you bozo?" Danny snarled. "What I want is everything you can tell us about Mr. Collins in apartment 26."

The rental agent relaxed, happy to deliver the bad news. "You missed him by six days. He moved out last Monday, no forwarding address."

Carol and I looked at each other. Fuck! I hadn't realized until that moment how jacked up I was. How much I wanted to get this guy. Carol's expression mirrored mine. We really thought we had him. Now it was back to the drawing board. Like Sam said, that's why they call it police work.

"Is the unit vacant?" Danny asked the rental agent, somewhat oblivious to our pain. "Yeah, it's scheduled to be cleaned tomorrow and then put back on the market."

"Then let's go have a look see, shall we?"

After objecting to this request, the rental agent, realizing Danny was about to throw him out the window, relented and we headed for apartment 26. All of us except Carol who stayed back to contact Annie and tell her that Mr. Dodger Hat was on the loose. I asked her to call Sam too, although I sensed Dodger Hat was nowhere near SoCal.

Back to it. One of the officers in the surveillance van was a crime scene expert, so he got in first to dust the apartment for prints and look for other forensic evidence. He came up empty. So did we. The apartment was not only empty, it was sterile, as if nobody had ever lived there. The humming sound of the empty refrigerator was the only noise.

"What about his stuff?" I asked.

"A truck from an American Legion Post showed up on Tuesday and took his bed, sofa, TV, and a chair."

"Which post?" Danny asked.

"Post 8. Collins authorized it when he left on Monday and said to give them the security deposit too."

****

Mark Collins had vanished. We interviewed the general manager of American Legion Post 8, which was located near the Vegas strip. He and some Vietnam vets who were eating dinner there recognized Mr. Dodger Hat, sans mustache. "Yeah, he just showed up out of the blue last week, offered some stuff if we picked it up at the Palm Villas, and said they'd be mailing us a check too. It was like Christmas in May."

"Did he say why?" Carol asked, back with us.

"Just that the vets had defended our country and were taking a lot of shit for it."

"True enough," I said.

Next stop was the golf course. The pros at the Sahara-Nevada Golf Club spoke highly of Collins's golfing prowess. "The guy doesn't drive it that long but he's a wizard with his short game. Kinda like Gary Player." But nobody really knew him. We did gain another photo, however.

"This is from two weeks ago," the head golf pro told us. It was a clear shot of Collins on the eighteenth green, getting ready to putt. "Nobody has seen him since, but that happens from time to time since he travels on business."

There was no doubt in my mind now. Collins was Mr. Dodger Hat, the guy who got me to eat shag carpet. He kept up with the times though. The Lakers had just won the NBA Championship, beating the Knicks. He'd switched. His hat in the golf photo said "LAKERS" on it in large letters.

"Did Mr. Collins need a sponsor to join your club?" Danny asked.

"Actually, I sponsored Mark," the pro said, looking a little embarrassed. "He'd started playing at the club as a paying guest maybe four years ago, but was real quiet, shy in fact. Didn't seem to have any friends. We get some noisy show-biz types here, they can get on my nerves. Mark was different. We never socialized away from the course, but I enjoyed playing golf with him, so I got him in. He's an investment banker with plenty of money so it was easy. He showed me his brokerage account once. Dude was loaded."

"Does your membership office have that, or a file on Mr. Collins?" Carol asked.

"Nope," the pro said. "Mark shelled out a bunch of cash upstairs, and the business office printed his membership card. He pays his dues a year in advance. It's not that unusual in this town, people flashing lots of dough, you know what I mean?"

Danny Sofos nodded, knowing exactly what the man meant. "Could I borrow this photo for a day or so, get copies made?" Danny asked the pro, who agreed and handed him the picture.

It was time for us to leave Las Vegas, empty-handed, with a near miss to our credit. We thanked Danny for his help and also for the fun evening. He promised to expedite the processing of the photo and to mail us copies ASAP.

Carol, ever the optimist, saw the glass as half-full. "We've got a photo, a name, and a face. And Collins very likely has no idea we're on to him, which is a very big deal."

"A car nut assassin with a soft spot for vets and who needs to play golf." I shook my head. "He could be anywhere in the world."

"If we're right, he killed Jason Phillips about three

weeks ago," Carol said, "and earned a good payday. But he's loaded with dough according to the golf pro, which means he doesn't need to work."

"So?"

"He likes challenges. Maybe that's what gets him off."

"What's his next challenge?"

"Maybe it's us." Carol grimaced as she spoke. "But I've got an idea what to do about that," she said with a bulldog look on her face, flooring the Nova as we crossed the border back to California.

CHAPTER TWENTY-EIGHT

SAM FULLER WASN'T BUYING it. It was the Monday after the Vegas trip, and Carol and I wanted to move quickly on Jack Green. "You guys are asking me to piss off the Orange County Task Force," Sam said, shuffling some papers on his desk while he considered our idea, "including the DA, a guy who may become governor or senator someday. At least he thinks so."

"Orange County has been dicking around with this Brotherhood of Eternal Love thing for months," I said. "At best, they get a bunch of hippies for drug felonies. Big deal."

"Actually, it is a big deal," Sam said. "Millions of dollars of drug sales. Kids' lives ruined. I'm for getting those criminals."

"Me too, Sam," Carol said. "But we've got Jack Green cold on kidnapping and sexual assault. Violent crimes. He's one of many in the Brotherhood. Orange County will still get them."

"Our big problem is Doc Green. We've got suspicions, inferences, but nothing firm on him," I said. "The LASD cops are right about that, and still ready to jump ship on us."

"So, what's the plan?" Sam asked.

"Simple. We bust Jack Green, transport him to San Luis Obispo, and get him to flip on his father." I tried my best to sound confident. It was a gamble. Jack Green likely would lawyer up and clam up, but Carol and I believed that we needed to take the shot.

Sam told us to wait outside his office while he made a couple of calls. Ten minutes later he waved us back in. "The simple answer to your request is 'No.' The Brotherhood Task Force is going to hit them on Wednesday at dawn, probably the biggest single drug bust in history. We need to stand clear. After Jack Green is in custody, we'll see if we can move him up to San Luis Obispo to face the felony charges."

"Wow, all because the Orange County DA wants—"

"Dammit. This isn't politics, Jimmy. Come on, you know better. It's logistics," Sam said, giving his world globe a slightly fierce spin. "This operation is being run by professionals, the Orange County Sheriff's Department. And it goes down in less than forty-eight hours. So go home, get some sleep, and figure out how to find this Collins character." The meeting was over.

****

I spent the rest of Monday grocery shopping, washing my clothes, and practicing my fiddle, trying to figure out some tricky descending note chords that Byron Berline, my favorite fiddler, had played with the Flying Burrito Brothers. It took my mind off Jack Green. Then I slept another twelve hours. I hadn't realized how wired I'd been, and exhausted. Too much adrenaline kicking through me. Sometimes I had to remind myself that this was, after all, a job—just like my father had worked at a defense plant, or doctors worked at hospitals, or lawyers did whatever the hell they did. I put in my time and got paid for it. Trying to convince myself, unsuccessfully.

On Tuesday I went down to visit Melody at Pacific State. Damned if I didn't hear *American Beauty*, my favorite Grateful Dead album, playing on the record player. Melody and Delores were sitting at the kitchen table playing cards.

"Gin rummy," Figueroa said. "She's winning."

Melody looked up at me. I nearly choked up. She was doing so much better, coming out of the darkness. "Probably cheating," I said to cover my emotion. Melody saw through it, thanked me with her eyes.

"No way, man. Fair and square. Sit down and rest your bones." She patted the chair next to her. I sat. Meanwhile Jerry Garcia was singing "Friend of the Devil," with these great, skittering mandolin notes framing the lyrics. Our band needed to add this song to our set list. I was itching to learn it and play it with the guys.

I watched the card game for a while, then convinced the nurse to let me take Melody for a short walk.

"Are you up to visiting your son in Los Angeles?" I asked Melody as we walked in the grass field among the fragrant eucalyptus trees. It was cool and overcast, a typical Southern California May morning.

Her face turned sad. "He probably hates me for never coming."

"His lawyers know what happened to you. With your permission, they'll tell Richard before you go in. They aren't bad guys, the lawyers, just real lefties," I said.

"Hell, I like lefties. Okay. Go ahead and set it up." Melody hesitated. "Give me a few more days to get my feet under me. I'm nervous about it."

I agreed. We went back inside. I had a cup of coffee with them and also briefed Sergeant Figueroa in private, telling her that if everything worked right, we might get Jack Green up to San Luis Obispo in a week or so to face felony charges. That made Figueroa happy. I could tell she was ready to get back home.

****

I stayed clear of the Orange County operation as instructed, not sure it was really going to happen after all the false starts. My negotiations with Manning's lawyers for Melody's visit, cleared by Sam and the DA's office, were going slowly. Some nut had shot George Wallace at a campaign rally in Maryland. He was alive but badly hurt. It had everybody concerned and distracted. Politics by assassination was happening way too much. Nixon was going to cruise to a second term no matter what, beating anybody to either the left or right of him, politically, unless he got shot too.

I was in my office on Thursday morning, drinking coffee, and reading the newspaper, when I saw it. "Joint Force Raids Drug Cult," the headline blared. It stated in the article that over fifty members of "the Brotherhood of Eternal Love were arrested or indicted, and large quantities of LSD, hashish, cocaine, and marijuana were seized in dawn raids in California, Oregon, and Hawaii."

It sounded good, until I called Sam. "Jack Green got away," he told me. "They found underage hippie girls and lots of dope in his Huntington Beach house, but he'd slipped away in the night."

"How come you didn't call me yesterday?" I groused.

"Hell, they didn't tell me until this morning. Strictly an Orange County operation. Anyway, they'll get him, just a matter of time."

But, at present, Jack Green was gone, just like Dodger Hat. Now what?

****

My answer came an hour later. I was catching up on some paperwork when Laurie told me there was a guy here to see me. It was Wilcox, the California Bureau man, the one with the frizzy hair who looked like the Eagles' drummer. He was wearing the same flannel shirt, except in the daylight I could see that it was expensive and wool. Lucky I hadn't torn it during our earlier encounter.

"We need to talk, off the record," he said—an ominous beginning, reinforced by the expression in his small, squinty eyes.

I nodded and offered him a chair in my small office. Wilcox sat down and then spun me a tale. The Bureau knew things, confidential things, about Doc Green and his relationship with the hitman. "I can't tell you how we know, and we can't directly act on this information," he said.

Jesus. That was pretty clear. They'd probably wiretapped the dentist, or broken into his home. It happened more than ordinary citizens knew, cops taking matters into their hands.

"Keep talking," I told him, guessing where he was going.

According to Wilcox, Doc Green had been in touch with a Mr. Collins on the telephone. He'd agreed to Collins's proposal, whatever it was, and had further agreed to wire $100,000 to US Bank of Portland, Downtown Branch, Account No. 7371004. But there was one complication for Collins. Since this was a new account, he'd been informed by bank officials that he must personally go to the bank and sign an authorization for a deposit of such a large amount. It was a State of Oregon law.

It was now Wednesday. Green had agreed to wire the funds by close of business Friday. He'd said he needed some time to get the money together. Collins would go to the bank the following Monday, first thing, and authorize the deposit. That was their business deal.

"You've got him," I said to Wilcox. "Go pick him up

next Monday."

"Except, like I said before, we don't know any of this," Wilcox said, grimacing. "We applied for a search warrant and got turned down. Doc Green is smart. Everything actionable went through the late Jason Phillips or Jack Green."

"What about Annie Hoover? Does she help you?"

"Nope. She's confirmed that Doc Green is some sort of weirdo and probably calling all the shots, but no concrete evidence."

"So, you figured out a way around your little legal problem," I said to Wilcox. "Me."

"It's not your problem," Wilcox said, trying to look innocent.

"Bullshit. You want me to just happen to visit Portland, and just happen to visit this bank, don't you? All off the books, and you don't know about it. You must think I'm pretty stupid."

Wilcox stood up. "It's entirely your choice, Sergeant Sommes, but you seem pretty gung-ho about catching Mr. Collins." He handed me a card. "Call me later at this number if you want additional particulars."

****

"Fruit of the poisonous tree," Annie said. We were eating dinner at Carol's bungalow. "If this Collins guy is arrested by the Bureau, or by you, all the evidence leading law enforcement to him is inadmissible in court on account of the unconstitutional wiretap, or whatever it was. And Collins walks away, a free man."

"What the hell does Wilcox expect me to do?" I asked, frustrated by the situation. So near and yet so far.

"Simple." Carol twirled up a forkful of noodles. "He expects you to go rogue and get the guy."

"You mean kill him? That's nuts."

"Or maybe arrest him based on an anonymous tip," Annie said. "The Bureau wants to put Collins out of business. Once he's identified, he's done as a hitman, even if he beats the charges. Nobody will hire him, and, who knows, one of his former clients might take care of the problem."

"I don't see much we can do about it," Carol said. "The Bureau screwed up." She went back to her spaghetti.

We ate in awkward silence. "I think you're right," I finally said, "nothing we can do, although I hear Portland is nice this time of year." Neither Carol nor Annie responded to my half-assed feeler. We moved on to other topics, not having a great evening.

Carol walked me to the door. "I can tell you're tempted. Be careful."

Damn right I was tempted; I was beginning to plan my trip, talking myself into a covert surveillance mission, no rough stuff. But halfway to my cabin, it hit me, so obvious it was embarrassing. Wilcox was setting me up, playing me for a patsy. There was nothing remotely useful I could accomplish in Portland, except to kill Mr. Dodger Hat, which I wasn't going to do. I played it straight as a cop, no exceptions. And like Annie said, any arrest would be tainted on account of the illegal search. Wilcox knew that too. He was no fool.

I changed course and headed for Sam Fuller's Cucamonga house, hoping he was home. On work matters, I trusted him completely. Mrs. Fuller fussed over me a little, brought us beers, then left Sam and me to talk. I laid it out for him.

He listened silently, nodding now and then. When I was done, he frowned and drew a deep breath. "I've been a lawman for twenty-six years," Sam said, "since the end of the Second World War, and most of it has been straightforward. I don't do politics except when necessary. But maybe four or five times in my career, I've gotten a sense of something lurking in the shadows, dark and sinister. The Marilyn Monroe overdose was one of them. The LA Sheriff's Department brought me on as a consultant, worried some of their officers were corrupt. The Feds were sneaking around. You couldn't tell the good guys from the bad guys. It was spooky as hell."

"Marilyn Monroe?" I couldn't help myself.

"Maybe someday I'll tell you the story, but not tonight," Sam said, smiling. "It'll take more than two beers. Back to your issue, these Bureau guys, Nichols and Wilcox, feel all wrong to me. They should have just blown into town, pulled rank, and taken the Mr. Dodger Hat case away from us. Sure, I would have been pissed off, complained like hell, but the Bureau ultimately wins those battles. Instead, they 'suggested' that you and Carol go to Las Vegas, even gave you their dossier on the hitter. And now Wilcox is dangling Portland at you like a shiny new toy. It's ringing false."

"Do you think they're impostors?" I asked him.

"Nah, I checked, discreetly. Nichols and Wilcox are agents, all right. But remember, the Bureau reports directly to the State Attorney General, who works for Reagan. We all know Ronnie wants to be president one day. Also, significantly, you know J. Edgar Hoover died two weeks ago. The FBI is adrift, and every agency in Washington is jockeying for position."

"So?" I was lost in this intrigue.

Sam took a big pull of his Budweiser. "I think the Bureau guys are working with the CIA to eliminate ex-CIA assassin Luther Simmons, aka Mr. Dodger Hat, aka Mr. Collins, and somehow saddle us local cops with the blame."

"Boss, if I brought that theory to you at work, you

might throw me out of your office."

My attempt at humor failed. Sam didn't laugh, just looked troubled.

"Remember how I started this conversation, son. Some bad shit is going down, outside your frame of reference."

We talked further and made a plan. Of sorts. Then he worked the phone as only he could, putting resources to work. I also called Carol and told her of the plan. "It better work," she said, "but I'm in."

I left Sam's house at close to midnight. Back at my cabin I called Wilcox for the particulars. He picked up after one ring, as if expecting my call.

CHAPTER TWENTY-NINE

CAROL AND I FLEW to Portland on Friday night, arriving close to midnight. We picked up a Chevy Impala at Hertz and drove to our airport motel, a Motel 6. It was a dump. I found Carol the next morning in the cramped lobby, eating a stale donut and drinking oily coffee out of a paper cup. She gave me a dirty look.

"You're gonna like me better soon," I told her. "I found a bargain rate for two rooms at the Benson Hotel for the weekend. Laurie helped me, said it's a really good hotel right next to the US Bank of Portland building. There's even a Trader Vic's next door, with a tiki bar. Might as well enjoy ourselves on this mission, right?"

Carol and I had decided not to discuss the true operation, even between ourselves, in order to project the right attitude. Instead, we were living our cover story; namely that this was an unsanctioned freelance operation to surveil, identify, and photograph Mr. Dodger Hat. Our superiors had no idea we were in Portland. It had the advantage of not being too far off the mark.

We drove toward downtown Portland on a sunny, cool Saturday morning, snow-capped mountains all around us. Neither Carol nor I had been to Portland before, but we had a Hertz rentals map to guide us. Wilcox had provided me with a name. We were meeting with "Jerry" at 10 a.m. at a coffee shop in the Imperial Hotel, near the US Bank of Portland.

In the city, parking was easy and free since it was the weekend. I looked north and saw the back of the sturdy old marble bank building as we entered the hotel and found the coffee shop. The aroma that drifted toward me made me realize I was hungry. Jerry saw us and knew who we were. Wilcox must have briefed him, maybe sent photos of us.

"The eggs Benedict are good here, maybe the best in town," Jerry told us as we got settled and drank coffee. "Sound good?" We nodded and he beckoned the waiter and made the order. "You guys want Bloody Marys?"

I said yes. Carol said no. Jerry was a goofy-looking guy, maybe thirty years old, with unruly reddish-blond hair, a scraggly beard, and brown eyes. He was dressed like a hip lumberjack in his Pendleton shirt and designer jeans. "How do you know Wilcox?" I asked him, since they looked like members of the same jug band.

"I worked for the California Bureau after college, kind of a gofer. It wasn't to my liking, the job or California. Portland's my hometown, so I came back. I freelance now, have a private investigator's license. But Wilcox called me, asked me to check out the bank building,"

Jerry's story was interrupted by the arrival of our food, and we dug in. It was tasty, especially the perfect home fries, not an easy thing to do just right, I'd learned, in my extensive breakfast-eating experience.

Jerry unfolded a hand-drawn map of about four blocks of downtown Portland and laid it on the table, moving coffee cups and silverware aside. "Here we are, at the Imperial, the Bank of Portland is one block north of us. Broadway, the main drag, is one block west."

"We're staying at the Benson for the weekend," I told him. That's on Broadway, right?"

He raised his eyebrows and whistled. "Big spenders,

huh. Yes, it is." He located it on his map for us. "Anyway, there are two entrances to the bank building, one on Sixth Avenue, and one on Broadway."

Jerry paused. "Your man, the object of your search, made a mistake in that regard. There are plenty of banks in downtown Portland that have multiple entrances and exits, and some have underground parking entrances. US Bank of Portland, by contrast, is a box canyon. He must be very relaxed about this deal."

"Good," Carol said. "We're taking photos, that's all. Then we split."

"Not my concern," Jerry said, "but you're in luck." He pointed to a structure on the other side of Sixth Avenue, directly across from the bank. "This is your best vantage point, a four-story parking garage. It's new. They tore down a tavern I really liked and put this in its place. Progress, right?" He gave us a grin that didn't match his eyes. "Anyway, the garage is open-air and you can park directly facing the bank. You can see both entrances. Perfect for your purposes."

Jerry paused, then looked at Carol. "I assume you have telephoto capacity on your cameras. It's maybe a fifty-yard distance from a south-facing parking spot to the Sixth Avenue bank entrance, which opens an hour earlier. Who knows why, banks, right?" Jerry added with another cold grin, reaching for his coffee cup. This guy was definitely playing us, and thought we were dumb as hell, I thought while glancing at Carol. She knew it too.

"Anyway, the third floor would be best," Jerry continued. "You'll need the height. I suggest parking there Sunday night. The garage gets busy during the work week."

I was studying his map. "The guy we're watching has a car he loves, a blue Corvette convertible. Do you think he'd park in this same garage?"

Jerry shoveled some poached egg in his mouth, considering the question. "I've got a BMW, and I wouldn't park there. Too many tight turns and small places. I'd probably valet park at the Benson, whether I was staying there or not, even if it meant eating at their steak house, or something. They take good care of the cars." He looked at his watch. "I've got to go. The map is yours. Good luck with your work. I've got this." He took the bill with him.

"Courtesy of the California Bureau," I said, as Carol opened her mouth to protest. She liked fighting for checks. "He'll expense it."

"I like the map," Carol said, "and he's given us a clear path in and out of this job." Keeping to the cover story. Even so, as we left, I gave a slight nod to the watchers, a man and a woman three tables away, part of our new Portland team.

After arid Southern California, it was nice to see so much greenery, even downtown. Carol and I took a long walk, ending up in a big park with statues of pioneers. I breathed in the scent of the pine trees. This was a nice city. Then we went back to work, returning to our rental car and driving to the third floor of the parking structure, to see how it worked.

"Jerry's right," Carol said. "This is almost too good. I wonder if Mr. Dodger Hat will notice this spot too."

"I'm sensing his guard is down. The guy is arrogant. I like that." I could see the Benson Hotel from here as well as the bank. A Cadillac pulled in front, and a valet quickly opened the doors for a well-dressed couple and handed them a ticket. The kid then drove the Caddy one block south and turned into a driveway that went underground. Carol was watching too. "Let's go snoop a little," she said. We left the car and found the stairs down.

There was room for maybe thirty cars down that

driveway where the Caddy had gone. A sign said, "Parking for patrons of Benson Hotel only. Valet only. All other cars will be towed." It gave a phone number for the towing company. Carol was scanning the cars. "No blue Corvette," she said.

It was time to check in at the Benson. We each had a small bag and resisted all attempts by several bellmen to carry them since our sidearms were in the bags. The elevator took us to two small adjoining rooms toward the back of the hotel. The windows faced a small interior courtyard, not glamorous at all. I could hear noises coming up from the kitchen. No wonder the rooms were cheap. Carol and I agreed to meet later and go to Trader Vic's for dinner. It was on Broadway right next to the hotel. We'd go early, at six o'clock.

The bed was comfortable. I decided on a nap. Drifting off to sleep, then waking again, restless, ruminating about the day... suddenly I saw it, with Technicolor clarity... half dream, half vision. It happened to me sometimes, but I wasn't clairvoyance or any of that nonsense. More like an extreme shot of logic, of knowing what bad guys were going to do. It had kept me safe on occasion. Anyway...

...It was Monday morning. I raised the hood of the Impala, as if I had engine trouble, shielding Carol and her telephoto camera from view. The small plaza fronting the bank building was busy, office types bustling about, some buying coffee and donuts from a small portable stand with a big parasol umbrella off to the right of the bank. At 9 a.m. we saw him, the Hitter, Mr. Collins—brown hair, mustache, nice sports jacket—walking toward the large metal door just as it opened. Carol was snapping photos murmuring, "This is good, this is good."

Then the man's head exploded, his hat blown against the door. One shot, then another, striking Collins as he went down. People turned and pointed at the parking garage, just as a pickup truck rumbled down from the fourth floor and stopped in front of our car, hemming us in. Jerry jumped out of the truck, placed an evil-looking sniper's rifle by the Impala's left rear tire, and yelled, "Nice shooting, Jimmy." A sedan screeched up, Jerry jumped in the passenger seat, and he was gone. Collins lay in a bloody heap on the plaza. I heard sirens. The cops were converging on us...

I shook myself out of this vision, pretty freaked out. This was how it was going down, more or less, and I didn't want to be Lee Harvey Oswald at the Texas Book Depository. I called Carol. "Let's go to that tiki bar now. I need a drink."

****

Collins was sitting in a Howard Johnson's off I-5 near Salem enjoying coffee with a slice of blueberry pie a la mode on Saturday evening. He was also getting used to his disguise, a bushy brown mustache, longish hair over his ears, and clear, rimless glasses. It was a good look for Portland, maybe a graduate student at Portland State. He was, however, dressed nicely, wearing dress slacks, a Van Heusen shirt, a sports jacket, and shiny loafers. Appropriate for the Benson Hotel, his home for the next two nights. The Benson wasn't the best hotel in town anymore, but it was perfect for this trip. He'd requested an upper-floor room looking east, which he knew faced the US Bank of Portland building.

Collins hated going to banks—too many cameras, too much identification, even if his was fake. But Oregon had a law about authorizing accounts. Nothing he could do about it. They'd laugh at such a law in Nevada. It would keep the mob money out. Perhaps he should have chosen Seattle, a larger city, maybe easier laws, but he liked Portland, had spent some time there between assignments.

He didn't know the US Bank of Portland, had never expected to see the inside of it. Early Monday morning he'd check it out, figure out the entrances and exits. All he knew at present was that the bank was old and distinguished, his kind of place. And Doc Green, bless his heart, was coming through with the money.

Collins took another bite of the pie—not bad although he preferred apple—and considered his future. What Green didn't know was that Collins was going to stiff him. He had no intention of ever returning to Southern California, no intention of doing any further business with Green, and no intention of killing those cops, a hit Doc Green desperately wanted. This hundred grand on Monday was his final reward for surviving in a tough business, and a final "fuck you" to characters like Doc Green. He'd done their dirty work long enough. Maybe he would go to Maui and drink mai tais, get a house on the slopes of Haleakala, and watch the glorious sunsets. Play golf on oceanfront courses.

Collins paid the bill and walked to his new set of wheels, a forest-green BMW convertible. He'd bought it used in Medford, Oregon, after disposing of his Corvette in a nearby landfill. He'd paid the junkman an extra hundred bucks to watch the Vette get compressed to an unidentifiable metal square. He felt relief rather than regret. That car had been an unnecessary entanglement. This Beamer, with its Oregon plates, was a good fit for the current version of Collins. He enjoyed the freedom of shedding identities at will, like throwing out old clothes. He'd kept that car too long as it was, but he seemed to have gotten away with it.

He'd be in Portland in an hour, going a conservative sixty miles an hour. A certain kind of tension, which had possessed him for so many years that he thought of it as part of himself, was starting to diminish. Maybe, just maybe, he could escape his assassin's life, which was darker and more confining than any prison cell.

CHAPTER THIRTY

TRADER VIC'S WAS A bust. I took two sips of my rum drink, pushed it away, and ate my teriyaki steak quickly for the fuel, hardly tasting it. Too much was going on. Carol agreed. We paid the bill and left, a waste of money. It was a short walk to the parking structure where we were to meet with the special Portland Police Department team. It was 7 p.m. They had commandeered the entire parking operation for the next two days—the regular workers were getting a paid vacation—and about eight of us were crammed into the small office on the ground floor of the facility.

The head man, Matt Greenstein, was intense and surprisingly young. He looked like he'd missed at least one night's sleep. He started the meeting with a firm warning: "No assassinations on my watch, or the mayor will have my ass." That set the tone. The team knew the basics from earlier conversations with Sam, namely that rogue law enforcement professionals, possibly Federal, were planning to kill a known hitman most recently going by the name Mark Collins, at the US Bank of Portland building on Monday morning.

I started to apologize in case nothing came of this, but the team leader interrupted me. "Look, if nothing happens, we'll all go home happy. Not to worry."

A BOLO had been issued for a 1969 blue Corvette with Nevada plates, number CF0175. Nobody named Mark

Collins was registered at any of the nearby hotels, but we knew the man traveled under many names. As for "Jerry," who'd pointed us to the third floor of the parking garage like lambs going to the slaughter, nobody had heard of him. They were still checking the list of licensed Oregon private investigators, but the group doubted he was local.

"Any surveillance on him?" I asked.

"That was a tough call," Matt said. "We didn't want to spook him and mess up the operation, so we had a team operate at quite a distance and they lost him."

I then offered my theory regarding how the hit might go down on Monday, not telling them it was the result of a mystic, half-waking vision, and definitely not mentioning Lee Harvey Oswald. Carol had told me not to, since she disliked my Kennedy conspiracy theories. But the scenario I laid out continued to make sense. The team agreed, but also discussed some other possible firing locations, complicated somewhat by the two bank entrances.

"What about Collins?" Carol asked the team leader. "Do we let him walk into the ambush?"

Greenstein shook his head. "My boss talked to your boss. We are to use our best efforts to apprehend him prior to Monday morning, even if it creates evidence problems down the line. Collins, your 'Mr. Dodger Hat,' needs to be taken off the street, as a matter of public safety as well as his own. Photos of him are being distributed as part of the notice to police officers. There will be increased police presence in the area near the bank, starting immediately."

The team leader stood up, stretching his back. "Now I suggest the two of you get some sleep. We'll meet here at nine o'clock tomorrow morning to review our contingency planning. Enjoy your evening."

Carol and I were being told to get the hell out of there, which was okay with me, at least for tonight. I could tell this team was highly competent. "Let's valet park at the Benson tonight," I said to Carol as we left them. "I want to scope out the area." Carol agreed and we retrieved our car. The plainclothes cop at the toll booth waved us through for free. I turned left on Broadway and pulled up to the hotel entrance.

"We're hotel guests waiting for others to join us for dinner," I told the valet. "Can you give us a few minutes here before you park the car?" He said sure and we waited and watched. It was Saturday, cool but no rain. Lots of people on the street. The entrance to the hotel lobby was busy, many well-dressed Japanese businessmen milling around, maybe heading for that steak house.

"Police cars on both corners," Carol noted, "increased security like he said, but keeping it low-key."

Feeling more relaxed, I was thinking about revisiting that tiki bar, if we could get in. There was a line in front. A sporty BMW convertible pulled up to the Benson's porte-cochère.

And then I saw him. Dodger Hat behind the wheel. Since he was driving a different car, the Portland team would not have spotted him from the garage, and we had no radio contact with them. It left us on our own.

I moved the Impala forward and angled it toward the street, not wanting to attract Dodger Hat's attention. It also gave me an opportunity to watch him through the side window on the passenger side. He'd only seen me once.

Dodger Hat was sitting there, calm as could be, engine running, waiting for the valet, a half-smile on his face. Maybe he was listening to music. His longish brown hair was pulled back. He looked so young to me, and harmless, which was so far from the truth. Maybe some kind of weird innocence marked assassins. He'd taken me down in seconds at our only other meeting. My heart was beating fast.

"Carol, I need you to look out the rearview mirror without moving your head," I said to her in my dullest possible voice. "Dodger Hat is sitting behind us in that convertible. It's different, not his Corvette."

One glance was enough to convince her. "Holy Mother of God," she exclaimed. "You're sure, right?"

"Yes. Only the glasses are different. It's him."

I could feel Carol's crackling tension. She wasn't going to wait. "Our best chance is right now," she said, reaching for her weapon.

Since I had a better angle and more cover, I started to do the same. "Do you think—"

Carol gave me a quick look. "No. Too many nightmares. I've got to do this."

Gun drawn, she opened the door and started for Dodger Hat. I got out on the driver's side of the car, trying to cover her. No good. Her movement attracted the hitman's attention. His eyes went feral. The beast in him emerged. He was out of his car in one lightning-fast motion, going straight for Carol.

I should have shot him then. Carol should have shot him as he hurtled toward her. Neither of us were stone killers, so advantage to Dodger Hat. Maybe if we'd game-planned it better, one of us would have taken him down. Now it was too late.

Instead, Dodger Hat used that split second to grab Carol. With a circular motion like a baseball pitcher, he pulled her right arm forward, almost tearing it from her shoulder, then jerked it upward. Carol's gun fell to the pavement, her bones breaking like brittle sticks. Then the man pulled her to him with his right hand, using her to shield his surprisingly small frame. A lethal-looking automatic pistol was in his left hand.

My gun was still leveled at him. Did I have a head shot? No. Carol was too close to him now.

Dodger Hat looked past her and recognized me. "You again," he said. Then his voice lowered. "Follow me and she's dead." Reaching across his body he hit her again, this time in the head, with his gun. Carol cried out in pain. "See what I mean, cowboy?" he said.

Keeping her body in my line of sight, and giving me no firing angle, he somehow slipped back into the convertible, snakelike, keeping Carol as his shield. I felt helpless. Dodger Hat gave me a sneering glance, then threw Carol into the passenger seat as he sped off, almost running me down, and then turned right, accelerating down Broadway.

It had taken less than thirty seconds. A policeman ran up to me. He must have been close by. "How can I help?"

"Get in the car," I said, my engine already revving. I glanced across the street. The Portland police squad car was empty. Shit! No help there. Running over the curb, avoiding a pickup truck, we gave chase down Broadway. The BMW was faster than our Impala but was staying within the speed limit, not wanting to attract any more cops.

My hands were shaking. God, I was such a failure, a coward. I should have fired on him. I froze instead. Was Carol already dead? And we couldn't even call it in for officer assistance.

"Tell me to keep it together, tell me not to fuck this up," I said to the young cop, trying to steady myself.

"Don't fuck this up, sir," he yelled in my ear. Then he yelled it again.

I think it was the "sir" that actually worked. Almost made me laugh despite everything. This kid was good.

I could still see Dodger Hat's taillights, maybe a hundred yards down Broadway. Traffic was fairly light, but I could keep at least two cars between us. We both stopped twice for red lights. There were no sirens or other police activity. Broadway changed. It was mostly office buildings now, dark on the weekend. I ran one traffic light to stay within sight of his distinctive taillights.

"Okay, where's he gonna try to lose us?" I asked the cop.

"Maybe Lake Oswego," he said, keeping his eyes on those taillights. "No, that's too far. He'll make for Council Crest Park, dark winding roads. From there he can sneak west to the Sunset Highway and head for the coast."

"Okay, I'm putting all my money on you, pal," I said.

Broadway curved to the right, then to the left. We kept driving for maybe five minutes, but it felt like forever. Then I lost sight of the BMW. Coming to the next intersection, I was going to go straight through it, trying to catch up.

"Turn left," the kid yelled at the very last moment. I did so with squealing brakes, fishtailing around the corner and hitting the concrete curb, barely keeping the car under control. In the distance we saw taillights again.

"That's him," my new buddy said. "I was right," he added with evident satisfaction. "The guy's heading for Council Crest Park. Use your parking lights now if you can."

I was happy to oblige and take his orders. It was quiet now, a residential area with narrow streets, some leading to cul-de-sacs fronting large old houses. "The road to Council Crest Park is another tight turn," the Portland cop said, and I slowed down. "Turn here." It was more like an alley. A very dark alley, and I had no idea where I was. Up ahead, my enemy might be relaxing. He must know Portland. Christ he'd hit Carol hard. Now we were following a narrow road of hairpin turns through a forest, right in the middle of the city. "Pretty close now," the officer warned me. "All lights off after this next turn."

****

Collins was calm. "Stay focused, live in the moment, and execute," his first CIA handler had always preached. The BMW traveled down Broadway, as fast as possible without attracting other cops. He heard no sirens. He knew that damn cowboy in his Chevy was behind him somewhere, but he mostly was concerned with other police cars. He figured the entire Portland Police Department was on alert, looking for a blue Corvette. Something had gone terribly wrong, but that was the past. Nobody knew this Beamer. He could get out of this if he stayed cool. He'd been in worse spots before.

The turn was coming up, and it was tight. He downshifted and pulled the steering wheel sharply to the left, skidding but keeping his wheels under him. The urban landscape quickly disappeared. He saw no headlights behind him. His hostage moaned in the passenger seat, but she was too hurt to move. He wouldn't need her much longer. He felt his first hint of elation. This was going to work. Good, because Collins had decided long ago that he'd never be captured alive. The life expectancy of a hitman in prison is measured in minutes and hours, not days and months.

He'd had a shot at Sommes back at the hotel, could've blown him away. He'd passed on it, thinking only of escape. There was something about that cop that unnerved him, made him hesitate. And now he had the guy's partner in his car. What a mess. Collins didn't want to kill her either, just dump her somewhere. But maybe he should break her neck first. Finish it. Filled with indecision, he felt his mood begin to darken. He didn't want to do any of this anymore. He hadn't even needed the extra money from Doc Green, since he already had plenty, some of it lodged at the Maui Branch of the Bank of Hawaii. No. It had been a matter of ego and greed, and the client had turned the tables on him, sold him out. There was no other explanation.

Collins turned into the city park, easily skirting the closed gate, and drove up the entry road, looking for the right spot. He found it and slid the BMW into a clearing behind a clump of bushes. Good enough for present purposes. No doubt about his future now. It had to be Maui. Images of islands ran through his mind as he sought to steady himself: Elvis singing corny hula songs on the beach, waterfalls in the jungle, his golf ball soaring over a corner of ocean and landing softly on a tiny green fringed by lava.

He scanned the park and saw an old railroad car up the hill. That looked good for stashing a body. He climbed out of the convertible and made himself pause and breathe deeply, cutting the tension. He loved the smell of the woods. It reminded him of his childhood, hiking in the Kentucky Appalachians, until everything back there turned to shit.

No time for memories. Stay focused, live in the present, and execute. He pulled the semi-conscious woman from the passenger seat and began to drag her up the hill, still not sure what he was going to do with her. Stay focused, live in the moment... and execute.

CHAPTER THIRTY-ONE

AFTER THE LAST SLOW, dark turn, we came to a straightaway, and I turned my headlights off. Ahead there was a closed gate to the park. I drove around it. The only illumination came from two small, dim light standards. The park appeared to be deserted. I could see benches, swings, a jungle gym, and something else—it looked like an old railroad freight car mounted on a frame with windows cut into it. Fun for kids. It was further up the hill, maybe fifty yards. The BMW was nowhere to be seen. I rolled the car to a stop and then saw movement.

Dodger Hat was dragging Carol toward the railroad car, illuminated by the half moon like a scene in an old horror movie and he was Frankenstein's monster. She was struggling, fighting him. They disappeared into the old metal car. My spirits lifted. Thank God she was alive. Now, if I could just keep it that way.

The young cop and I got out of the car, weapons drawn. His was a .44 Magnum. "What's your name, son?" I asked, speaking softly.

"Jim, sir. Jim Krueger."

"I'm Jimmy too. Anyway, if this slimeball gets past me, blow him to hell with that Dirty Harry gun of yours. He's a killer. Wait for me here. Copy?"

"Yes, sir."

I started up toward the railroad car, slanting to the left, which appeared to be a blind spot from the freight car, since I could make out windows that faced the other way. The moonlight helped me to find my way up the hill. Was Dodger Hat a werewolf? I was scared to death of him but knew this was my only chance. He was planning to finish Carol here, ditch the BMW, and then make his escape.

I crept closer, cutting my hand once on a thorny bush, making my own trail as I tried to avoid making any noise. When at last I got to the freight car, staying just left of its open door, I could hear their voices. Carol was baiting him, playing on his insecurities. A gutsy move, but maybe a fatal one with this type of killer.

"We call you Mr. Dodger Hat, because you're stupid or vain, or both," Carol was saying, contempt in her voice. "Always wearing a hat. You going bald or something? Having manhood issues? Can't get it up?"

"Do you really want to be spewing silly little insults at me in your last moments on earth?" the man asked. "You hear that glorious silence? I lost them all, including your partner."

"Don't be so sure," Carol said, slurring her words. I could tell she was hurting badly. "The entire Portland PD is on your ass."

Dodger Hat laughed, an ugly mirthless sound. "Lady, I've had entire fucking armies on my ass." A pause. "The funny thing is, I'd decided to let you live, you and Sommes, and then, here you are. It must be karma."

"No, it was a parking ticket, you moron," Carol said with desperate effort. She was slipping away.

I had to move now. What did I have available? Not much. I reached for the rental car keys, held by a clunky metal key ring. It had some weight to it. I threw the keys as hard as I could through the open door into the far right corner of the freight car. They clanked off metal as I moved forward. Dodger Hat fired three rounds at the open window closest to the noise. He'd fallen for it! The rounds illuminated the interior just long enough for me to see Carol lying on the floor, not three feet away from him. Realizing his error, Dodger Hat swore, turned toward me, and aimed. Too late.

I shot him twice in the chest, jumped into the railway car, and kicked the gun out of his hand. Officer Krueger arrived almost at once. He shined his flashlight into the car. Dodger Hat was down, bleeding badly. Carol lay motionless.

The killer was still alive, but just barely. I crouched over him, and he looked up, right through me, a half-smile on his face, already on his final journey. He said, "Maui," then sighed a single long exhalation, and he was gone. I felt his neck, no pulse, then moved quickly away, disquieted by him even in death.

"You didn't wait below, did you?" I said to Krueger.

"No sir," he said.

"I wouldn't have either," I said, liking him a lot. I found my keys, as Krueger lifted Carol carefully and carried her down the hill. I staggered behind him.

"We're going to Sisters of Mercy Hospital," he said, taking the keys. "It's close. I'll call in the crime scene from there. He's not going anywhere."

I felt my left shoulder. There was blood. Mine. Dodger Hat must have squeezed off a round as I was shooting. I sat in the back seat with Carol in my arms, holding her together as best I could, tears in my eyes, feeling relief and the beginnings of pain.

****

They stitched up my shoulder—the bullet had gone right through it, missing the bone—and put my arm in sling. It hurt, even with painkillers. I went to find Carol after they were done with me. The nurses wouldn't let me see her or even tell me how she was doing. I fell asleep in an ugly yellow plastic chair in a hallway.

Finally, a nun shook me awake and took me to see Carol's surgeon. The good news, he told me, was there was no concussion. The second blow, which looked so vicious, had been glancing. The rest of it was brutal.

Dodger Hat had dislocated her arm with that vicious pull. Her right arm, elbow, and wrist were broken. It had the doctor shaking his head. "Like she was hit by a train or something," he said.

"Can I see her?" I asked.

He said okay, but just for a moment. I went into her room. She was in some kind of traction device to stabilize her shoulder and arm. She had a black eye from his second blow. I sat down next to her, not sure what to do.

Carol opened her eyes. I squeezed her left hand. She was residing in a different world, floating on some kind of opiate cocktail, unable to speak. But I saw one question in her eyes.

"Yeah, we got him," I said. She gave a tiny nod and drifted away to sleep. I called Annie to give her the news. It was a terse exchange. She said she'd get the first available flight.

****

I met with Greenstein on Sunday. He apologized again for missing Dodger Hat's new car and expressed concern about Carol. I let him off the hook. No way they could have tracked a completely different car. In fact, Carol and I were lucky, if you could call it that, to have met up with Collins at the Benson.

"Not good enough," Greenstein said. "That empty squad car on Broadway, they both were getting coffee.

Accordingly, both of them were suspended without pay for a week to drink as much frickin' coffee as they want. If one officer had stayed on duty, as required, he could have called in and reported the BMW, and Collins would have been apprehended earlier."

And maybe gotten Carol killed, I thought, but stayed silent.

"At least Jim Krueger did his job," Greenstein added.

I agreed. "He saved Carol's life. Give him a big raise."

Greenstein did point out a silver lining to the radio silence, namely that the rogue Feds were not alerted to Dodger Hat's presence, or his death, if they were monitoring the Portland police radio traffic. Krueger had used a telephone at the hospital to alert his superiors.

So, the Monday operation to trap the rogue Feds was a go. I got to observe it from the mobile command center located, ironically, in a room on the top floor of the Benson Hotel. It had a sweeping view of both the parking structure and the bank building. As the operation unfolded, the details didn't exactly match my earlier vision but were close. A man and woman, dressed like Carol and me, never left the ugly brown Impala after they parked it on the third floor. The assassination squad, two men in Portland PD uniforms, set up on the second floor, below where Carol and I would have been. That was smart and gave them a quicker getaway path after they'd planted the rifle on us. Fortunately, the Portland team had anticipated this possibility and had it covered.

Just as the bank opened, a man with longish brown hair, a bushy mustache, and a Lakers hat took his first steps toward the elegant bronze doors of the US Bank of Portland's Sixth Avenue entrance.

Jerry the sniper, our breakfast friend, was tucked behind a concrete building column on the second floor of the garage, using the railing to steady his rifle and preparing for the shot. He flipped up the sight on his weapon, zeroing in on the target. That's when three officers jumped him before he could fire, smashed him to the pavement, and cuffed him. The getaway driver, none other than the California Bureau man Wilcox, was quickly surrounded by other cops holding guns to his head. Neither suspect offered any resistance, acting more like captured soldiers than criminals. Name, rank, and serial number. The FBI, finally part of the act, led the two men away.

There was jubilation in the Command Center. "That was a little risky," Greenstein said to me as we watched together, "but I wanted to nail the bastards in the act. No ambiguity. We've got a special jail set up for them on Hayden Island. That'll give the suits in DC time to figure out what to do with them. There will never be a trial or anything public. This is internal spook type stuff. Good riddance." Greenstein didn't look tired anymore.

Down in the bank plaza, the man playing the part of Dodger Hat walked to a van parked on Sixth Avenue, took off his sports jacket and the ball cap. Then he calmly shed his body armor and head gear, threw them in the van, and departed.

****

I stayed in Portland a week, keeping in touch with Sam by phone. Annie was still in Portland too. I figured she'd be furious with me for dragging Carol into this. Not so. Carol had told her that the images of the horrific Claremont bombing, the crime scene, had lodged in her mind and weren't going away until the murderer was found.

"I couldn't have prevented her from coming here," Annie said, mostly relieved that her lover was going to survive, and be good as new according to Carol. Annie was planning to split her time between Portland and Claremont until Carol was released, probably in a month. Annie and I respected each other but were not friends, so we didn't spend time together during that week. I couldn't figure out why we didn't get along and stopped trying. By unspoken agreement, we alternated our visiting times with Carol.

During my last visit with Carol before I flew back to California, she dropped a bombshell. "I'm thinking about resigning from the Claremont PD."

I was floored. "Is it because of Dodger Hat? Your injuries? You did great, distracting—"

"Just wait, Jimmy, let me explain this my way. It's not because of him, at least not directly." Carol took a sip of water through a straw. "I know I could easily put in my twenty years, be a small-town cop, and never face anybody like him again. But guess what? I'm not sure I want to. With that guy gone, a switch flipped in my mind. I realized that I don't need to be a police officer anymore."

"You solved this case," I said, trying to talk her out of it. "You found that Green and Phillips owned the drug house, getting us on the right track. Then you discovered the parking ticket. That led us to the car, which took us to Dodger Hat. Sam Fuller told me he's going to use your work as a teaching example to the new detectives, showing them there's no substitute for brains in this business."

Carol smiled as much as her injuries allowed. "Hey, I said I was thinking about resigning from the Claremont PD, not retiring to some rest home. I appreciate the compliments. I might need them as references."

"What?" I was confused.

"How does 'Carol Loomis, Private Investigator,' sound? Most of the old geezers working as PIs in the Pomona Valley are close to worthless. And you just said it yourself, I'm a damn good investigator." Carol paused for more water.

"I'd hire you in a minute," I said. "Can you swing it, the business side of things?"

"Annie and I have talked about it some. The Justice for All Clinic is pursuing some big voting rights cases, trying to overcome the obstacles Chicano voters face. You heard about it some at that Sycamore Inn dinner. Man, I could sink my teeth into that work. It's no charity or sweetheart gig, either. She'd clear it with her ethics committee if we get that far. It would get me started with some income while I develop other work."

"Boy, you and Sam Spade. I like it, but it's mostly divorces, you know."

"Whatever," she said. "I don't mind tracking a philandering husband from time to time." Wincing, Carol rearranged herself in the hospital bed. "This assumes I can get my body to function again. Everything still hurts. And I've got to get licensed. None of this is a sure thing, so don't say anything, even to Sam."

Knowing Carol, it was going to work. I told her how happy I was for her and hugged her on the undamaged side of her body, saying that it all sounded great, which was true.

Leaving the hospital that day, I felt like I was losing my best friend. I'd had this idea, or hope, that she and I might partner up one day, work together full-time as cops. That wasn't going to happen, and, mulling it over, I decided that it was probably for the better. Hanging around with me was too dangerous. I intended to keep fighting monsters like Doc Green and Dodger Hat. It was my calling.

I flew back to California that afternoon, with Richard Manning and Doc Green very much on my mind.

CHAPTER THIRTY-TWO

"DO YOU NEED ANY counseling?" Sam asked me over the phone. "It's fairly standard when a police officer is required to use deadly force."

"No. The dude was well on his way to killing Carol, and I was next. It was an easy call."

"Regardless, you're flying a desk for the next two weeks, no weapons, no rough stuff. See you tomorrow for the meeting. Eleven a.m."

Actually, I was reliving the Portland scene with dizzying intensity every hour or so, the noise, even the smells, the look on Dodger Hat's face as he died... But I believed it would pass. My main concern at the moment was whether I would be able to cradle my fiddle against my sore left shoulder. So far, so good, with extra padding. The sling was off, and I was running through scales, no problem with fingering the strings. Lucky I was a righty.

I knew occupying myself with such matters was the best therapy. Our band had a practice session soon and a gig in early June. I couldn't wait. After working through "Orange Blossom Special," I pronounced myself good to go. Time for some sleep.

A call from Annie Hoover woke me up. It was close to midnight. "Can we meet soon?" she asked. "Before your meeting." How did she know about that?

"Sure, you mean now?" My shoulder was aching like hell.

"How about 7 a.m. at Walter's?"

****

The next day dawned hot and bright, even in the early morning. Summer had arrived. Annie had gotten to the restaurant before me, grabbed a booth, and ordered a pot of coffee. We each ordered scrambled eggs and toast. I wasn't that hungry, but it paid for the booth.

Before I could ask her, Annie told me that Sam Fuller had invited her to the meeting this morning and was asking her to consider wearing a wire to entrap Doc Green. The two of them were meeting prior to the larger meeting today to go over the plan.

"No way," I said. "Carol damn near died in Portland, and now Sam wants to endanger you? Let me wear a wire, for Christ sake, not you."

"That makes no sense, Jimmy, but I appreciate the sentiment. Carol, by the way, thinks I should do it. She says we've got to put these bastards away. Sam Fuller says I'll be fully protected every step of the way, and that this creepy dentist is a coward who hires other people to do the violent stuff."

That was true. I knew the type. I agreed to at least listen to Sam's plan later today. Annie was a tough cookie. I was coming to the reluctant realization that I needed to let this play out with me partly on the sidelines. And nobody but Annie had total access to Doc Green.

Annie hesitated as I prepared to pay for breakfast. There was something on her mind. "Listen, I'm no good at talking about personal stuff, but you and Carol, I'm not trying to break up your friendship or anything."

"I know that. I'm no good at personal stuff either," I said. "I'm real happy for Carol and you. I just want her to be happy." An awkward silence followed. Carol and I had

never been lovers, but our level of intimacy was close to that, and that put Annie in the position of replacing me to some degree, whether I liked it or not. I sighed. "Don't worry about it," I said. "We'll figure it out." We parted ways out on Yale Avenue.

Putting on my shades, I elected to drive to San Bernardino on Baseline, taking my time. As I passed Doc Green's compound, I slowed, thinking about Annie's involvement and the next steps in the case. But my mind was drawing a blank. Carol usually got my brain started, and it wasn't working that well since Portland.

****

The 11 a.m. meeting got underway. It was Sam, the LASD men, Figueroa from Paso Robles, Annie, and me. I was asked to summarize the Portland operation, the results of which they knew, but Sam wanted my personal play by play. Afterwards, even the ever-cool LA guys were impressed.

Then Sam took over. "Exactly what's going to happen to Jerry the sniper and Wilcox is being determined at Federal levels far above me. The long-slumbering FBI is finally getting involved. Annie, your other Bureau contact, Nichols, has disavowed all of the dirty tricks. Regardless, he has been suspended and is under house arrest in Sacramento."

"Is the rest of the California Bureau clean, the big-shots?" Al Sevilla asked.

Sam shrugged. "The attorney general himself called me to apologize. He and the leadership of the California Bureau were totally in the dark. We may never know for sure, but we'll make the assumption for now that Nichols, Wilcox, and Jerry the sniper were freelancing. The Bureau is out of this anyway, since Luther Simmons, aka Mr. Dodger Hat, is dead, thanks to Jimmy, Carol, and the Portland team. The CIA, of course, isn't talking. Par for the course.

"Our focus now," he continued, "is Dr. John Green, the wayward dentist. There has been no media coverage of the Portland operation, and we managed to get the Bank of Portland to tell Green that Mr. Collins had received the money. That's all the dentist knows, and he's sitting there at home, assuming, but not really knowing, that everything's okay. And he's waiting for Dodger Hat to contact him. That means we have a narrow window for moving on him before he finds out that Dodger Hat is dead." He now turned toward Annie. "Miss Hoover has agreed to wear a wire and confront Doc Green at his house. She'll be protected."

The operation was straightforward. Annie would call Doc Green and threaten to quit the clinic unless Green cut her in for a greater share of the drug proceeds. With Jack Green on the run, Jason Phillips dead, the Brotherhood rounded up, and the hitman absent, there was nobody to run their drug operation. Doc Green always left these gritty details to others. Money was already owed to their suppliers, primarily a Mexican cartel not known for its patience. Doc Green needed to step up fast, and Annie was available.

The operation was set for the following Tuesday, the day after Memorial Day.

****

I was with Annie that morning when she made the call to Doc Green. "They came to the clinic, some goddamn gangsters," she said to him. "They demanded to see Gringo Jack saying they needed their money, or they would burn down the building! Help me, please," she cried, her voice a

mix of panic and anger. "Some of the staff is fed up, ready to quit."

We were recording the call. Doc Green told her settle down, that he didn't give a rat's ass about the staff or the legal clinic. He suggested they meet at Bank of America. He could get her some money.

"Not enough. No banks, no dribble of cash. We need a complete plan or I'm out. And you need to pay me more for doing all this shit. I'm coming to your house at seven tonight," Annie said, then ended the call. It was perfect.

Wilcox had lied about the search warrant. The Bureau men had not even tried to get one. So, once Green incriminated himself on Annie's wire, all the legal processes were set to roll.

After the techs fitted Annie with the wire, I gave her a pep talk. She was nervous. "You're a Stanford lawyer, for God's sake, and he's a crooked dentist. I've never met a dentist I liked anyway," I chattered away, "even the ones who aren't criminals." It drew an odd look from her.

Time to move out. Everything was in place as Annie drove to the dentist's compound. It was still daylight. Neighbors in the houses adjoining the Green compound had been asked to vacate for the evening. There was some danger to her, but armed men were thirty seconds away when she entered Green's house—not including me on account of Sam's light duty commandment. But I was close by.

Green and Annie met for about half an hour inside his house, then walked over to his office. They both looked serious, but under control. We actually had better eyes on them in the office, more windows. Soon after, a message from a forward observer: "Signs of a struggle, chair tipped over."

"Move in now," the tactical commander ordered.

Three tense minutes later, "All clear," came over the radio. "Suspect in custody, witness unharmed." I ran to Green's office and went in just as the dentist, escorted by Al Sevilla, was getting marched out the door in handcuffs. Annie was sitting in a chair, a blanket draped over her. A nurse, part of the team, was already with her. I sat down.

"I'm okay," she said before I could ask. "It went like this. Green and I were talking, I was explaining how the accounts were set up. Then I asked another question about his son." Annie grimaced. "Maybe one too many questions. He jumped me, knocked over my chair, and started clawing at my shirt, tearing it off, scratching my chest. Then he saw the wire, yelled 'You bitch.' That's when the deputy," she pointed out the window to Al Sevilla, "tackled him."

The nurse got up. "We're taking her to Pomona Valley Hospital, just as a precaution."

Annie looked scared, but happy. "You did great," I told her.

Once outside I congratulated Sevilla, clapping him on the back. He'd come through in the clutch, a good lawman. Green was sitting motionless in the back of a squad car, staring straight ahead, acknowledging no one. What a twisted son-of-a-bitch.

****

Listening to the tape later, I learned that Doc Green performed just as we needed him to, cursing his son, talked about hiring a "professional" to run the entire drug operation, and agreeing that Annie needed to be well paid for her role. He'd offered to write her a check for $10,000 right away. That's why they went to his office. Doc Green also complained about all the cocaine and hashish hidden in his garage, filling it up. The new manager needed to get the damn drugs into a warehouse.

It was unclear whether it was just Annie's questions or if something else also triggered Doc Green's attack on her, but his actions cemented the case against him. He was arrested for assaulting Annie. The drug felony charges were added after the San Bernardino DA's office listened to the tape.

Later, as I was hoping, the crime scene techs found an unusual account book in the back of the dentist's desk. Although it was disguised with weird hieroglyphics, a LASD forensic expert was able to break the code. It turned out the idiot had kept a record of his transactions with a certain Luther Simmons, our Mr. Dodger Hat. A considerable sum of money had been wired to a Las Vegas bank account belonging to "Mark Collins," on the afternoon of May 25, 1970, at 5:30, the day Rebecca Meadows was murdered. Bingo.

Al Sevilla—LASD had taken the lead in the case after some bureaucratic infighting—discovered another key piece of evidence: Doc Green's Appointment Calendar for March, 1970. It showed a four o'clock appointment on Friday, March 6 for Miss Rebecca Meadows. She was complaining of serious pain at the site of an old filling. A follow-up appointment was shown for Friday, March 20. A small star was handwritten next to it. I called Carol in Portland and gave her the good news. As usual, she had been the first to think of it.

It would take some time, but Doc Green was going to sing. I knew the type. Since there was a mountain of forensic evidence accumulating against him, Dr. John Green was certain to be convicted. Given this, maybe he would choose to brag about his clever plan to kill Rebecca. It might save him from the gas chamber.

Annie had reeled him in. She could get back to her life, and her work, joined soon by Carol as a part of both. All of us were damaged, Carol the worst, but Dodger Hat was dead, and Doc Green was likely jailed for the rest of his life. It gave me grim satisfaction.

We never talked about it much later, the three of us. Like returning World War II soldiers, it was better to move on. Triumph voiced often tasted bitter.

****

Two days after Doc Green's arrest, Melody Manning and I were sitting in a small room at the Federal Detention Facility in downtown Los Angeles with one of Richard Manning's lawyers. "I'm sure you understand that we won't allow you to interview Richard Manning," the man said to me. "Among other things, the US Attorney's Office has jurisdiction, and they don't recognize you as having any role in this matter."

I waved him off. "I know all that. I'm here to support your client's mother."

"Okay. I'll escort her in now. I'll give them as much privacy as I can," he gestured toward the walls and ceiling, "but you never know in this place."

Melody looked small and frail, but she bravely went through the clanking metal door without looking back. I waited, my mind going back, as it often did, to the gunfire in that freight car. The terrible noise. The smell of blood. And the word "Maui."

Melody returned after an hour, tight-lipped and pale. We'd already agreed I was not to ask her any questions about her visit. If she wanted to talk, fine, but it was strictly up to her. I took her to lunch at my favorite LA restaurant, an unpretentious, noisy joint near Dodger Stadium that featured the best roast lamb and roast beef sandwiches on the planet, served with potato salad and pickles. I had a beer and Melody had a Coke.

"No booze for me while I'm on methadone," she said, plowing through her lamb sandwich. After a while she said, "The lawyers say I can't talk to you. It could harm Richard's case," she said.

"I know."

"I'll say one thing, though. Richard still strongly believes in the revolution, no wavering at all. It's just the, uh, specifics of how things went down that weren't what he'd imagined."

"Got it. Let's get you home." As we drove east on the San Bernardino Freeway, Melody fell asleep. I was intrigued by the nugget of information she'd provided. It might be nothing. Manning had previously expressed some remorse, in his weird way, about the secretary who'd been hurt by the first bomb. But maybe he now was referring to the second bomb too. Had he played a role? I had an idea about how to find out.

****

"Just look at the photo when it comes through. See if it rings any bells," I said to Allie over the phone. She was at the *Village Voice* office in New York City. They had one of those fancy new facsimile machines. So did the San Bernardino District Attorney's Office. "Call me if you recognize the man."

"Okay, but don't expect any miracles," Allie said. "It'll be later though, I'm on deadline." She hung up. I liked this journalist version of her... tough and independent as ever, but with focus.

I worked with a technician at the DA's office to slowly feed our sketch of long-haired, mustachioed Dodger Hat into this magic machine. Everything had a green tinge to it. Five minutes later, the picture was in New York. Wow.

Allie called me late that night, waking me up, practically morning her time. God, did the woman ever sleep? "This is really weird," she said, "but I think I remember seeing that man, the one in the sketch, back in those crazy days. He was with Jason Phillips. I never talked to him, but I noticed him because he was really good-looking." She laughed. "Even us revolutionary types had hormones, you know what I mean?"

Did I ever. An image of Allie, naked in my bed—her olive skin glowing in the candlelight—so vivid it hurt. "Go on," I said, harsher than I'd intended. "When and where did you see him?"

"You sound like my editor. It was after the Kent State shootings—we were really angry—probably outside the chaplain's building. That's where we worked. Jason was serving as our conduit, talking to everybody, the straights, the freaks, the professors, even the ROTC guys. He was good that way. I figured the handsome guy was just another one of his contacts. Poor Jason."

Yeah, poor murderous Jason Phillips, but I kept my thoughts to myself. "Thanks, Allie. One last question. It's important. Did you see the man in the sketch before or after the first bombing?"

"That's easy. It was after, because that first bomb almost ended our negotiations with the administration. When I saw this man, it was when things were back on track, later in May. That's as much as I can remember about it, given all the sleepless nights and Benzedrine."

"Your memory's good," I said. "I'll pass the information along to our lawyers. It will help place the hitman in Claremont at the right time. Thanks." Then I stopped talking. So did she. There was nothing else either of us could think to say. Just a business call.

"Bye, then," Allie said, softly. The line went dead. Was there a catch in her voice? Or did I just imagine it?

Wide awake now, remembering the way we were, I put Coltrane's *My Favorite Things* on the stereo, filling my mind and heart with sweet torture. All alone, at 2 a.m.

CHAPTER THIRTY-THREE

TWO WEEKS LATER ONE of our assistant DAs called me. "Richard Manning copped a plea," he said, "second degree murder." In a confession statement, Richard Manning admitted that he'd built the second bomb, the one used to murder Rebecca Meadows. It was attorney Jason Phillips who'd hooked Manning up with another member of the Che Guevara Brigade, a man he knew only as "Kurt." The plan was to plant the bomb in the Claremont Graduate School mail room and detonate it at midnight on May 25, 1970, when nobody was there. Manning stated that this "action" was necessary to regain the revolution's momentum. His colleagues were selling out, co-opted by the Establishment, working with the university pigs on meaningless liberal reforms while Nixon's Fascist Police State continued unabated. This new bomb would show the world that the movement for universal justice would continue. Power to the People!

On the night of May twenty-fourth, Manning met Kurt in a grocery store parking lot in Claremont and gave him the bomb. It was in a cardboard box and not yet armed. Kurt had assured Manning that he was an experienced operative and knew how to rig the device to explode at just the right time, using a simple alarm clock as its timer. Richard Manning drove away, secure in his belief that they were about to strike another blow for the revolution. As he found out the next day, it hadn't worked out that way.

Kurt, of course, was Collins. In an addendum,

Manning's lawyers stated that their client never intended to harm anyone with either the first or second bomb. They claimed he was a victim of the reactionary and counter-revolutionary murder plot hatched by Doc Green, Jason Phillips, and the other drug dealers. It didn't matter. Manning was knee-deep in Collins's murder of Rebecca Meadows, regardless of his intent. That's why he took the plea. But I was happy for Melody's sake that her son might actually get out of prison in twenty years or so.

"I'm planning to meet him at the gate," Melody told me later. "He's my boy. Nothing changes that."

Driving home that night, thinking about Manning's plea, I reflected on the case, and what a long, strange trip it had been, which led my mind to Acid Bill Dixon. He'd gotten me started on this, in that funky bathroom at Baldy Village, five months ago. It seemed longer.

Had it changed me? Maybe. I was better at work, more patient, not so damn cocky all the time. Humility is a powerful thing. I was still haunted by that moment in Portland at the Benson Hotel, when I'd failed to protect Carol. Sam Fuller had told me that my prudence was correct. That I didn't have a clear shot. Carol agreed. I didn't buy it, never would. She'd almost died. I needed to live with that. Focus instead, like the shrink told me—I'd gone once—on the fact that Carol was okay. That ultimately young Jim Krueger and I *had* rescued her from that evil bastard. It did help some.

Carol was due home next week. She was going to work half-time for several months, while she prepared to become a private investigator—the plan was still a deep dark secret. Annie and I were going to surprise her by picking her up at the airport in her beloved cherry red Chevy Bel Air. The City of Claremont had finally replaced the windshield. It was about time.

****

It was a late summer weekend gig at The Corral, about two months after Manning pleaded out. The college kids were drifting back to town, the joint was packed, and our band was hot. We were playing *White Bird*, really whaling on it, revving up the crowd. Sokoloski's lead guitar was growling with lots of distortion, while I played some Duane Allman slide guitar riffs on my fiddle, the strings practically smoking. Our drummer, who loved to rock, was propelling us ahead. No country twang tonight.

That's when I saw her, standing at the same post in the back of the club where she'd been that first night. Allie. The thing is, I wasn't surprised. Her presence felt right, almost preordained, especially in the midst of this song. The notes sparked off my fiddle as I gazed at her, thrilled out of my head, but playing slower now, out of rhythm with the band. Sokoloski looked at me like I was crazy, then he saw her too, nodded, and began to match me, note for note, the tune getting jazzier. We were chasing the moon. The bass player followed, then the drummer. The singers were lost, but it didn't matter. Allie was watching us, swaying gently.

This music, I realized, was for the entire cast of characters: Allie for sure, but also for innocent victim Rebecca Meadows, plus for the cops, the crooks, the bomber and his hippie mama, even the hitman. And, of course, for Carol. Just this once, our band was playing like Coltrane, wheels within wheels, beyond words, at this little joint on Baseline Road where time sometimes played tricks, blending past, present, and future. I looked down at the crowd in front of the stage. Acid Bill Dixon, surrounded by his usual young acolytes, was grinning up at me. He nodded his head. I'd gotten it right.

EPILOGUE

Thursday, August 8, 1974

AN ORANGE COUNTY DEPUTY sheriff called me with a tip. Jack Green had shown up at a bar in Huntington Beach earlier in the day, acting crazier than usual, raving about competitors poaching his turf, flashing weapons and cash, and threatening the patrons. He was all gangster now. Any vestige of the Brotherhood of Eternal Love guru who'd scattered Orange Sunshine LSD tabs like candy among the faithful was long gone. It was cocaine now, maybe some heroin. None of it was free, and there was no love to be found. Plus, Green, a champion surfer, barely touched the water these days, too addicted to his product to care, according to the Orange County deputy. There was also a rumor that Jack had stiffed his Mexican supplier, a dangerous thing to do. Cocaine made people crazy. I'd seen that plenty of times in my work.

Curious, I drove down to Green's sprawling compound that night and parked just out of sight. I was sitting in the dark in my rental car, since Green's guards, patrolling the perimeter with their AK-47s, knew my Dodge Charger by sight from previous visits. Tonight, like always down here, I was a private citizen. Nobody knew about these nocturnal vigils, not Sam Fuller, not Carol. My mission was unclear. It had something to do with bearing witness, since the law couldn't touch Jack Green. He'd beaten all the charges against him, even the assault on Melody Manning. I didn't know how. During my last visit, a woman in baggy shorts and a tie-dyed surfer t-shirt had seen me. She'd come outside the compound, called me a fucking pig, and threatened to release the dogs on me. I'd left, but couldn't seem to stay away.

The sky was littered with stars on this warm August night. A west wind carried the sound of the waves breaking on the beach. It was almost midnight and quiet at Green's place; even those damn Rottweilers of his must be sleeping. Maybe he'd come down off his coke high, or whatever was fueling him, and crashed. I'd give it another half an hour, then split.

Five minutes later, the lights came on in the compound, accompanied by noise and all manner of commotion. A car engine started. "Open the fucking gate," a man bellowed. Was it Green? Then a black Porsche convertible roared out, heading south on the coastal road. I drove to the corner and started to turn right to follow him, almost getting broadsided by a souped-up Camaro, driving just as fast. I saw a rifle extending out the Camaro's window pointed toward the Porsche, a gunman in the passenger seat paying no attention to me. They were after Jack Green.

I couldn't match the speed of the two cars but could see the beams from their headlights, and then muzzle flashes from the Camaro. Why in the world had Green left his compound? His protection? Maybe he thought he could make it to one of the old Brotherhood hideouts in the canyons above Laguna. Or maybe he was just too paranoid to think straight.

We were driving in a deserted shoreline preservation area, the only break between the beach towns. Perfect for an ambush. The coastal cliffs loomed ahead, and the road became a series of curves. No other traffic, just me trailing them. Both cars slowed to make the first tight turn, more gunshots from the Camaro. The Porsche accelerated, trying to gain an advantage over the curves. Too fast. I heard the squealing of brakes, then metal on metal, a hellish noise even from a distance. Jack Green had missed his turn. I slowed down, considered a U-turn for my own safety, and then kept going instead. I needed to know.

The Camaro was parked in a small pull-out area. Two men wearing bright flowered shirts, their guns now held loosely at their waists, were looking at the mangled guard rail, and beyond it toward the Pacific Ocean. I drove by, too slowly, almost hypnotized by the tableau. One of the men turned to look at me, the other grabbed his arm, seeming to restrain him. I came to my senses, hit the gas, and got the hell out of there. They didn't follow me.

Laguna Beach was the next town. I found a pay phone near the Taco Bell and called the local police, providing details about the two cars, the chase, and the accident. I did not give my name or identify myself as law enforcement. I told them all I knew and hung up, not wanting to spend all night talking to policemen in a dingy interview room. For one thing, they'd certainly be curious about why I was there in the first place. I departed Orange County and all the drama.

There was no elation, but I felt some relief. Jack Green hadn't killed Rebecca Meadows, but he'd been part of the vicious cover-up. I looked forward to Melody Manning's reaction. She'd likely dance a jig, maybe break out one of her favorite Grateful Dead albums to celebrate.

But bad guys killing other bad guys—which this surely was—was a zero sum game, and becoming a daily and depressing occurrence in Southern California. Merging onto the I-5, still crowded after midnight, I thought about sunny Atascadero in uncluttered Central California, where life seemed more settled and ordinary, maybe better. Not a war zone. I could call Chief Alvin Rhyne about a job. But no... that was nonsense. My job, my band, my family, my cabin, Carol, even Allie for our stolen moments; it was all here in messy, dangerous Southern California, not in some idealized place. I got home at 3 a.m. and fell into a deep sleep.

****

Two days later, I was reading the Saturday *San Bernardino Sun*, preparing to start a weekend shift; all of us were working due to a mini-crime wave in Alta Loma. The front page was all Richard M. Nixon. He'd finally quit in disgrace and was on his way back to California, to San Clemente, not that far from where Jack Green had driven off the cliff.

"Jimmy, you've got Carol on line two," Laurie yelled out, earning her overtime pay. Our intercom never did get fixed.

I picked up. "Did you see the newspaper?" Carol asked.

"Yeah, I know, asshole Nixon."

"No. Not that," Carol said, sounding impatient. "Look on page six, toward the bottom."

The article stated that there had been a fatal one-car automobile accident north of Laguna Beach early Friday morning. A drug kingpin named Jack Green had driven his Porsche through a metal railing off a cliff into the Pacific Ocean. He'd been seen in a bar earlier in the day with weapons and a suitcase full of cash. The police estimated that the car must have been traveling over one hundred miles an hour to break through the railing and fly thirty yards into the ocean below. The article reported that there were rumors that a vehicle was chasing Green at the time of his death, but the authorities found no evidence of this.

"You didn't do it, right?" Carol asked.

"Nope."

"Good." She hung up.

My new partner, Jim Krueger, who'd relocated from Portland, was reading over my shoulder. "Jack Green. Weren't you after that guy?"

"Not anymore, dude," I said, getting up and grabbing my battered old Stetson. We had work to do, a string of burglaries on Baseline Road.

Author's Note and Acknowledgments

This is a work of fiction. Fortunately, no bombs were set off at the Claremont Colleges in May of 1970 following President Nixon's invasion of Cambodia and the student unrest it unleashed; which intensified when news of the deaths of student protesters at Kent State and Jackson State swept across college campuses throughout the country.

I was a witness to and participant in the protest activities in Claremont during that wild month, all of which were peaceful but also highly disruptive to the status quo. I refreshed my recollections by researching those events via the special collections at Claremont's Honnold Library.

I want to thank several people who helped move this book from vague notion to reality. Tommy Hays, Vicki Lane, Stanley Dankoski, Tena Frank, Heather Dickmeyer, and Mary Munter all read drafts of the manuscript at different stages and provided critical feedback. I'm particularly grateful to Scott Reckard for steering me toward San Bernardino County as a key location and for providing me with wise counsel throughout the writing of this novel.

All of the teachers and students at the Great Smokies Writing Program in Asheville, North Carolina deserve special mention. It was there that I learned how to write fiction.

Finally, my heartfelt thanks to Rosemary Zibart for putting me together with Geoff Habiger at Artemesia Publishing, and to Geoff for finding a place for me and *Baseline Road* at his remarkable small publishing house.

About the Author

Orlando Davidson graduated from Claremont Men's (now McKenna) College and UCLA School of Law in the 1970's and headed west to the Hawaiian Islands. After a thirty-five-year career in Hawaii working as an attorney, planner, lobbyist, and public official, Orlando relocated to western North Carolina and began to write fiction. *Baseline Road* is his first novel and was shaped by his experiences during the Kent State protest days. He now resides in Portland, Oregon.